Dark Storm

Dark Storm

SARAH SINGLETON

SIMON AND SCHUSTER

First published in Great Britain in 2012
by Simon and Schuster UK Ltd, a CBS company.

Simon Pulse and its colophon are registered
trademarks of Simon & Schuster UK Ltd

www.crowmaiden.plus.com
www.simonpulse.co.uk

Simon & Schuster UK Ltd
1st Floor, 222 Gray's Inn Road, London WC1X 8HB

This book is a work of fiction. Names, characters, places and
incidents are either the product of the author's imagination or
are used fictitiously. Any resemblance to actual people living
or dead, events or locales is entirely coincidental.

A CIP catalogue record for this book is available from the British Library.

PB ISBN: 978-0-85707-075-3
EBOOK ISBN: 978-0-85707-558-1

1 3 5 7 9 10 8 6 4 2

Printed and bound by CPI Group (UK) Ltd, Croydon CR0 4YY.

www.simonandschuster.co.uk

For Marc, my Beloved

The shop stood at the end of the seafront, wedged between a fishmonger's and a place selling beach clothes and post-cards. A poster in the window caught Ellie's attention, advertising a summer youth theatre project, something her grandmother had urged her to try. She stopped to look, although she had no intention of joining.

Fairies decorated the left-hand side of the poster, a man with a donkey's head on the other side.

'It'll be good,' said a voice, to her right. Ellie jumped. She'd been so lost in thought she hadn't noticed a young man approach.

'You should join,' he said. 'You should do something. You're going to be here all summer.'

'What? I mean . . .' Ellie was flustered and annoyed. Who was this guy and how did he know anything about her? She glared into the face of this intruder who stood beside her, offering unwanted advice. He was about eighteen, tall and strongly built with thick, rumpled, golden hair and brilliant blue eyes. He returned her scowl with a grin, running a square hand through his hair.

'Really, it'll be fun. You'll meet some cool people. Like

me,' he teased. It was impossible to take offence. His eyes twinkled with humour. Ellie looked at him properly. Big scruffy boots, jeans splashed with white emulsion, a red T-shirt, faded to pink.

'I'm sorry, do I know you?'

'I'm Alex,' he said, thrusting out his hand. 'You don't know me, but I've heard a lot about you. This place,' he gestured, 'You know what it's like. My mum does yoga with your grandma. You're here all summer, right?'

'Yes.' Ellie reluctantly shook his hand then turned her face away, studying the shop window. What else did Alex know? Presumably the reason she was here – about her mum? She folded her arms, held herself tight. *This place.* Of course everyone would know. She felt the sting of exposure and humiliation. She didn't want to be wondered about.

Ellie stepped towards the shop door, simply to escape. Alex, thankfully, didn't follow her.

'I'm signing up,' he said to her back. 'It'll be fun. Take a chance, why don't you?'

Ellie stepped into the shop, giving him the merest glance as a goodbye. She shut the door, leaned back against it and closed her eyes. Then she took a deep breath and stood up straight.

A second-hand bookshop. A dark, old-fashioned place crammed with wooden shelves, like a maze, with piles of faded paperbacks, baskets of maps fifty years out of date and boxes of ancient postcards. Ellie hadn't been here for years but a memory unfolded in her mind, a summer morning with her mother, seeing a display of books about the sea in the window and buying a little volume full of beautiful illustrations – seashells and creatures from rock pools. Then they'd spent the afternoon at the sea's edge, identifying anemones, goose barnacles and a tiny tan-coloured porcelain crab. She savoured the memory, the pain and pleasure of it.

'Can I help you? Are you looking for anything in particular?'

People never left you alone for long in this town. Now it was the shop assistant, a middle-aged man with a beard.

'Uh, no. Just browsing.' She fixed her attention on the shelf of books in front of her – a collection of children's novels – aware the bookshop man was still staring.

The man returned to the counter. Ellie plucked a book at random from the shelves, something by Enid Blyton, eager to look like a real customer. She was the only one in the shop.

Ellie slid the book back into place and moved past sections on history and warfare to a shelf of misery memoirs. She'd read a few when she was fourteen – for some reason they'd been all the rage amongst the girls at school. Then real misery had come knocking and these tales had lost their savour. She moved on again. Poetry and drama. Ancient volumes in green hardcovers impressed with gold. Then something caught her eye – a manila folder pressed against the back of the bookshelf. She reached out for it but half the books on the shelf shifted dangerously when she tried to pull it free. Suddenly the bookshop man was back by her side.

'Let me help,' he said, levering precarious volumes out

3

of the way, pulling others aside. 'There, I think you can take it. Hmmm . . . It's amazing what junk turns up in this place. The manager picks up all sorts of stuff.'

Ellie lifted the folder. For a moment she held it aloft, this unlikely package of old brown cardboard, its unknown contents making it bulky. A puff of dust hung on the air, creating a halo. Ellie wrinkled her nose.

'What is it?' Still she held the folder at arm's length, unwilling to bring it closer. She turned it around. Nothing written, no indication of what might be inside.

'No idea,' the bookshop man said. 'Bring it over to the counter and have a look.'

Ellie didn't move. Something seemed to run along the length of her arm, from the folder. A curious sensation – chilly, prickly – beneath her skin, something seeming to bite. Her fingers opened and the folder dropped to the floor with a crash. She gave a sudden, violent sneeze.

'Oh, I'm sorry, I didn't mean to.' Ellie bent down to pick it up.

'Don't worry, I've got it,' the bookshop man said, squatting, corduroy-clad knees splayed, pale hands reaching out. 'My goodness, look at that. Fancy. Can you see what it is?' Pieces of richly coloured cardboard lay across his palms.

'What is it?' she said.

Bookshop man didn't answer. He swiftly herded up the remaining pieces, the pile of old printed paper and hand-written notes, then spread them out across the counter.

He peered. He picked something up, examined it and put it back.

4

'Well I never,' he said. 'Well, well.' He didn't look at Ellie at all. She had ceased to exist to him.

'What is it?' Ellie repeated, raising her voice. She leaned over the counter, to see for herself.

Although faded, the card pieces of different shapes and sizes were richly coloured: blood red, royal blue, emerald green. A pair of golden cherubs frolicked on one section. A deep scarlet curtain emerged from another, and then columns, and a painting of a scene in a palace. The puzzle resolved itself.

'It's a model theatre, isn't it? You could put all these pieces together,' she said.

The bookshop man looked up from the counter. 'Yes, exactly. How exciting! I'd no idea. It looks old. Perhaps it's Victorian? These model theatres were all the rage then.'

Ellie felt twin surges of emotion. For some reason she wanted the model theatre – more than she'd wanted anything in a very long time. The pieces were so utterly lovely. Even its agedness added to the allure of this mysterious, unexpected thing. She wanted to snatch it away from the bookshop man, to hold it to her chest and run away home with it. At the same time she felt a terrible fear. She could see he wanted it too, this fabulous find. She was scared he wouldn't sell it to her, or perhaps only for a sum she couldn't afford. And she had to have it. She had to.

'How much is it?' she said.

'What?'

'How much is it?' This time her voice was strident.

'Oh, I don't know.' He shook his head, annoyed and distracted. 'There's a play script here too, can you see?

Romeo and Juliet. Someone's written notes – see?' He gestured at some scribbling in the margin of the text.

Ellie picked up one of the pieces of paper. A name sprang out at her, written in heavy black ink, the letters looped and flowing – the handwriting of an earlier age. Harry, it said. The tail of the 'y' looped up with a strong flourish.

Harry.

'How much is it?' She stood as tall as she could for this, the third and final time of asking. Her voice was clear and ringing. He couldn't ignore it. The bookshop man looked at her, his hand still caressing the pieces on the table possessively.

Did he know who she was? About her loss? Would that make him more generous, and compassionate? It had sometimes worked that way, over the last eighteen months. She sent out an invisible appeal, to the gods, angels, the conscience of the bookshop man.

The shop door blew open with a bang, bell jangling. A breath of cool, sea-salty air filled the room, carrying a whiff of dead fish from next door, a hint of ice cream, the sound of people from the street outside. The mood of the shop altered in a moment.

The bookshop man stood up, backed a step away from the counter and rubbed his face with the palms of his hands as though he'd just woken up.

'What, what was I saying?' He blinked twice and shook his head. 'Oh, I don't know, I don't suppose it's worth much.' He gathered the pieces together without even looking at them. 'A fiver, how about that?'

'Okay, well yeah. Sure.' Ellie helped him stow the last

pieces into the manila folder and rummaged in her handbag for a purse. She handed over five one-pound coins and grabbed her prize. She didn't want him to change his mind before she'd left the shop.

'Thanks,' she said. 'Thanks a lot.' And she dashed outside into the street, through the crowd of holidaymakers, along the front and up the High Street, home to her grandparents' house.

2

The heavy front door slammed shut behind her. Ellie kicked off her flip-flops and padded along the cool, chipped black and red tiles in the hallway.

'Ellie? Lunch is ready. Come and sit down.' A voice from the kitchen.

Ellie ignored her grandmother and ran up two flights of stairs to her attic bedroom. She dropped the folder on the end of her bed before racing back down the stairs and into the dining room.

'You've plenty of energy. Are you hungry? It'd be good to see you with an appetite again.' Jean, Ellie's grand-mother, was tall and willowy, with thick, purely white hair in a plait. She'd laid the table with fresh bread, cheese, pickles, ham and salad. David, Ellie's grandfather, stepped in from the kitchen with three bowls of steaming soup on a tray.

'Lentil and vegetable. I made it this morning,' he said. 'While your grandmother was writing.' They were cheer-ful and chatty, as usual. Beyond the window Ellie could see the little sloping garden, with its fig tree and fuchsia bushes, beyond which stood a wall and then a steep drop down to the river. Once the old house had been a mill, and now, with four floors and a multitude of steps, no two rooms were on the same level. You could see fossils in the exposed stone.

Ellie loved the house. She'd always loved it. Her mother and uncles had grown up here and, during her own growing up, she'd come to stay every summer. Arriving on the coach the previous week, she'd felt she'd travelled not only in space but in time, back and back, to the enchanted seaside place where she'd spent so many happy holidays with her parents and grandparents, a place where nothing seemed to change. But it *had* changed. There was no mum here now to share stories with, and her dad was a long way away and probably not thinking about her at all.

Ellie tucked in to her soup, shaking off the maudlin thoughts. Her grandfather cut a slice of bread and dropped it onto her plate.

'Grandma, you remember that book Mum bought years ago, a little book about the seaside? Do you still have it here?' Ellie was eighteen, just, but she spoke with her mouth full, enjoying the chance to be a child again.

'Gosh, I've no idea. I don't remember. How long ago was this?'

'I wasn't very old. Maybe ten years ago?'

Jean shook her head. 'If it's here, it'll be on the shelves in your room. Have a look.'

After lunch Ellie disappeared into the attic. One window looked out over the garden and the river, the wild bank of trees beyond, and then more houses. At the front, she saw the descending jigsaw puzzle of rooftops and pastel-painted houses, a tiny corner of the sea just visible in the distance. Varnished floorboards, fresh white walls. On a broad shelf under the eaves stood pictures, odd china ornaments, stones from the beach, a vase full of seagull feathers and an old doll's house. This had been her mother's room, her mother's doll's house, and, later, Ellie's. She peered into the windows of the doll's house, at the unchanging interior world with its miniature furniture. The family of dolls were sitting stiffly at the table in the dining room. Mother, father, son and daughter with faded, still-smiling faces and plates of cracked plaster food in front of them. She felt a sudden urge to disturb the tiny tableau. To change its symmetry to reflect her own family upheaval. She sighed at her ridiculousness and went to pick up the manila folder. She sat on the bed, which was large and squashy with a curly white iron bedstead and a lush patchwork quilt of green, scarlet and amber, stitched with glittering threads and quirks of decorative embroidery, another of her grand-mother's creative projects. Ellie opened the folder and took out the contents piece by piece, placing them on the quilt, relaxing and beginning to savour the pleasure of locking herself away and having this wonderful discovery all to herself.

Slowly she worked out how to put the pieces together. It wasn't easy, without instructions, but Ellie was patient and canny. The parts had numbered slots and tabs. The stage floor slid into place. Three sets of wings to left and right, a tall arch and columns at the front, a beautiful backdrop painted with a city scene, grey towers around a courtyard with a fountain, and statues painted on the wings: gods and nymphs in various poses, some twined with wild roses.

Oh, it was beautiful. When she'd placed the last piece, Ellie carefully lifted the theatre and put it on the table by the front window. Then she stepped back and stared, feasting her eyes. About fifty centimetres high, and well proportioned, the theatre led the eye into its depths, the world within a world She'd found half a dozen cardboard characters, guessed which was Romeo, which Juliet. Ellie had studied the play for GCSE and she'd watched the film version with Leonardo di Caprio several times.

She picked up Juliet, a miniature figure in a white dress with long, copper curls, and placed her in a balcony, stage right. Then she stood Romeo, in a black coat, dark hair to his shoulders, in a slot on the stage gazing up at his love.

Ellie took a step back to gaze at the spectacle of the theatre, the little scene she'd created. She stared intently, focusing her attention, wanting to be inside it, part of it, leaving the world behind. She wanted . . . wanted what?

A peculiar, unsettling feeling.

A shadow passed across the theatre – an unseen seagull flying past the window, perhaps. Ellie stood up straight and gave her head a shake. She remembered the moment in the bookshop when the door had blown open and the atmosphere had altered in just the same way – as though a current of energy had been turned on. The play script and various sundry papers still lay on her bed. She gathered them together and placed them on the table by the theatre, to study later.

'The seaside book,' she said aloud. She left the theatre on

the table, opened her bedroom door and clattered down the stairs to her grandmother's study, where she spent her days writing about gardening. Books were heaped on numerous shelves along the walls.

Ellie searched for a long time. Perhaps the book had been lost, donated to Oxfam, loaned to someone who had never given it back. She looked again. For some reason it was tremendously important for her to find it. Why was that? To confirm her memories?

It had to be here. She needed it.

At last, there it was – a neat little volume at the end of the shelf, tucked between fat paperback novels. It was just as she'd remembered, with exquisite little sketches of seaweed varieties and creatures from rock pools.

Ellie sighed. She glanced around the room. She wanted to go out again, to get away. She was never comfortable anywhere for long these days.

'I'm going out, Grandma!' she called, galloping out of the front door before her grandparents could ask where she was going. The door thudded closed behind her, and she hurtled down the hill, along the path and through the narrow, winding streets to the seafront.

3

'Don't worry, I'm not stalking you.'

A shadow had fallen over her notebook. Ellie looked up to see the blond boy, Alex. She was sitting on a slab of warm, bluish rock, the cliff behind and in front the damp sandy beach and the sea running in long, repeating lines. A view now broken by the unwelcome shape of Alex.

She squinted up at him, closing the notebook to hide what she was doing.

A glossy, whip-thin black and white dog bounded up to them, gave one short, encouraging bark then hurtled off across the beach and into the waves.

'Walking the dog,' Alex said. 'It's my neighbour's, but he's too old to walk her much. Can't let her off the lead on the main beach in high season, so I come here instead. So, really, *you're* stalking *me*.' He grinned, teasing, seemingly oblivious to Ellie's prickly mood. The sun had tanned his skin the colour of honey, though the hair on his forearms was pale.

Without asking, he sat on the rock next to her. The breeze tugged at his hair.

'So did you sign up?'

'What?'

'For *A Midsummer Night's Dream*.'

Ellie stared at him. Then she shook her head. 'No.'

'But you like acting and arty stuff, don't you? So why not?'

'How do you know that?' Ellie demanded. Then: 'Grandma, obviously. Yoga class. This place. Right?'

Alex nodded slowly. 'Right.' The dog was bouncing into the sea, a piece of leathery seaweed trailing from her mouth. Alex gestured to the notebook. 'What were you drawing? It looked good.'

'Oh, the sea.' She indicated the landscape. The journal was her private world. Between the black leather covers she wrote, sketched, stuck pictures, tickets, poems and various other bits and pieces. She slid the book into her bag, along with the seaside guidebook, pens and pencils.

'So you know a lot about me,' she said. 'Tell me something about yourself. It isn't fair otherwise.'

Alex grinned. He had a wide, sunny smile. She noticed, for the first time, that he had a bag as well; a faded khaki canvas bag. Various sticks protruded from the top.

'Not much to tell,' he said. 'I was born here. I live with my mum and dad. He does fishing and boat trips and makes stuff.'

'Work? College?'

'Done my A levels, same as you. Though I'm not as smart as you, at least not from what we've heard from your grandma.' He eyed her, gauging her reaction, then leaned back on the rock, shading his eyes with his arm. 'In the autumn I want to do an art foundation course at the college in town. Why do you look surprised?'

14

'I dunno. You don't seem the arty type to me.'

He wasn't insulted. In fact, he laughed. 'You think you have to be thin and fragile and flaky to be creative? You need to widen your horizons.'

The conversation lapsed. The dog raced towards them again, then veered away at the last moment, scattering them with grains of sand. She leaped over the rocks, up and down, and onto a huge clump of clay soil at the bottom of the cliff.

'So you'll join, won't you – the theatre group? I won't take no for an answer.' Alex sat up again, propping himself on his elbow.

'Why's it so important to you?'

'Self-interest,' he said. 'We need someone for Titania, Queen of the Fairies.' He studied her face. 'And you've got the right look.'

The remark was cool and matter of fact, but Ellie blushed.

'We've got a meeting tomorrow night – seven thirty in the Marine Theatre. Come along.' Alex stood up. The dog gambolled over, now carrying a stick, which she dropped at Alex's feet. He picked up the stick and hurled it over the sand, to land, just, in the fringe of the sea. The dog barked for joy and galloped off in pursuit. Still watching the dog, Alex said, 'Seriously, come along. Or I'll stalk you all summer long.'

'Why do I find that so easy to believe?' Ellie said. 'Okay, you win. I'll be there. Just for the meeting. If I don't like it, I won't join.'

'Fair enough,' Alex said. Then, with a sudden, animal bound, he began running across the beach after the dog.

Three white gulls swooped down, over his head. Alex looked back. 'See you later!' he shouted, his words almost snatched away by the wind.

Ellie watched as he disappeared around the headland, then she took out her journal and opened it again. She'd sketched the shoreline, its cliffs and rocks, and described the incidents of the day – the discovery of the toy theatre and the rediscovery of the seaside book she'd bought with her mother. She took out her pen and wrote: *I'll go to the meeting. Maybe that'll stop them nagging me. I'll give it a try. Alex seems nice enough, though I hate that they all know so much about me.*

The wind blew Ellie's hair into her face. She sucked the end of her pen. The lure of rock-pooling had faded, despite the guidebook in her bag. She didn't want to do it on her own.

But she *was* alone, no getting around it. She'd lost her mother, and her dad had abandoned her. Grandparents, sure, but she was a visitor in their lives. Welcomed and loved, certainly, but it wasn't the same.

She clamped her teeth against the pen. On the beach, an elderly couple walked arm in arm. The breeze fingered their silvery hair. A tan-coloured dog trotted sedately beside them. Far away, across the glistening sand, a family with two little children paddled in the tiny waves. Ellie could hear their excited voices, the cries of the children when miniature waves washed over their knees.

What was her dad doing now? Was he thinking of her?

Probably not. He was preoccupied. He had his own life to get on with. She pushed the image of him from her mind, squashed it down and locked it away. Another gust of wind. Ellie shivered. She thought of the holidaymakers on the main beach, all goose-pimply beneath the sunscreen, reaching for their shirts and jumpers – the joys of the English seaside holiday.

She stood up, dropped her pen and journal into her bag, and began to walk home. At least her grandma would be pleased if she went to the meeting.

4

In bed, back propped against pillows, in a pool of light from the lamp on the bedside cabinet, Ellie pondered the script and papers she'd found in the manila folder. In the night-time quiet she could hear the river beneath the garden and the closer sounds of her grandparents getting ready for bed.

Romeo and Juliet. The ultimate teen romance.

Various notes had been scribbled in the margins of the script – reminders of stage directions, comments on the delivery of particular speeches.

Ellie traced her finger over the name written at the top of the script – the letters formed by a strong, confident hand. Harry, it said. No surname. Judging by the notes, Harry had played Mercutio, Romeo's friend.

How long ago had this happened? The bookshop man reckoned the model theatre was Victorian. One hundred and fifty years ago? One hundred? Either way, Harry would be dead by now. His performance of Mercutio, whether brilliant or mediocre, was done and gone, consigned to the past. Where did it go, the past, visible only through the clouded window of memory, or letters, pictures, diaries and books? What was that expression she'd heard? Something about the past being a different country. A place you'd once lived in but could never, ever go back to, no matter how much you wanted to.

And now this script, like a postcard from that different country. From Harry, whoever Harry might be.

Ellie put the script to one side and picked up the other papers. A typed schedule of rehearsals; a black and white photograph of a Victorian family – mother, father, two sons and a daughter, all posing stiffly with solemn faces; a programme and tickets for a music recital in Dorchester, on 21st September, 1896. The tickets were unmarked, suggesting Harry hadn't attended the event. At least she had a date now. More than likely, the model theatre was at least one hundred and twenty years old.

Thinking about it, this stretch of time past, of Harry and his play, Ellie felt a shiver of pleasure. How exciting to have uncovered this little treasure, to have a mystery to unravel.

She picked up the family photograph. Judging by the clothes, the family had been well off. The father looked stern in his dark suit, whiskers on his face, hand clamped on the shoulder of the woman sitting in a chair in front of him. She wore a dark, silky dress. Her face was beautiful, clear-eyed, and she held the hand of a pretty girl who stood beside her, aged about fifteen perhaps, with curls of long dark hair – hard to tell its colour in the black and white picture. Two boys – the younger one about sixteen, with pale blond hair, the older one . . . Ellie drew a breath. Standing straight, a touch of arrogance evident in his posture, he glared directly into the camera. Dark hair, a strong, angular face.

Ellie stared at him, the boy. The other family members seemed to fade away. He was the dominant figure. For a moment, the others lost definition, receded, while the boy grew bolder and stronger, staring out of the photograph, staring directly at *her*.

Ellie dropped the picture. She'd been holding her breath. She rubbed her eyes. The photo lay in a pool of royal blue velvet, on the quilt her grandmother had made. Ellie yawned. She needed to sleep. She bundled script and papers together and stacked them on the table beside the theatre. Then she climbed into bed and turned off the light.

In a moment, she fell asleep. Outside, the river ran, unheard. On the floor below, Ellie's grandparents settled into bed. On the chimney stacks the gulls scratched and fluttered. The moon, three-quarters full, rose over the sea and poked fingers of fragile light through the chink between the curtains.

Ellie opened her eyes, instantly wide awake.

She was lying in bed, flat on her back, arms away from her sides, as though stranded, left by a sudden swell of water.

The house was silent. It was night still, but the darkness seemed to shine. Ellie breathed deeply. A scent flooded the room. Strong, thrilling, exotic – a rich, spiced smell, something like incense, but clean and natural, not like the cloying, chemical smell of so many commercial products

Where had it come from?

The scent poured into the room, like water, filling it from floor to ceiling so she was immersed in it, breathing it in.

Slowly her eyes adjusted to the darkness, noticing the familiar form of the bed, the furniture, the room. Her gaze moved to the theatre.

This was the source of the scent, she knew at once. In some peculiar way she could see it, rolling out of the theatre's open front in slow waves.

She didn't move, body heavy, limbs like stone. A voice in her mind suggested this was strange and unnatural, that she should be afraid, but she wasn't. A minute passed, and another. Ellie wondered if she was still asleep and dreaming – if the scent was something conjured by her imagination. She forced herself to move, levering her arms into action, turning over in the bed, she reached for the switch on the bedside lamp.

Light filled the room. The scent vanished.

Ellie sat up in bed. It had disappeared without trace. She sniffed, trying to catch it again, even the merest hint. Had it been a dream? Could you dream smells? Was that possible? She couldn't remember having done so before. People didn't usually feel physical pain in dreams either. Someone can hit you or stick a knife in you during a dream and you don't feel a thing. Feelings, though – emotional pain, terror, loss, grief – oh yes, you could feel those . . . She remembered her weeks of bad dreams when her mother was sick, all the nightmares of loss when she'd died.

So had Ellie dreamed this too?

The clock ticked quietly on the cabinet beside the lamp.

21

It was just after midnight. Ellie thought she'd been asleep for a long time but in fact, it had only been an hour. She turned off the light.

Outside the house, in the street below her window, people walked by. She heard a loud, jovial male voice, probably someone on their way home from the pub.

On the table the model theatre glimmered. Its sharp edges – roof, columns, proscenium arch – glistened as though someone had painted them in silver.

Ellie heard a sound like a sigh. The pile of papers – script, photograph, postcard and the rest – slid from the table and landed with a crash onto the floor.

Her heart beat hard, the blood tingled in her veins. She felt a slow, icy prickle over her skin, on the soles of her bare feet, the backs of her legs, her fingers, her scalp.

She waited, not daring to move, eyes fixed on the ceiling, taking slow, shallow breaths. Time passed. She counted to a hundred, and then a hundred again. Nothing else happened. Nothing moved.

The moon had passed from the window now, taking its light away, making the theatre a mass of shadows.

Ellie turned on her light a second time and climbed out of bed. She grabbed her dressing gown, wrapped it around her and then picked up the fallen papers from the floor. Why had they fallen? A draught, maybe. She hadn't put them on the table with enough care and they'd overbalanced. No use letting her imagination run away with her. In the real world, only ordinary things happened.

Ellie put the pile on the table, more carefully this time, further from the edge, and returned to bed. Just as she was about to climb in, she noticed her journal, lying open on the other side of the bedside lamp.

She was sure she hadn't left it open. The book was too private, too precious to leave open, even in her bedroom. The journal was her secret place, her one true companion.

Now it was open and exposed. Her old fountain pen, a long-ago gift from her father, lay across the book, top off, a drop of ink glistening on the golden nib.

Ellie pulled her dressing gown tight around her, folded her arms, and slowly crouched down. The paper was bare, except for two short sentences written across the top of the left-hand page, the ink drying even as she read it. No mistaking the handwriting: the bold, archaic style, the strong returning loop on the 'f'. She'd seen it before, on the script for *Romeo and Juliet*.

'*You are beautiful,*' it said. '*What is your name?*'

5

'Your grandmother tells me you're joining the theatre group. I'm so pleased. It'll do you the world of good.'

Ellie flinched. She and her grandfather were sitting in the back garden, in the dappled shade of the fig tree, drinking cups of strong coffee. The sun-heated air smelled of rosemary and lavender.

Her grandfather had worked in the local authority's planning department before he retired. Now he was a volunteer warden at the town museum two days a week, a keen gardener, and carrying out research for a local history book.

'I haven't joined,' she said. 'I'm just going to a meeting.' She realised how sharp her voice sounded, so she drew a breath and added in a more amiable tone, 'I'll check it out – see what it's like.'

Her grandfather nodded slowly. 'Excellent idea,' he said. Ellie picked up a section of the newspaper lying on the garden table. He was looking at her and she knew what he was thinking because he'd said it so many times before: that she looked like her mother, that she reminded him of her. Occasionally, absent-mindedly, he called her by her mother's name.

In one way she liked this. In another way – well, she was Ellie, her own distinct self. She didn't want to be a walking memorial to someone who'd died. Then why come and spend the summer in Lyme-on-Sea, asked a nagging internal voice. Because I had no choice, she thought. There is always a choice, the voice nagged again. Of course you had a choice.

'Are you okay?' her grandfather asked, putting his paper on the table. 'What're you thinking about? You look quite cross.'

'Oh, no, I'm fine,' she said. Everything seemed to irritate her these days. 'I mean, thanks for asking.' She picked up her coffee and rose to her feet. 'I'm going inside. It's too hot out here.'

She sensed his gaze. She knew her grandparents worried. From time to time her grandma would initiate some kind of conversation about Ellie's life, her future, her mother – and Ellie would always refuse to respond. They wanted her to open up, share her feelings, seek closure, find a way forward – and all those other fake, annoying things people said. Of course they meant well, but Ellie wasn't going to be badgered into anything. She'd deal with things her own way.

Now though – well, something else had happened.

Something huge, and strange, and utterly impossible. Someone had written in her journal.

She walked through the house and up the stairs to her room. The theatre looked smaller this morning, less significant in the bright sunlight, colours faded. She scarcely glanced at it. Instead she slid her hand under her pillow and drew out the journal. She flipped through the pages. There it was – the sentence she'd read a hundred times.

You are beautiful. What is your name?

Even after so many readings, the words gave her a rush of intense feeling. Shock, yes. And affront, because her most personal space (bedroom, journal) had been invaded; fear, because the source of this message was unknown – and a terrible, dizzying pleasure, to be told she was beautiful.

She'd run through so many explanations for what had happened. The most likely was this: overwrought with emotion, she'd written the message in her sleep. One part of her mind clung to this rational analysis. Another louder part knew this wasn't true. She hadn't written the message, asleep or awake.

Someone had been in the room with her. She'd felt his presence.

It was Harry.

Harry.

The boy in the photograph, who'd written on the script for *Romeo and Juliet* in 1896. And he was dead.

Of course all this was impossible, but nonetheless it was true.

Ellie read the message again. *You are beautiful.* Beautiful. No one had told her she was beautiful before, except her mother – and what mother doesn't think her child is beautiful?

Still holding the journal, Ellie stood in front of her mirror, trying to see what Harry could see. She narrowed her eyes. Her first emotion was displeasure. Was that the same for everyone? Some uncomfortable difference between what she thought she looked like and the reality in the mirror.

So. Moderate height, slender, boyish build. Tiny chest (she wished it were larger), long brown hair the colour of dark chocolate, blue eyes and pale skin. Too pale, she thought, prone to looking grey and transparent when she was tired or fragile; bluish shadows under her eyes, occasional outbreaks of spots on her forehead, which she hated. Elfin face with high cheekbones, pointed chin and slanting eyebrows. From time to time she wondered if this made her look exotic. Mostly she thought she looked odd. Was that why Alex had said she had the appearance of a fairy queen? Ellie shook her head and frowned. She'd lost it, her attempt to be objective. She could only see the individual flaws, not the overall picture.

Certainly she'd never felt beautiful – only gawky and awkward. She was eighteen now, officially an adult, but this seemed like a trick. How could she be grown up? She had no particular sense of style, no strong feeling about who she was. Shouldn't that have happened by now?

Having failed to find beauty, Ellie abandoned the mirror. She flopped onto the bed and gazed at the writing in her journal.

What is your name?

She picked up the fountain pen, unscrewed the top, and wrote: *Eloise Winterson. People call me Ellie. Are you Harry?*

She felt foolish, and excited. She closed the journal and stowed it back under her pillow.

*   *   *

Baked fish and mashed potato for tea, with a bowl of salad from the garden. Fresh fish from the town's fishermen, tasty and salty, sweetened with tomato, a melted cheese topping. Her grandparents talked about the birds they'd seen in the garden. Her grandfather told them about an old railway line into the town, now vanished, that he'd read about in his researches.

Ellie found it hard to concentrate. She ate her dinner absent-mindedly, paying scant attention to them. The world was one step away. Her mind played over and over the events of the previous night, the perfume filling her room, the boy's commanding eyes staring from the photograph, the moist ink in her journal. Would he return this evening? Would he answer her question?

'Ellie. Ellie? Isn't it time you left?'

'What?'

'The meeting. Didn't you say it was half past seven? You'd better go now or you'll be late. Don't worry, Grandpa and I can clear up.'

The theatre group. She'd forgotten all about it.

'Oh. I don't think I'll go. Really, I'm not that keen.'

She saw a look pass between her grandparents. Her grandma took a deep breath and straightened up. 'Really, Ellie, I think you should go. Didn't you say you'd told Alex you'd give it a try? You can't let people down like that. You've spent far too much time on your own. I'm sure you'd enjoy it.'

Ellie noticed a flicker of something in her grandmother's face. Hurt and worry. She didn't know how her granddaughter would react to this galvanising speech. Everyone treated Ellie gently now.

She scowled, wanting to hide away in her bedroom and wait for the night, but her grandparents were looking at her, wanting to push her out into the world.

'Sure, I'll go. Anything to keep you off my back,' she said ungraciously. Her grandmother flinched. Ellie knew she sounded like a stroppy thirteen-year-old but hated being bullied. She stood up, leaving her plate on the table, and stomped out of the house, slamming the door behind her.

Fresh air, a sky of scarlet and gold. Ellie paused on the doorstep, breathed deeply. Despite herself, she was enjoying the touch of the cool air on her face. It *was* good to be outside. Streamers of cloud spun away from the declining sun. Light shone on the roof tiles, on angled walls of pastel blue and pink and the golden weathervane on the church steeple. A seagull, white-breasted, swooped above her head and landed on the narrow road in front of her. Well, the meeting would pass the time, wouldn't it?

An illuminated stained-glass sign above an archway announced: Marine Theatre. Beyond the archway, a large courtyard overlooked the ocean and led to the theatre itself, right above the seafront. One long-ago summer holiday Ellie had attended a workshop here, with twenty other children, making mermaid and pirate costumes. This memory surfaced as she passed through the door and into the gloomy interior, which smelled of dust and beer.

Posters on the wall advertised forthcoming concerts by tribute bands and almost-forgotten pop stars from the seventies and eighties. Although the door was open, the place was quiet. Ellie wondered if she'd made a mistake. Had the meeting been cancelled? She pushed hesitantly at the door into the main auditorium and stepped inside.

Nobody. It was not an inviting place. A plain stage, with tired, mauve curtains and rows of plastic seats.

'Excuse me – are you here for the meeting?'

Ellie whipped round. A girl was standing at the entrance to the auditorium.

'Uh, yes. Have I come at the wrong time? I was told seven thirty.'

The girl smiled. Her face seemed to twinkle, making her very appealing. She was about Ellie's age and remarkably pretty, with smooth, bright blonde hair (probably dyed) and big brown eyes.

'The meeting's upstairs, in one of the little rooms. It's cosier up there, and we've got a kettle so we can have coffees. And I brought cakes. Meetings are so boring. We wanted this one to be fun. My name's Daisy, by the way. You're Ellie aren't you?' Daisy chattered on as she led the way upstairs. She was short and curvy, dressed in a little candy pink dress with lime green leggings and a flowery cardigan. She had half a dozen brightly coloured plastic clips in her hair, all sorts of quirky bangles and a necklace made of lemon yellow silk flowers. Ellie felt decidedly shabby and dull in comparison.

'Here we are! Come in – I'll introduce you to everyone.'

Ellie felt a moment's shyness when she stepped into the room. A dozen unknown faces turned to look at her. Everyone stopped talking. Then she saw Alex at the back of the room, sitting on a table with another girl. He gave

Ellie a big, warm smile. What a relief, to see his known, friendly face.

'Great to see you, Ellie. I'm so glad you've come!' He stood up and gave her an enormous, unexpected hug, then backed away. 'You've met Daisy? She's a dream, you know. A complete star.' Alex gave Daisy's arm a brief squeeze and she grinned back at him.

'Everybody! This is Ellie!' Daisy said. 'Will you have a cupcake? I made them myself. It's another of my summer projects. What do you think? The rose ones are my favourites, but my mum reckons the black and white ones are more original.'

It was hard to get a word in edgeways. Ellie didn't speak, only followed Daisy to some old but comfy-looking armchairs, all mismatched and crowded about a low table. Mugs of tea and coffee surrounded a large china plate where a dozen gloriously colourful cupcakes waited.

'You made these?' Ellie marvelled, breaking into Daisy's stream of talk. 'Wow, they're amazing.'

Daisy blushed with pleasure. 'Oh, I want to do better,' she said modestly, looking at the toes of her cute pink shoes. 'Try one – please. And d'you want tea or coffee?'

Ellie picked up a cupcake decorated with black and white stripes while Daisy made her a hot drink. The other people in the room had resumed their conversations, though Ellie knew she was still an object of interest. From time to time someone would glance over. How much did they know about her? Would they ask difficult questions, or be embarrassed? More often than not, it was the latter. Even after a year and a half no one outside her family dared ask her anything about the loss of her mother. It was too hard to deal with grief. Too scary and dangerous. At times, during the last year at school, she'd felt like a leper, as though she had a brand on her forehead – D for death. The other girls had drawn away. Her only real friend had moved to sixth form at a private school, and when Ellie's mum's condition spiralled, Ellie hadn't had the time or energy to maintain the connection or make new friends. She'd spent a lot of time alone.

A tall, skinny man of about twenty-five called the meeting to order. Ellie scanned the rest of the group. They looked to be about her own age.

'Thanks for coming along this evening. Most of you know me, but for those who don't,' a glance at Ellie, 'my name's Mike and I'm producing and directing the play this summer. We've secured some funding from the town council and a charity supporting youth summer projects, and we're all set to start rehearsals. First I'd like everyone to introduce themselves – tell us something about yourself, and why you're here.'

The introductions began. Most of them were locals and knew each other already, judging by the laughter and teasing. Two lads, who'd come together, were also new to the group, and a girl of about sixteen, the youngest. Carly was painfully shy and very overweight. Mike had to ask her to repeat her name three times before she spoke loudly enough to be heard.

Then Daisy introduced herself. How pretty she was, with her big wide eyes and narrow chin, cherry-coloured lipstick applied to her perfect lips.

'You now, Ellie.'

Daisy had finished and squeezed Ellie's arm reassuringly.

Ellie hesitated. She was the centre of attention. Everyone was silent, waiting for her to speak.

'I'm Ellie,' she said. 'I'm spending some time with my grandparents before I go to university. Well, if I get my grades. They live in the town. I've been coming here every summer so I know the place pretty well.' She spoke in a rush, wanting to get it over with.

Mike nodded. 'Welcome, Ellie. So, why have you come along tonight?' He was a bit irritating, she thought, with his down-with-the-kids manner. She decided to be blunt.

'Alex asked me.' She shrugged, her voice flat. 'That's it.'

Mike nodded encouragingly and waited a moment longer, giving her an opportunity to share. When she didn't respond, he moved on to the next person.

Once the introductions were over, Mike plonked a large canvas bag on the table, drew out scripts and handed them round.

A Midsummer Night's Dream. Ellie had seen it on the television, the one with Rupert Everett as Oberon, King of the Fairies, and Michelle Pfeiffer as his Queen Titania. She'd watched it with her mum, and they'd loved it, the atmosphere of magic, the strangeness of the fairies. This happy memory carried in its tail, as they so often did now, the sting of loss. She wished her mum was alive to share the adventure of the play, to sit in the audience and watch the final performance. *Stop it*, she admonished herself. She was feeling sorry for herself in advance, and they hadn't even started rehearsals.

'This session I'd like to hear you all reading, and then I'll decide who gets which part,' Mike said. 'Try not to be self-conscious. I'd just like to get some idea of your voice, your presence. Would everyone stand up please?'

So they all read. Some were better than others. Several struggled with the language. Daisy giggled. Then it was Ellie's turn. She thought she did okay. Alex was confident and funny, as Ellie would have expected. The surprise performance came from Carly. She'd been so shy when she'd introduced herself, but armed with the script, everything changed. She stood up straight, threw back her shoulders, and read with a clear, sensuous voice.

The atmosphere in the room completely altered. Everyone was mesmerised, caught up in the voice and the words. Carly lowered the script, and seeing everyone staring, she returned to her old self, rounding her shoulders, dropping back into her seat. A moment of silence – then Mike jumped in.

'Wow, that was great, Carly, really special. You've got a talent, no doubt about it. Good stuff! Right – who's next?'

The meeting finished at ten. They spilled out of the theatre into a chilly, clear night of brilliant stars, the sea spreading darkly to the horizon. Ellie could hear the waves breaking over and over on the pebbled shore. She thought of the name written in her journal. *Harry*. Harry who thought she was beautiful. A tremor of something, pain and pleasure, passed through her body.

'Fancy a drink?' Alex stood beside her, by the wall, over-looking the sea. 'A few of us are going to the beach.'

34

Daisy stepped forward, slipping her arm through Ellie's. 'Oh, do come.' She blinked, fluttering her lush, made-up eyelashes. Some part of Ellie wanted to run home, to her room, to check her journal, to find out if the events of the previous night had been created by her disturbed imagination. (Of course they had, what was she thinking? A ghost? Don't be an idiot.) Out in the fresh air, after the unexpected pleasure of the meeting, and the hours distracted from her thoughts, the possibility of a ghost seemed stupid, a moment of madness.

'How can I resist?' she said. Daisy grinned happily, looped her other arm through Alex's and guided them along the front to a quiet end of the beach. Several people were already there. Two girls were standing at the water's edge, dodging the waves and shrieking with laughter.

'Come on,' Alex called to them. 'We're going further along the beach, the other side of the harbour.'

They were a lively bunch, about twelve altogether, some from the meeting as well as those they'd collected on the beach. They all seemed to know each other, with much teasing and laughing and sharing of old jokes. But Ellie didn't feel like too much of an outsider as Daisy's arm was still looped through hers and she kindly introduced her to the others.

The beach beyond the harbour, beyond the reach of the lights on the promenade, was a wilder place, with great mounds of pebbles with seaweed strewn over, the wooded cliff rising behind them like the wall of a ruined fortress. A big bright moon dusted the place with light, though occasionally rags of cloud would pass across its face, casting them into a deeper darkness. The waves seemed bigger too, this side of the harbour wall. They crashed onto the pebbles, rushed back with a hollow roar, then crashed again. Ellie felt a thrill of excitement. Some of the boys started building a fire with pieces of driftwood and dried seaweed. Soon flames rose up, red and gold in the night, wood crackling as it burned. Alex returned to Ellie and Daisy and handed each of them a can of beer. The three of them sat on the pebbles, Daisy hugging her arms around her legs.

'So, how long have you two known each other?' Ellie said.

'Oh, a long time. We went to the same school,' Daisy beamed. Ellie studied them, envying how relaxed they were together. Were they an item?

'He's my best friend,' Daisy added, glancing at Alex and patting his arm. 'I love him to bits.'

Best friend. Not going out then. Ellie felt a tiny bit relieved. She didn't want to be a gooseberry, did she?

'So, what did you think?' Alex said. 'You going to be in the play?' He took a mouthful of beer, keeping his eyes on her.

'If I get a part, yes. Why not? That Mike guy is a bit annoying, but the rest of the group seem pretty cool. And that girl Carly – wasn't she a surprise? D'you know her?'

Alex shook his head. 'Nope. Don't think she's a local. Maybe a visitor, like you. A lot of students come and stay here for the summer, getting holiday jobs for the high season. We should have invited her along for a drink.' He nudged Daisy. They're kind people, these two, Ellie thought.

'It did cross my mind, but she slipped away,' Daisy said. 'Maybe next time.'

They were silent for a moment. Ellie took a sip from her can, enjoying the fresh fizz on her tongue.

'Are you enjoying your stay?' Alex said. 'It must be difficult, coming back to your mum's home town.' He and Daisy both looked at her. She knew what they were thinking. Alex had offered her an opportunity to talk. Ellie's guard went up.

'I'm having a great time. And this theatre group – well, I think it's going to be interesting. Thanks for inviting me along.'

'My pleasure,' Alex said, raising his beer in a toast.

The drink started taking effect. Daisy dragged Ellie to her feet and they climbed over the banks of pebbles and down to the sea's edge. Spray from the waves landed on their faces and hair. Daisy walked precariously in her little shoes, teetering like an ungainly bird as pebbles shifted under her feet. The girls shrieked with laughter. Ellie glanced back. Some of the boys were feeding larger pieces of wood into the fire. The flames rose up, sending sparks into the sky. Someone shouted out and the others laughed.

Ellie picked up a pebble and flung it into the sea. She didn't see where it landed. It disappeared into night, and the greater blackness of the water. Daisy scooped up another stone and did the same. She threw awkwardly, unbalanced and dropped onto her bottom.

'Are you okay?' Ellie asked. But Daisy was laughing. Ellie helped her back to her feet.

'I'm fine. But my leggings are wet and I'm getting cold. I'll ask Alex if I can borrow his jacket.' She hobbled back up the beach, glancing back at Ellie, expecting her to follow. But Ellie lingered a moment, staring out at the wild sea, the waves with their froth of foam.

Another shred of cloud covered the moon, blotting out the pale light. Ellie shivered, wrapping her arms around herself. She glanced over her shoulder all of a sudden, thinking one of the others had come to join her – she had a sense of someone behind her. No, she was alone at the sea's edge. She tensed her shoulders. It was getting cold. The wind pulled at her hair.

She looked around again, still feeling a presence, as though someone was staring at her – perhaps one of the boys, buoyed up by drink, checking her out? But they were all up by the fire. Ellie glanced to left and right. She was alone. Nonetheless she called out, in a low voice, 'Hello?'

Silence, except for the waves. Ellie edged back, towards the others, peering through the dark. A cloud of smoke drifted from the fire and engulfed her. Ellie blinked, her eyes stinging. She stopped, waving her hand in front of her face.

'Ellie?' Someone said her name aloud. The smoke cleared. She saw the fortress cliff with its fringe of ancient woodland looming over, and the lights of the town, seemingly far away.

Cloud passed from moon and silver light rained on the beach, making a shining path on the sea. Where were the others? She turned around, disorientated, trying to see where they were, momentarily afraid. Which of them had called her name?

'Daisy?' she said. A pebble slid beneath her foot and she fell, as Daisy had. A stone bruised the bottom of her spine and she squeaked in pain. She glanced up – a figure above her. One of the boys come to help? A beam of moonlight brushed against his face, painting in pale skin, a straight nose, shadowed eyes, a mouth of strong, sensuous curves. This arresting face moved forward and she looked into intense eyes, a gaze that seemed to scorch through her, through skin and bone into her heart. She held her breath . . .

The face disappeared. She blinked. It had lasted a single moment. Had she imagined it? A trick of smoke, moonlight and imagination? Now she could see no one. As she scrambled to her feet, the fire became visible again beyond a bank of pebbles. The other party-goers were sitting beside it in twos and threes. Daisy was on her feet, donning Alex's jacket.

'Ellie? Is that you? You okay?' he called out.

'I'm coming,' she called back. 'It's cold!'

What had she seen? Ellie welcomed the warmth and normality of the gathering by the fire. Her pulse was racing. That face. She'd seen it before. Was it . . .?

'Sit by me!' Daisy said, breaking into her thoughts. Ellie shook her head to clear it. The strangeness of the moment passed. She was stressed, overtired and imagining things. She took her place with Daisy and Alex and took another swig of beer.

*   *   *

Ellie got home at midnight. She ran all the way up the hill to her grandparents' house. She'd had a second beer and felt the tiniest bit intoxicated.

'Ellie, is that you?' Her grandmother, Jean, was standing on the stairs, wrapped in a red silk dressing gown, white hair cascading voluptuously over her shoulders. Ellie blinked. It wasn't right for someone so old to look quite so alluring.

'You shouldn't have waited up,' Ellie said. 'You don't have to worry about me. I am eighteen, now.'

'I'll always worry about you, even when you're forty,' Jean said. She tipped her head to one side. 'You had a good time? You look like it.'

'Yes,' Ellie nodded. 'We've got another meeting tomorrow. It was good.'

She ran upstairs. Jean backed into the doorway of her bedroom, but Ellie stopped to give her a hug before continuing up to the attic room.

Ellie stopped outside her door. At the meeting with Daisy and Alex, the events of the previous night had seemed absurd – perhaps the result of her own mind and overheated feelings. Now, standing on the threshold, she remembered the flood of scent, the ink drying on the page in her journal and the awareness – so intense – of a presence in her room. She felt a swimming in her legs and stomach. She closed her eyes, afraid and at the same time wanting – wanting what?

The image of the boy's face floated into her mind: Harry. Had she conjured him up on the beach too? The boy in the photograph she'd glimpsed only briefly. Was it wish-fulfilment? Perhaps her mind had painted him on the elements of night.

What *did* she want? Nothing made sense. Was she losing her mind? She leaned her head against the door, pressed the palms of her hands against the wood. She could hear her pulse, the drumming of blood in her ears, behind her eyes, in the tips of her fingers. What lay beyond the door? Who was there?

With shaking hand, she reached for the handle, which was smooth and oddly warm. She turned it, and slowly pushed the door open.

Darkness. A flutter of white at the window, air touching her face. The window, Ellie thought. It's only the curtain blowing. Someone had opened the window. She stepped inside and turned on the light.

The room looked disconcertingly normal. The bed had been made, clothes picked up from the floor and folded – her grandmother, no doubt. Ellie pulled out the journal from under her pillow. Harry's writing (or was it her own?) and then the question she'd left: nothing else. She felt a plunging disappointment. What exactly had she been expecting? Ellie closed the window. Like an automaton, she went down to the bathroom, cleaned her face and brushed her teeth. Then she put on her pyjamas and climbed into bed.

Ellie lay in the dark. The shadowed walls seemed to lean. Was she more tipsy than she'd thought? She closed her eyes.

A moment later, she opened them again. The scent. She could smell it. Ellie trembled. Her mouth was dry.

She swallowed, but otherwise kept still, afraid to move. A whisper of perfume – not the overwhelming tide of the previous night – a mere thread of scent that teased her nose.

She wanted to speak, but didn't dare.

The journal lay on her bedside table. Had he answered her question?

She longed to look, but didn't dare do that either.

Something crashed on the floor. Ellie's heart leaped into her mouth. She gripped her duvet, pressing deeper into the mattress, trying to hide. Minutes passed. Nothing more happened. Her fear cooled. Ellie counted to ten then sat up in bed. She turned on the bedside light.

The *Romeo and Juliet* script lay scattered on the floor – again. She reached for the journal. Beneath her question, something new had been written.

Eloise. Ellie. You have a lovely face.

You know who I am.

I want to talk to you, Ellie.

I've woken up. I have waited a long time.

6

Ellie sat outside the café. It was nine, too early for the crowds of holidaymakers. She had a cappuccino and a half-eaten croissant. Her journal lay open in front of her, and she was writing up the events of the previous evening, the meeting at the theatre, her second encounter with Harry.

I have waited a long time.

Had he been waiting for *her*? The note implied as much. She hadn't managed to sleep after this second visitation. Once she'd read the note, written in the same archaic handwriting, the tension in the room disappeared. The perfume faded. Ellie lay awake a long time, trying to get comfortable and to sleep. But she had too many questions running through her mind.

Who was Harry? How could they talk?

At seven, she got up, dressed and went for a walk along the beach. She had the place to herself, except for the gulls, and a single cormorant drying its black wings in the early sunshine.

She wanted to share this adventure with someone, but didn't know who to tell. Her grandmother? Daisy or Alex?

They would think she was mad, wouldn't they? Even if she showed them the writing in her journal, they wouldn't believe her. Anyway, another part of her wanted to keep it close, this strange, unsettling happening. She was afraid the adventure would vanish if she shared it – exorcised, perhaps, by an obvious, rational explanation. If she opened the lid, exposed her ghost to others, maybe she'd lose the extraordinary intensity of the experience. It might be spoiled.

So, who was Harry? What was he like? She drew out the family photograph and stared at it.

'How do I talk to you?' she said aloud. 'Tell me what I have to do.'

The photograph stared back at her. Harry wasn't helpful.

'Ellie?'

She pushed the photograph between the pages of her journal and closed it up. Daisy was standing in front of her.

'Oh, I'm sorry, are you busy? Shall I leave you to it?'

'No, no. It's okay, honestly. You surprised me, that's all. Please, sit down. Can I get you a coffee?' Ellie didn't want Daisy to go. She'd spent such a long time alone these last months, and she'd enjoyed the party on the beach with Daisy, Alex and the others. She'd forgotten how nourishing good company could be.

'I'll have a latte. With lots of sugar.' Daisy smiled and sat down. Ellie dashed inside to the counter, now unaccountably afraid Daisy might run away and leave her on her own.

They talked for an hour. Daisy had finished her A levels too, and had a part-time job at another café in the town, serving cream teas, coffees and cakes to tourists. She told Ellie she wasn't sure what she wanted to do next. She had nothing lined up.

'I love cooking,' she said. 'I'd be quite happy carrying on where I am for a bit. I've got a whole lot more I want to learn.'

They finished their drinks. Daisy said, 'I'm going to the Marine Theatre. I have to start thinking about costumes. D'you want to come?'

They walked along the seafront. Now holidaymakers thronged the path. The sea glittered and the air carried the scent of frying chips. Seagulls perched on lamp posts. Families crowded the single sandy beach by the harbour. Ellie felt a rush of pleasure, to see it all, and to feel the sunshine on her face. Daisy smiled and slid an arm through hers.

'You're cool, Ellie,' she said. 'I'm glad we're friends.'

It was strange walking beside Daisy. She was so cute and colourful, with all her quirky clothes and accessories. People looked at her as they went by. A couple of boys grinned and one, having passed, shouted something incomprehensible. Ellie felt dowdy in comparison. She always dressed simply and today was no different: skinny black jeans, white T-shirt, no make-up. Her only adornment was a plain silver ring her mother had given her.

The theatre was open. Half a dozen young teenagers were hanging around outside, two of them messing about on skateboards in the courtyard. Ellie heard rock music from inside. Some kind of kids' summer holiday activity was going on.

'Can we go in?' Ellie asked.

'Sure, don't worry.'

A long-haired young man in a tie-dyed T-shirt shouted out something to the kids outside, perhaps calling them in. Daisy chatted to him briefly, and he gestured them into the auditorium.

The interior of the theatre was even less appealing in the daytime: an anonymous place – beige, tatty and plastic. Ellie surveyed it without pleasure.

'How are we going to make this place magical?' she said. 'Impossible.'

'We'll think of something,' Daisy said. She sat on one of the seats in the middle of the auditorium, took out a sketch-pad and pen, and stared thoughtfully ahead of her. Ellie mooched to the front and clambered onto the stage. Purple nylon curtains hung to left and right. In the wings she found storage cupboards full of props and stale-smelling costumes from various amateur productions. Some steps led down into a floor beneath the auditorium.

Ellie looked back. She could still see Daisy, all alone in the sea of seats, head down, focused on her sketch. The rock music had stopped. She couldn't hear the skateboarders either, though distantly, through some unseen open window, came the sound of the sea.

She looked again at the stairs. Ellie wondered if it was right to go poking about without permission but she felt nosy. She wanted to explore. With a final glance at Daisy, she grasped the banister and stepped lightly down.

A hallway with doors to left and right, dimly lit by a single electric bulb. This part of the theatre was older than the auditorium and the front of house. She saw flaking pale green walls, ornamental plaster mouldings on the ceiling painted over and over with layers of paint. Two carved wooden faces on either side of the arch at the bottom of the stairs – covered in thick, gloss paint, making the features indistinct – and the unmistakable smell of damp.

Five doors, two on either side and one ahead. She tried the first door to her left – a room full of junk, reels of plastic-covered electrical cable, broken lights, an old water cooler. The second door opened onto a cupboard full of brooms, mops and cleaning chemicals. The third was locked, and the fourth. The last door revealed an odd-shaped room, with a sloping ceiling and a single tiny window, like a lozenge, high up on the far wall. The window was open. Was this how she'd heard the sea?

Ellie stepped inside. The door closed behind her and the sound of the sea grew louder, as though the waves were just beneath the window. Nothing in here – just a stained, sticky carpet under her feet, walls panelled with dark wood and more plaster mouldings painted almost to obliteration. Nothing to stay for – but she stayed. Why was that? The perfume of damp was stronger here – dust, decaying plaster, stone and earth. And something else. Her body reacted before she realised what it was.

A wave of heat rose from the pit of her belly, burning through her limbs. She started to tremble.

A scent, floating on the air – the mellow-sweet resinous smell that had flooded her bedroom these two nights past.

'Harry?' she said aloud, without thinking. 'Harry?' Her voice sounded noisy and out of place. She turned around suddenly, afraid someone might be standing behind her. No one there. The door was shut. She whipped round again, to face the little window, then back slowly to the side of the room.

'Harry?' she whispered. The fragile perfume disappeared. Ellie took a deep breath. Had she imagined it?

A thunderous bang on the door.

Ellie's heart missed a beat. She jumped away.

'Ellie? Ellie where are you?'

Ellie pulled the door open, onto darkness. Daisy stood outside, just visible in the gloom.

'Are you okay? What are you doing? Did you see what happened?' She was pale and breathless.

'I'm fine,' Ellie said. 'I was just, well, having a look round. What's the matter?' Her voice was calm but her pulse raced.

Daisy took her hand and pulled her out of the room, up the stairs and onto the stage. The auditorium was also dark.

'What happened to the lights?' They stood side by side, staring out into space. A faint dusting of daylight leaked in through the two sets of open doors at the back of the room and brushed the tops of the seats. They could hear loud voices and complaints from elsewhere in the building, the holiday activity kids evidently power-cut too.

'It was dead weird,' Daisy said. 'The wind seemed to cut through the room, and then the lights went out.' She shivered. 'And then, just after, I heard something on the stage.

48

I thought it was you. Like an actor – reading something from Shakespeare. Was that you?'

The lights came on. Someone cheered from beyond the auditorium.

Daisy shivered again, playfully this time. Light restored, the episode had become a pleasurable adventure.

'I was a little bit scared,' she said, widening her eyes. 'Weren't you?'

Ellie shook her head. 'I didn't notice the power cut. I don't think the light was on in the room anyway.'

Daisy looked over her shoulder. 'So what was down there?'

Ellie shrugged. 'Storage. You've never explored this place?'

'I've never been here before. Well, except to see shows. Never backstage.'

'Come and see.' Ellie led the way back down the stairs. Daisy peered into doorways. Ellie went straight to the crooked room with the little window. The place was ordinary now: no sense of a presence. She noticed dust on the skirting boards, the tatty carpet and old panelling. Something had changed. What was it? She ran her hand along the wall, taking slow steps, intrigued. There – that was it. On the right hand wall the panelling had separated from the wall. Ellie pushed it gently. The wood shifted. She pushed a little harder. The panel gave a little bounce then popped open.

Ellie was worried and intrigued. Had she broken something? She pulled the loose panel away and found a small, white door with an ornate metal handle. She held the handle and tugged, but the door didn't budge. A small keyhole winked underneath.

'Ellie? Where are you?' Daisy stepped into the room. 'What are you doing?'

'A door. Look – behind the panelling.'

Daisy too tried to open it. 'We need the key,' she said. 'Mind you, if the door's been blocked off it's not exactly likely to lead anywhere.'

'No,' Ellie said. She replaced the panelling, hiding their discovery. She had to find that key.

7

Ellie dreamed of Harry. She lay on the cool grass in the garden, eyes closed, arm covering her face, while the sun soaked into her body. She wasn't asleep: she could hear the sound of the stream beneath the garden, the distant cries of the seagulls and the occasional quiet murmur from her grandparents, talking in the kitchen. Neither was she entirely in the real world. She drifted off into long flights of fantasy, Harry's written words floating through her mind.

You have a lovely face.

I have waited a long time.

She drew him in her imagination, playing Mercutio in *Romeo and Juliet* so many years before. What would his voice sound like?

Her imagination didn't need precise details. She knew it was crazy to be obsessing about someone she hadn't even spoken to but the painful pleasure of it, the fantasy, this longing, was too delicious to stop.

I want to talk with you, Ellie.

He'd seen her. He'd thought she was beautiful. So her thoughts revolved, conjuring up scenes in which they met, or walked together. She imagined him wrapping his arms around her, this mysterious man who'd singled her out. No doubt the lack of tangible information made it easier to build these fantasies. In her mind, Harry was beautiful and perfect.

Would he return tonight?

She'd written a new question: *How can we talk? What must I do?*

'Ellie – dinner's ready,' her grandmother called through the back door. Ellie had pins and needles in her arm and her neck ached. She sat up slowly, rolling her head to loosen the muscles. The sun was lower, filling the garden with pale golden light.

'Are you're out again this evening?' Jean asked. Fish pie for dinner, served with crisp green beans from the garden. Ellie ate greedily, realising she'd had no breakfast or lunch, too preoccupied to notice hunger.

'Yes,' she nodded, with her mouth full. 'We'll find out what parts we'll be playing.'

'Oh, how exciting! I'm sure you'll get something good. Queen of the Fairies, maybe. Yes, proud Titania! You have the look. And they'll have spotted your talent.'

'Sure, Grandma.' Ellie frowned at her plate, pleased and embarrassed at once. She was the only grandchild, and understood all too well that her grandmother was far from impartial. Ellie was less confident about the impression she'd made.

She helped her grandfather wash up. He chatted about goings-on in the town but Ellie's attention wandered. She thought about the meeting, but most of all, she thought about Harry. How could she find out more about him?

'Grandpa,' she interrupted. 'You know your local history stuff? How could I find out about people who used to live in the town a hundred years ago?'

He was surprised by this sudden interest and lifted his hands from the washing-up bowl. 'Oh! Various ways. Census information. Church registers of baptisms, weddings, that sort of thing. And we've got several books about some of the town's Victorian characters, collections of old photos. What's this about? Is it something to do with the play?'

Ellie shrugged. 'Nothing in particular. I'm just interested.'

He rambled on about research and Ellie's attention drifted. She wanted to find out more about Harry.

Mike welcomed them into the theatre. A large Victoria sponge in a veil of caster sugar waited in the middle of the table. Daisy was sorting out mugs for tea and coffee.

'Hey, Ellie!' Alex stood up and greeted her with a hug. She sat down beside him. Glancing round the room she saw they had gained a couple of new people, two more boys, dressed in Jack Wills shirts and long shorts. Mike bustled around self-importantly then went through the long process of introductions for the benefit of the newcomers, who were spending the summer holidays working in Lyme. At this second meeting, Ellie felt like an old-hand. She wasn't the newbie anymore.

'Right, I'm sure you're all keen to know who's going to play what,' Mike said. He'd tied his hair back today, revealing a hoop earring. He drew out a typed list, pausing a moment, enjoying the suspense.

'Right,' he said again, eyeing them all. 'Shall we begin?'

Alex was given the part of Bottom, the weaver. The name alone caused hilarity. Alex stood up, grinned, bowed, and treated them to his impression of a donkey braying. Daisy ruffled his hair good-naturedly as Mike continued with the list. Daisy next – she was playing Hermia, one of the two pairs of lovers. When they came to Titania, the Fairy Queen, Ellie held her breath. She realised she did want this part, just as her grandmother had suggested.

'Carly,' Mike beamed.

A moment's stunned silence. No one cheered, as they had for Alex. Ellie felt a moment's cold, bitter disappointment. This was a surprise. Carly blushed and shrank in her seat. How could someone so shy perform this significant part? Daisy clapped her hands together, 'Oh you'll be wonderful. You read so beautifully!'

And then they recalled, all of them, how Carly had been transformed with the script in her hand. Could she take that to the stage?

Ellie's mood sank. The main parts were going, one by one. Had she read so badly the previous night? Didn't Mike rate her talents? Then, at last, he said her name.

'Ellie Winterson. Ellie – I'd like you to be Puck. Robin Goodfellow. He's the troublemaker, the mischievous fairy. He's a male character, but there's something about you – I think this could work. I think you could do wild and fey very well.'

Applause again, for her this time. Ellie's pride was restored. It was an interesting role.

Some members had more than one part. Mike explained

he'd abbreviated the play just a little. Discussions ensued about stage set and costumes. Daisy shared her first ideas and showed some sketches and Alex agreed to come up with further ideas by the next meeting. They began to read through the play, all excited and inspired. At ten thirty, Mike ushered them out with instructions to learn lines and passed round a printed rehearsal schedule. They had only four weeks to bring the production together.

'I've heard the theatre's haunted,' Warren, one of the new boys, said to Daisy. 'Is that right? My mate was here this morning. Said the lights went out and everyone was scared.'

Ellie and Daisy exchanged glances.

'They did go out,' Daisy said. 'Me and Ellie were here when it happened.'

'Blown fuse,' said Mike. 'Place like this, with all the lights and some dodgy old electrics.'

'No,' Warren shook his head. 'Nothing like that. Nobody fixed anything and the lights just came on again.'

Mike gave a wry, challenging smile. 'Power cut?' Everyone looked at him. Mike added, 'You believe in ghosts then?'

'No. Course not.' Warren grinned back, feeling foolish with everyone looking at him. The moment passed but Ellie didn't relax.

Daisy invited Carly and the two newcomers to the pub. It turned out Carly had moved to the town only a few weeks before, with her parents. She hadn't made any friends yet, so Daisy took her under her wing. They went with Alex and some of the others to The Mermaid but this time Ellie declined. Now the meeting was over, she could only think of one thing. She had to get back for Harry. Would he return tonight? She yearned to know more about him.

'I'm sorry, I'm really tired. I've got to get back.'

Daisy looked disappointed. Alex shrugged and said, 'Sure, okay.' But he reached out for her forearm, held it gently and said, 'Could we meet up tomorrow? If you've nothing else on. Come round to my place?'

'Sure,' Ellie nodded. She stepped away from him.

'Don't you want the address? Give me your mobile number, I'll text it to you. Come round in the morning. About eleven?' Alex said.

Ellie was eager to leave but she gave Alex her number and hurried off home, running past the lighted windows, the closed shops full of clothes and gifts, past the fish and chip shop with its handful of customers, and up the little hill to her grandparents' house.

Ellie dumped her bag in the hall. Her grandparents were already in bed but the light was on in their bedroom. Jean called out a goodnight as Ellie crept up the stairs.

The attic room seemed flat and ordinary. Nothing had moved. Ellie sat on the bed, still dressed, left her journal on her bedside and waited for something to happen. She'd wound herself up tight over the course of the day, building up for an encounter, adding fuel to her feelings with imagining.

An hour passed. Nothing happened. And then another hour. Her excitement drained away and was replaced by a chilly, empty misery. Ellie got ready for bed and slipped under her duvet. What had happened to Harry? This obsessing had pushed to one side any thoughts about her mother and her father but now her sense of isolation increased. Even the imaginary ghost had lost interest in her.

8

Eloise –

I have waited at the Marine Theatre for a long time. I have waited nearly a hundred years. When you set up the model theatre, you gave me a new window on the world. You woke me up. I made the theatre with my sister Violet. I hope you like it. It took a great deal of work and thought.

Seeing you, I'm greedy. I want to know more. Your family, your life. You seem sad. I haven't seen you smile. I would love to see you smile.

So, shall I tell you something about myself? My name's Harry. I'm nineteen years old. I live at North Hill House, a mile out of town, with my parents, my brother and Violet.

I followed you in the theatre – did you know? I think you did. I want you to see me. I want to talk with you. I woke up when you touched the model theatre. Perhaps if you found another of my belongings the connection would be stronger.

You will find the key in the old cabinet in the office. Look in the bottom drawer.

Harry

Ellie was sitting in bed. The journal lay on her lap. She read the letter over and over. She lingered over certain particular phrases. *You seem sad. I would love to see you smile.* She'd slept though Harry's visit. He'd come and gone – but what a trove of information he'd left. She felt excitement and intense frustration. So he was nineteen. (Or had been, when he'd died. How had that happened? How could she possibly ask that question?) She knew where he'd lived: perhaps she could find the place. And he'd confirmed what she had suspected, his presence in the theatre the day before.

It was ten already. Ellie had slept late and could hear the sound of her grandparents moving around downstairs. She ran her fingertips over the beautiful handwriting, wondering how he'd written the words. Was the pen guided by an invisible hand? Evidently he was able to manipulate objects in the material world – she thought of the papers falling from the table, the loss of power at the theatre. He'd done that too, hadn't he? Or at least, his presence had triggered it. Could he touch her? The mere thought of it made her shiver. What would that feel like, the fingers of a ghost? She ran her own fingers over the soft, bare skin of her forearm, seeing how the fine hairs stood on end. She turned her hand over and touched the silken skin between the inside of her wrist and elbow, delicately tracing the path of the turquoise veins, just beneath the surface.

Her mobile bleeped from the bedside cabinet. Ellie dropped the journal on her bed. A text from Alex. Damn, she'd forgotten she'd agreed to see him. The message, and thoughts of Harry, had driven the meeting from her mind.

Fingers hovered over the keypad. Couldn't she cancel? Make up an excuse? Ellie shook her head. No. That wouldn't do. She'd said she'd go. Ellie had a swift shower, dressed and headed out of the house. It was only ten thirty. If she was quick, there was time to drop by at the Marine Theatre and still get to Alex's place without being too late. She ran most of the way there, past slow-moving families carrying beach mats, towels and brightly coloured buckets and spades. Some of them squinted at Ellie as she hurried by.

Cars nosed slowly along the High Street, where it turned to run along the seafront. Ellie dodged between the cars at the traffic lights and, out of breath now, up the pavement, under the sign and straight to the theatre's main doors.

Which were locked. She tugged at them, cursing under her breath. Overhead, three enormous seagulls, brilliant white against the blue sky, hovered on long wings. Ellie glanced at them then pulled on the door again, hopelessly hoping it would open and allow her inside.

'It's not open.' The voice came from behind her. Ellie whipped round, embarrassed. A middle-aged man with a bulging string shopping bag was standing in the courtyard observing her.

'Oh yes, of course, I know. You see, I wasn't – well, I'm not here for the activities, I, well, I forgot something. Left it here after a meeting last night. For the youth theatre group.' She blushed. The man was about ten metres away across the courtyard, still looking at her. Why had she babbled like that?

60

'You're Sophie's girl, aren't you?' the man said. His voice was calm and level. She lifted her chin and looked directly into his clear blue eyes. The name hung on the air between them. Sophie. Her mother's name. It was the first time anyone had said it aloud . . . for how long? Her dad referred to her as Mum, her grandparents as 'your mother'.

Sophie. The word seemed to hover, like the seagulls, on the breeze.

'Yes,' she said.

The man nodded. 'You look like her,' he said. 'When I saw you – well. I used to know your mum, a long time ago.'

Ellie blinked. The man came into focus – no longer anonymously middle-aged, but someone her mother had been young with. He had tanned skin, thick grey-blond hair and deep creases beneath his eyes and around his mouth, as though he'd spent years in fierce sun and wild weather. The string bag in his hand contained brown paper bags, probably containing fruit or vegetables. A baguette protruded from the top. They stood in silence for a few moments. Then the man said, 'Aren't you seeing my son this morning?'

'Your son?'

'Alex. He said something about it.'

'Oh. Yes. I'm on my way now.'

The man twitched his head. 'I'll show you the way.'

Ellie took one last, longing look at the theatre then walked over to this man, her mum's friend, Alex's dad. He was very tall.

'I'm Joe,' he said. 'I've seen you a few times – from a

distance – when you were little and Sophie brought you down in the summer.'

But Ellie was thinking about Harry, wondering when the theatre would be open and how she could get inside. She needed to find the key to the little door behind the panel.

'So how are you enjoying your summer?'

'Oh, it's okay.' She didn't encourage the conversation and Joe didn't insist. They walked up the long hill, past the church, and then down a narrow side road. At the end stood an odd little white house in a big, rambling garden full of long grass and flowers. Joe pushed open the gate and they walked down the path to the front door of this one-storey, makeshift, higgledy-piggledy house with painted wooden walls and a porch with a bench and pots overgrown with weeds and herbs. Beyond the house, the garden fell away to the sea. Joe opened the front door.

'Alex? Ellie's here.'

Inside, the house was comfortable but untidy. They stepped into a kitchen with a low ceiling, plants flourishing on the windowsill, a large ginger cat sitting on a long wooden table in the middle of the room. Plates, cups, pieces of driftwood and various curled sketches and paintings rested on a dusty dresser at the side of the room.

Alex appeared, in ripped jeans. He cleared a space on the table, shifting the cat to one side, and laid out a breakfast of oranges, coffee, croissants, bread and butter. He didn't ask Ellie if she wanted to eat but laid a place for her anyway. Somewhere in the house, music was playing – something of Alex's?

'So, it's been some time since you last visited your grand-parents,' Joe said. 'How many years?'

'Oh, I don't know. Not that long.' For some reason this innocent question made her defensive. It was true, she hadn't spent a summer holiday here for a few years. In her early teens, the prospect of weeks by the seaside away from her friends had seemed less appealing. And then her mother had been ill, and they'd not travelled anywhere very much. The last time she'd been here was for the funeral.

Joe gave her a quick, shrewd glance then took a large knife to the baguette, cutting off three generous pieces.

'How long are you staying? And how's your dad?'

All this while Alex didn't speak, too busy shovelling a croissant into his mouth.

'Till the beginning of September, probably. My dad's in the US till then.' It hurt to think of home. She'd had so much else to think about these last days – her memories of the town, the theatre group and, most absorbing of all, the arrival of Harry. She pushed thoughts of home firmly aside, sat up straight and said, 'I might stay longer – maybe till I go to university. If I get the grades, that is.'

She took a sip of strong, steaming coffee.

'Your dad's okay?' Another level question from Joe, as he sat down and plastered butter onto his bread. 'He must have had a hell of a time.'

'My dad? Oh yes, he's fine now. He's very happy.' She couldn't hide the note of criticism in her voice.

'A hell of a time for everyone,' Joe said. 'You. Sophie's parents. How are they, by the way?' His hands were strong.

Father and son were alike, she thought, looking from one to another.

'Oh, they're fine.' She took a deep breath, not wanting to be spiky but unable to give Joe more than these most perfunctory answers.

'Come on, let's go out,' Alex said, standing up and shoving a last piece of bread and butter into his mouth. Perhaps he was embarrassed by his dad's attempts at conversation, though he didn't seem it. The two of them were very relaxed with each other.

'I'll just grab my jacket,' he added.

Ellie swallowed another mouthful of coffee and headed out with Alex, leaving Joe at the table. He lifted a hand in farewell.

'Enjoy yourselves,' he said.

A cool breeze whipped across the garden from the sea, tinkling a chime hanging outside the door. Ellie rubbed her bare arms.

'What are we going to do?' she said.

'I thought we'd go for a walk. Is that okay?'

'Sure. Can I have a look around here first? You've got a lovely place.' The garden was wild, with long, soft grass that rippled in the wind. At the back several fruit trees stood, some with acid green baby apples, others with ripening plums. A huge hedge of lilac and honeysuckle grew over an old wooden bench, where Ellie sat down, enjoying the sunshine and sheltered from the wind. Alex sat beside her.

'Where's your mum?' she asked.

'At work. At the library.'

'Your dad's not working today?'

'He's got a fishing boat, does some tourist trips and stuff. But he does all sorts of things – bit of building, some teaching at the college in term time.'

Ellie shaded her eyes and stared out across the sea. The garden offered a tremendous view across the bay. The sea glittered in the sunshine. Far out, she could see the white sail of a little yacht.

'So what about you?' Alex said. 'Tell me what happened to your mum.'

'Everyone's heard about that, haven't they?'

Alex nodded. 'Of course. She grew up here and nearly everyone knows your grandparents. So naturally, yes, people've heard.'

'And everyone's too scared to ask me about it. Except you.' She looked away from the sea towards Alex.

Alex said, 'Actually I was scared to ask you too.' He leaned back on the bench, his big body relaxed, his legs crossed one over the other. Huge brown boots on his feet, the laces undone. 'Do you mind talking about it, or do you want me to shut up?'

Ellie looked at the sea again. 'It's fine,' she said. 'What do you want to know?'

'She had cancer?'

'Yes, she did.' Ellie looked back at the sea. It wasn't so hard to talk that way. 'It all went on for a long time. She had three operations, and months of chemotherapy, but nothing worked. She got sicker and older and weaker and thinner. Bit by bit the cancer ate her up, and then a year and a half ago, she died.'

Alex didn't answer right away. For a minute or two, they sat in silence. The only sound was the breeze buffeting the trees, and the distant clink of the chimes on the house. The garden seemed suspended in the air, caught between the sweeping blue of the sky and the darker, striped blue of the sea.

'And even though this time's passed, it doesn't stop hurting. I miss her so much, I think about her so often. I feel it's marked me – and I know this sounds dramatic – it's as though I've been mutilated by her death – and everyone can see it,' Ellie said.

Alex took a deep breath.

'I don't think you need to worry so much about what people are thinking,' he said. 'You seem to worry it's the only thing people have in their minds when they meet you. I know you're living with this loss all the time, but maybe you're over-sensitive about the extent to which other people are conscious of it? Does it help to talk to me? If you talked about it more, maybe that would help.'

Now she'd started, Ellie did feel an urge to speak again. She nodded slowly and said, 'When Mum got ill, really ill, I couldn't believe it was happening. You have this idea about what your life should be like, and then something terrible happens and it just seems utterly wrong and unfair. You think – it wasn't meant to be like this. This isn't right.

'One of the strangest, hardest things is how mixed up and contradictory your feelings are. I mean, most of the time I felt so sorry for Mum. It was horrible, seeing how she suffered and how hard she tried to hide that and be cheerful for my sake. But sometimes I felt so angry with her for being sick, and how her illness totally messed up my life and took it over. And then I'd hate myself for feeling that way.'

She hadn't admitted this to anyone before: neither her father, nor her grandparents, who were themselves caught up in the drama. Perhaps the space of time or Alex's lack of involvement made him a suitable confidant. He had a special quality about him, something she'd discerned even after so short a time – calm self-possession and kindness. She knew he wouldn't judge her.

'I don't think anyone would be surprised that you'd felt that way,' Alex said.

Ellie took a deep breath. 'Shall we go on this walk, then?'

Alex stood up. 'Sure. But if you ever need to talk about it . . .'

'Yes, I know. I mean . . . thanks.'

They headed out of the town, uphill across steep fields, past grazing cattle and clumps of giant thistles, then through a patch of shady wood of pine and holly trees. They talked about easier things – the theatre group and their parts, learning lines, the rehearsals to come.

They crossed a golf course and then descended into the next bay, through another wood and field, scrambling over a stile before taking the road to the beach, where a man was selling hot drinks and snacks from a shed. Alex treated them to cups of tea and slices of flapjack. Sweating from the walk, they sat on the beach, a wild place, sand and pebbles in broad stripes. Wreaths of seaweed lay at the sea's edge. The only other visitor was a man walking a dog, away in the distance.

Neither Alex nor Ellie had spoken for a while. They munched their flapjack in silence, tired by the walk.

'So where's your dad?' Alex asked.

'In America.' Ellie took a sip of tea, burning her tongue.

'For work or pleasure?'

'Both. He gave up his job when Mum got really ill. Now he's starting up a new business. He's travelling around, seeing clients, doing some sightseeing.' She kept her voice flat, struggling to quell the emotions stirred up by the thought of her father's trip.

'That sounds great! Wow, good for him. Didn't you want to go too?'

'No!' she said.

'Why?'

'Don't you know? Everyone here seems to know everything.' Ellie felt a familiar queasy feeling in her stomach, a mix of hurt and outrage.

'Ellie,' he said gently. 'No, I don't know. Remember what I said – people aren't thinking about you half as much as you believe they are. They have their own worries.'

'Okay. I know, you're right. I didn't want to go because he's taken *her*,' she said. 'He's taken this new woman.'

'Ah,' Alex said. 'He's got a new girlfriend. You don't like her?'

'I don't like her at all. I certainly didn't want to go on holiday with them. What – playing gooseberry with my dad and this woman?'

Alex said, 'But he asked you to go?'

'Yes. They both did. Lots of times. But I didn't want to.

68

Do you think they had a right to emotionally blackmail me into going if I didn't want to?'

'No. No, of course not.' Alex touched her knee very lightly. 'You've had a horrible time. It must have been incredibly tough, losing your mum.'

Ellie rubbed her eyes. She clambered to her feet, angry with herself for opening the lid on the subject. She didn't want Alex to feel sorry for her. He stood up too, brushing sand from his jeans.

'D'you want to head back now?' he said, good-natured as ever. Her anger seemed to make no impression. It washed off.

She studied him, feeling antagonistic, resenting the opportunity she'd given him for pity but wanting something from him at the same time. What? Some kind of confirmation?

'Sure, yes. Let's get going.'

Ellie was tired by the time they reached Alex's house, though he seemed as energetic as ever. It was two in the afternoon and they had the place to themselves. Alex showed her round. Next to the kitchen was a long, comfortable living room with a stone fireplace and a huge, comfy sofa, lots of paintings on the walls in bright, splashy colours, pictures of fruit and bottles and flowers and stones. His parents' bedroom led off the living room. A makeshift wooden staircase, little more than a ladder, led steeply up to Alex's room in the loft.

'Wow, it's lovely.' Poking her head and shoulders through the hatch, she surveyed the low, higgledy-piggledy room, with its beams, slanting roofs and low dormer windows. Ellie clambered up into the attic, catching a sea view through one of the windows. Alex slept on a mattress on the floor and had all sorts of pictures pinned to the walls – black and white photographs, old and new postcards, cuttings from magazines. And, balanced along the length of the two beams, all sorts of sea findings – pretty pebbles, pieces of wood, fragments of glass, old bottles, pieces of red-rusted iron. Across one triangular end of the room he had a long desk made of mismatched pieces of driftwood, in grey and the palest gold.

Ellie ran her fingers along its surface.

'Did you make this?'

'No, my dad did.'

'It's gorgeous.' The desk fitted perfectly into the quirky space, complete with shelves against the wall and half a dozen intriguing little boxes, also made of driftwood.

'I did make those,' Alex said, as she picked one up and marvelled at the complexity, the box like a jigsaw puzzle of pieces.

'Some are better than others,' he said. 'My dad taught me. D'you like them?'

For the first time, Ellie caught a note of shyness in his voice; was he worried about what she might think?

'They're absolutely amazing,' she said. 'God, you're so clever. I don't know how you do it.'

Alex blushed and grinned. 'You have to wait a long time,' he said. 'Wait to find the right pieces that fit together. Can I show you one last thing?' He seemed younger now, red-faced. More boyish and goofy, bright with enthusiasm. 'Here – have a look. Tell me what you think.' Shy again.

He opened a narrow cupboard at the other end of the loft.

Fairies. Sort of fairies. She stepped closer. The light in the loft was rather variable, patches of sun, pools of shadow. Ellie peered into the cupboard.

'Can I take one out?' The fairies hung on almost invisible strings. Puppets.

'Sure. Let me help you.' Protectively his hand dived into the cupboard, before Ellie could mess up the delicate procedure. He drew out a figure of tan, ochre and conker brown, about thirty centimetres tall, a narrow creature made of bark and sticks, furnished with fragments of sea glass and reclaimed oddments such as rusty nuts and bolts and old pearl buttons. Clothes of rags and ribbons. The face was driftwood, a bulb of pale grey with a tiny knob of a nose, a narrow carved mouth and eyes.

Ellie marvelled. Even the driftwood boxes paled in comparison to this. Alex grinned and blushed again, evidently delighted by her response.

'It's all recycled, everything,' he said. 'You know, stuff I've found on the beach or out walking, some of it from charity shops, the fabrics from old clothes. I've sold a couple in one of the shops in town. I sold it for forty pounds, though the gallery took fifty per cent. They take a long time to make, and it's quite hard to sell them, I fall in love with them, that's the trouble. But I can't keep them all. What would be the point of that?'

He was chatting on, words tumbling out, thrilled to

have an appreciative audience for his creations. Ellie stared at the fairy-creature, letting Alex's words wash over her. How extraordinary the way this assemblage of lost things had become a personality, a being imbued with character and quirks. How sombre this one looked, the wooden face shaped by the sea, the carved eyes seeming to enhance what was already present. He (certainly the puppet was a he, despite the long rag robes) was a creature of autumn woods, of moss and mist and twilight.

'Does he have a name?'

'Birch,' Alex said. 'Just because his body is made of birch.'

'It suits him.'

'What about this one?' He handed over a second puppet, a sleeve of blues with a moon-white face and long pale yellow hair. 'It's horse hair,' Alex explained. 'One of my friends collected it for me, when she trimmed her horse's mane. And the jewels on the dress and her hands – see them? Guess what they are.'

'I can't guess. I have no idea.'

'From tin cans. I punched out tiny circles, stuck them on.'

While Alex galloped on with an explanation of this particular technique, Ellie stared into the face of this second creature. If the first conjured up the spirit of autumn woods, this blue girl made her think of the sea on a summer night, all the layers of blue, the silver of stars and moonlight. Ellie glanced up at Alex, speaking with such animation, then back at his creation, the sea girl. The previous day she'd felt envious of Daisy for her style and her dream of cooking. Now she yearned to be Alex too, for this talent he had, to make something so strange and beautiful out of waste, and for his loft bedroom, for being the source of something, for knowing what he wanted, for his home and his intact family.

Ellie handed the blue girl back.

'Do you want to see the others?' he said.

'No, really I think I ought to be getting back.' She was more abrupt than she'd intended. The wind dropped from his sails.

'Oh, okay. Sure. But I'm glad you liked them.' This with a hopeful tone.

'Of course I like them. They're wonderful. You're really talented.' She couldn't rid her voice of a certain flatness. She didn't want to see any more of his marvels and wonderful life. 'I've had a great time – thanks for the walk.'

Alex rallied a little. 'Let's do it again sometime. Would you like to? I enjoyed it too. Anyway, I'll see you at the rehearsal tonight.'

Ellie was already climbing down the stairs. She heard a door open and a woman's voice called out a hello. Alex's mum? She didn't want to meet her. Ellie hesitated on the stairs, wondering how best to avoid seeing her.

'Are you okay?' Alex was staring at Ellie.

'Yes, sure. Tired, that's all. I really have to go. I'll see you later.' She dropped to the ground floor, looked around for Alex's mum, who was, judging by the sound of the kettle, in the kitchen. Ellie scooted through the living room, through the front door, out and away from all of them. She took a deep breath, hurried along the garden path and out of the gate, and down, down the long hill to the Marine Theatre.

9

The theatre door was open. Ellie stepped inside. Who was here? She couldn't hear anyone. A familiar stale smell: dust and damp, a hint of beer. She walked through the foyer to the ticket office, sweating, feeling like a criminal. If someone challenged her, she had an excuse ready. She'd come to check up on the rehearsal schedule.

The office door was open, no one inside. A tatty room, like the rest of the theatre, with a worn carpet and a battered Formica desk. Harry had said: old cabinet, bottom drawer. She scanned the room. Nothing looked old – at least, everything looked 1960s old, but not nineteenth century old. She looked around again. Her heart was beating fast. She felt a physical surge of excitement, in the pit of her belly.

Was that it? Beyond a grey metal filing cabinet, something crowned with a mound of old newspapers. She skipped over to take a closer look. Yes, surely. A tall chest, narrow, made of wood with three deep drawers. She tugged the ornate metal handle on the bottom one and drew it open.

Far away a door slammed and she heard voices. Ellie

swallowed hard. She had to hurry. The excuse of a rehearsal schedule wouldn't cover her rummaging around like this. She'd look like a thief.

Old cardboard files filled the drawer, along with a chaos of loose papers – invoices, receipts, bills a decade old. She rummaged through, then lifted out papers in clumps, listening out for the owners of the voices she'd heard. She had to hurry.

How could one drawer hold so much? Files sprawled over the floor, spilling their contents. At last she reached the bottom. Where was the key? She couldn't see anything and felt a plunging panic. Was this the wrong office? The wrong cabinet? What if Harry were thinking of the key's keeping place a century ago? What if Harry didn't exist at all and this was all a giant, self-created fantasy – about to culminate in her arrest for theft? Her thoughts ran out of control. In desperation she plunged her hand into the drawer and patted all over the wooden bottom. There – right at the back – not one key, but a small bunch of them: an odd assemblage, all ages and sizes, a collection of the lost and forgotten and not-needed. She scooped them up then dropped the keys on the floor beside her and stuffed the paper back into the drawer. It wasn't easy. How was all of this going to fit back in? Calm down, she told herself. Just do it. She dumped the papers back in, bit by bit, hands shaking. Now she could hear footsteps in the corridor outside. The theatre's main door opened too. People were coming from both directions. She grabbed the last files, stood up and shoved them in as an old woman stepped into the office: a very smart old woman with a chic bob, and expensive-looking clothes. She gave Ellie an odd look.

'Can I help you? What are you doing?'

Ellie tried not to look flustered. The bunch of keys still lay on the floor. She resisted the temptation to glance at them.

'Oh, I, well . . . I mean, I'm a member of the youth theatre group. We're doing *A Midsummer Night's Dream*? I'm looking for a rehearsal schedule.'

The woman glanced around the office then looked at Ellie again. 'I don't think you'll find one here. In any case, you shouldn't be in the office. Why isn't it kept locked? Any Tom, Dick or Harry could walk in.' This last comment to another woman who had appeared behind her.

'It is kept locked, usually. I'm sorry, it's my fault – I didn't realise the main doors were open.' This second woman fussed apologetically. Ellie took the opportunity to scoop up the keys and dash out of the office, as the two more people appeared – Mike and a young man, another member of the youth theatre group. She felt a surge of relief, because their arrival seemed to validate her presence in the theatre.

'Hey, Mike! Have you got another rehearsal list? I lost mine, really stupid I know.' She spoke loudly, for the benefit of the women. Mike looked puzzled. He said he'd email her a copy, waved at the women in the office then wandered into the auditorium. Ellie tagged along, asking him what he was doing. She needed an excuse to return to the little room with the panel and the locked door.

Mike and his friend climbed onto the stage and started

talking about scenery and a funding application. Ellie left them behind and walked purposefully down the little stairs and into the crooked room.

Everything was ordinary today. She had no sense of a presence and the room seemed tatty and dim. She found the loose panel, pressed it as she had before, and it popped open, revealing the little white door. How long ago had it been covered up? She considered the bunch of keys, found one that looked the right size and pushed it into the lock. No good. She tried a second. The third key slid into place. She felt a surge of excitement. As she tried to turn the key she felt the lock's resistance, the grating of its metal workings: she fiddled, then came a shift, and it turned. The door opened, with a little cough, and then a breath came from inside, smelling of dust and damp stone and age. Elle felt another flutter of intense excitement. She pulled the door wide open and peered in.

The cupboard was only a few inches deep. She saw an old brick wall, moist and mould-stained. No wonder it had been locked and boarded over. A few old scraps of paper lay on the floor. She picked them up, turned them over. Was that it? Surely not. She was missing something. Ellie stuck her head into the opening and scanned the interior. There – to the left, tucked in the side – a fat lump of something on the floor. She pulled it out.

Ellie spread the lump across the floor – revealing a heavy black jacket, damp and stinking, decrepit with age. Patched with mould, parts of the fabric had disintegrated. Ellie wrinkled her nose. Was this it? Had Harry sent her on a quest for this revolting thing? She could hardly bear to touch it.

Gingerly she poked at the jacket. Was something in the pockets, perhaps? She opened the jacket. No – there was something inside the coat itself: an old-fashioned white shirt with a high collar.

Time seemed to stop for a moment – as though reality had shrunk to one object, an old shirt locked away perhaps for a hundred years. Nothing else existed, except this. The shirt had been Harry's. She was certain of it.

She lifted the shirt from the old jacket, which had protected it from the ravages of years spent in a damp little hole in the wall, and held it aloft. Sunlight shone through it from the little window. Some speckles of mould, yes, but not much.

Harry's shirt. He'd worn it. Perhaps molecules from his skin still lingered on the fabric. Ellie slowly moved her face towards it, till the linen brushed her nose lightly. She caught the merest whisper of scent, beyond the must and mould, the low, woody notes of the exotic, masculine perfume that had flooded her room. She closed her eyes and breathed again. The fragrance seemed to play over her nerves, the key to a particular, intense emotional note. She trembled.

A noise from upstairs broke her trance. Ellie rolled up the jacket, stuffed it back into the cupboard, locked the door and replaced the panel. She folded the shirt, hid it inside her jacket and returned to the auditorium. Mike and his friend were still where she'd left them.

'I'm off home,' she said. 'I'll see you later.' Then she hurried off, aware they were still looking at her with puzzled faces. The two women had left the office and locked it, so Ellie decided to return the old keys another time. She hurried out of the theatre and all the way back to her grandparents' house.

'Grandma? Grandpa?' No one home. She ran upstairs to her bedroom, took the shirt out and spread it over her bed. Harry's shirt, surely. Harry had touched it, worn it, filled it with his warm body. She ran her hands over the fabric. She pressed the shirt to her face again, yearning for another hit of perfume. Nothing now – had it gone?

Ellie took out a wire coat-hanger and hung the shirt from a hook on the back of the bedroom door. She felt excited and disappointed at the same time. Why was that? What exactly had she been expecting? To be satisfied? But she wasn't – she wanted more. Her yearning to see Harry, to hear his voice, had only grown stronger.

10

Midnight. Ellie lay on her bed, still dressed. Moonlight poured through the window onto the model theatre. No sign of Harry. Still she waited. Each minute stretched out.

The shirt hung on the door, pale in the darkness, much like a ghost itself.

What exactly was she expecting? It was hard to say. But she was expecting something.

Far away the church clock chimed. One o'clock. Ellie must have dozed for a little while at least. The light had changed. The moon had moved from the window, and now only a pale light came slanting into the room. The theatre lay in shadow.

The bedroom was hot and stuffy. She climbed off the bed and opened the window, allowing in a little fresh air. Then she took off her jumper, enjoying the touch of cool air on her arms. She looked to the door, at the old shirt. Had it truly belonged to Harry? She walked over, touched the shirt with her fingertips then took it from the hanger. The shirt didn't open all the way down the front. You had to pull it on over your head then it had three buttons to do up. Without really thinking what she was doing, Ellie took the shirt from the hanger, raised it over her head and slipped her arms into the sleeves. The shirt dropped over her, musty linen brushing against her face and body. The fabric skimmeded her bare skin. She ran her hands over the front of it, wrapped her arms around herself

'Harry,' she said, very quietly. 'Have I got it right? Where are you?'

Something stirred, although the curtains at the window didn't move. The contents of the room seemed to shift – books on the shelves, bedclothes, the pictures on the wall – as though everything was coming into focus. Or perhaps, moving out of focus. Ellie's nose tickled, then she registered again the low note of the exotic, masculine scent. From the shirt or the theatre this time?

'Harry?' she said again, a little louder.

The room shifted again. Ellie rubbed her eyes trying to make sense of the scene. Although she hadn't moved, the room seemed further away and less substantial. Ellie rubbed her eyes. She could hear her own heartbeat. She didn't feel afraid but her senses were primed.

The air trembled, just in front of her. A mist appeared, fragile and hard to see. As the moments passed, the mist grew denser, shaping itself, curling around, to build up a torso, limbs, a face. A face she'd seen before – in an old photograph, conjured in the night on the beach.

Ellie stared at the emerging figure, her body shaking. She felt shocked, cold and afraid. Her nerves responded: she felt sick, hot, hysterical, furious and tearful in turns. Then all these feelings drained away, leaving her empty.

He stood before her.

Tall, slim, with longish, ink-black hair and milky skin. He wore a white shirt (like hers) and a dark waistcoat. And his face. Oh, his face! She knew it. He was utterly familiar – and at the same time, his beauty was a shock. She hadn't been prepared. The sight of his face blocked out her ability to speak and think.

Ellie and Harry stood as they were. Neither moved nor spoke. For a moment his body seemed to melt back into mist, then he grew solid again, more real than the ghostly, insubstantial room in which they stood.

'Ellie,' he said. His eyes were a deep brown. She studied his face, the individual features. Black brows; a strong, straight nose; well-shaped, sensual lips. Something intimidating about him. Although he was nineteen, he seemed a man and not a boy. He possessed a man's assurance. His body wasn't gawky. Although he was slim he had an aura of strength, suggesting he had spent hours walking and riding and hunting. And for all his beauty, she could see something stern in his face – suspected he might be proud, quick-tempered, headstrong, determined. Selfish? *Be careful*, she warned herself.

These thoughts played through her mind all in a moment.

'Ellie,' he said again, lingering over the word. His voice seemed to caress her name. 'So you found the shirt.'

'You're a ghost,' she said.

He didn't seem to hear this. The shadow of a smile crossed his face.

'I've wanted to ask you,' he said, 'why you never smile. You always look so sad.'

83

His accent was strange, his voice modulating oddly. Was this the way the wealthy spoke a hundred years ago? He wasn't difficult to understand, but nonetheless, he was a visitor from another land, the land of the past.

She looked into his eyes, not like any brown eyes she'd seen before. Illuminated, unnaturally bright. Ghost eyes. What had he seen in the kingdom of the dead? She had so many questions.

'But you look sad too,' she said. 'Why are *you* sad?'

'You are very direct.'

'No more so than you.'

He paused then said, 'That's true.'

'Is it because of the shirt that I can see you now?' Ellie said. 'You've been watching me, haven't you?'

'I have been watching you, yes. I was . . . asleep for a long time. In the dark. Dreaming sometimes. And then – you woke me. I connected with you through the model theatre I made with my sister. So – I caught glimpses of you. I think, sometimes, I heard your thoughts. But I couldn't see you clearly, until tonight.'

'Because I'm wearing your shirt.'

'My shirt. It looks strange on you. I like it. Yes. It belonged to me, like the theatre and the script. Bring them together, and I can step into this place – with you.'

'But you're dead, aren't you? How did you die?' The question was brutal, but Ellie couldn't resist asking. She felt oddly confrontational. Because she was frightened? In awe of him? She didn't like his manner – his pride. The phantom seemed to tremble on the air. The figure broke up momentarily and then assembled itself again. Dark eyes glittered.

'I'm not dead. How can I be dead?' he said. 'I'm here, talking to you. The dead don't speak.'

Ellie stretched out her hand and very slowly reached for Harry's arm. Her hand passed through him. She expected a sensation but felt nothing.

'You're not here,' she said. 'Not physically. Do you remember dying?'

His composure slipped again. He flinched, speared by some devastating emotion. His eyes blazed.

'I don't know what happened to me. There's so much I can't remember,' he said. 'My life. My memories. They're in pieces, all broken up. Like dreams. But this moment now, with you, is very strange. I think it must be another dream.' He gave her another intense look, as though he could see right through her eyes into her thoughts, her soul. She looked away.

'Why d'you think it's a dream? I'm real. As real as can be.'

'Are you? How do you know?'

'What a stupid question. Of course I'm real! I have a life, a world, friends.'

'Yes? Where are they?'

'My grandparents are asleep downstairs. And my friends are – out there!' She gesticulated at the window.

'And my sister's in the theatre rehearsing for *Romeo and Juliet* with my friends, and my parents are at home, in North Hill House.'

'No they're not. That was a hundred years ago!'

'I've woken in the future? Or have you stepped into the past?'

Ellie looked wildly around the room, dizzy, wanting something to hang on to. The room didn't look real. It was unfocused: vague and faded.

'Don't worry.' Harry held out a comforting hand. He reached for her shoulder but his hand passed through her. 'See,' he said, 'you're insubstantial – a ghost. I can't touch you. I didn't mean to scare you. Perhaps we aren't in my time or yours. Maybe our wish to meet one another created a place in-between.'

She thought for a moment. Then she said, '*Did* we wish to meet one another?'

Harry shook his head impatiently, as though she'd said something stupid. 'What have you been thinking about these last few days? Why did you read my notes? Why did you find the shirt? Do you think I haven't heard you calling me?'

Ellie blushed, to think he'd felt the intensity of her interest.

'And you wanted to see me too?'

'Yes,' he said simply.

'Why?' Her tone was fierce. She felt wrong-footed and vulnerable.

His eyes blazed again, the brown becoming black.

'How can you ask that?' he said. 'How can you not know?'

Ellie's lip trembled. A wave of something passed through her. She did know.

She said, 'It was luck – me finding the theatre.'

'Luck? Is that what you think?' The colour in his eyes dimmed. He gave her a calculating look. 'It wasn't luck.

The theatre found you. *I* found you. Do you know how long I've been waiting?'

'A hundred years,' Ellie said. 'You were waiting for *me* for a hundred years? Anyone could have found that theatre. It was just luck.'

'Anyone could have found it, yes. But I don't think anyone could have woken me.'

Again that sensation, of heat and cold, soaking through her body.

'I don't know how long it's been,' he continued. 'I only know I've been waiting – or perhaps, suspended. Like Sleeping Beauty.'

Ellie blushed again, remembering how Sleeping Beauty was woken, and by whom.

'Why were you waiting? What do you want?'

Harry shook his head. She could hardly bear to look at his face, and at the same time she wanted to eat him up with her eyes, to feast on him, on his terrible beauty.

'Perhaps to feel this.' The ghost flickered, as though he had burst into a thousand pale, trembling flames. He was consumed by them; face, body, hands all disappearing. Ellie felt a plummeting sense of loss.

'Harry! Harry!' she shouted. 'Don't go! Please! Don't go!'

The white fire consumed itself and disappeared.

Ellie stood alone, in the dark room. The very last rays of moonlight had passed from the window. She didn't move, shocked and overwhelmed. Her mind went blank.

'Ellie? Ellie, are you okay?' She heard a voice from the landing. Ellie bounded into bed and pulled up the covers as her grandmother knocked on and then opened the door.

'Ellie?' she whispered. Electric light spilled through the doorway. Her grandmother padded into the room on bare feet, long white hair spilling over her dressing gown. She sat on the side of the bed and lightly touched her grand-daughter's face. She smelled of sleep and lavender and familiarity.

'I heard you shout,' Jean said. 'Did you have a night-mare again? Were you dreaming about your mum?' She gently stroked Ellie's hair.

Ellie shook her head. 'No. It's okay. I did have a dream, but it wasn't about Mum, don't worry. I'm okay.'

'Are you sure?'

'Yes I'm sure.'

'Would you like me to stay with you till you fall asleep again?'

Ellie smiled, seeing her grandmother's lovely face above her own, enjoying this moment of being a child again.

'Go back to bed, Grandma. I'm fine, honestly.'

Her grandmother bent over and gave Ellie a light, dry kiss on the forehead.

'I love you, Ellie,' she said.

'I love you, too.'

Jean lingered a moment more, before leaving the room. She pulled the door shut behind her, leaving Ellie alone in the dark.

11

A shriek at the window woke Ellie.

A huge white seagull perched on the window ledge, glistening in the bright sunshine, its raucous voice filling the room. Ellie hadn't shut the window. From the pavement beneath came the sound of happy voices, families enjoying their summer holiday.

She couldn't remember falling asleep. Her grandmother had kissed her goodnight – and then, without a moment of thought, she'd slept. For the first moment after she woke, Ellie's mind was empty – and then, in a rush, came dazzling images of Harry, his miraculous appearance in her room, their conversation, and his face – *his face* – burning in her brain. He'd waited a hundred years. He'd waited a century, he said – *for her.*

In remembering she felt again the tumult of emotions. She played them in her mind, over and over, feeling each time the same rush.

She lay in bed for an hour. Outside, people wandered along the street. Dimly she heard children, the conversation of an elderly couple, a dog barking, the cries of gulls and the occasional car. But these were all distant, barely registered.

All that mattered was the drama of this first encounter with Harry, her drowning in a deluge of feeling.

Would she see him again? He hadn't said so. She had no idea when or how they would meet, but meet they must. They had to.

The clock unfolded time. Eleven o'clock. She could hear music in the house, her grandmother perhaps playing something in her studio as she wrote. Still wearing Harry's shirt, hugging it around her, Ellie climbed out of bed and went to the bathroom. She undressed and stepped into the shower. Hot water sluiced over her face and body and hair. She closed her eyes.

Ellie had never felt anything like this before – this burning, consuming intensity of feeling. More than anything, it felt like falling. These last months she'd been walking towards the edge of a cliff, step by step. These last days, she'd crept closer and closer to the limit. Now she'd dropped over the edge – not so much dropped as flung herself into the abyss. She'd lost her grip. She was plummeting, down and down. No end to this falling – no place to land, only the helpless, dizzying descent.

What would happen at the end?

She dressed and headed downstairs.

'Would you like something to eat? I've left the breakfast things on the table,' Jean said, sticking her head out of her studio as Ellie passed on the stairs. 'Grandpa's in the dining room reading the paper. He'll make you some tea.'

Ellie drank the tea but couldn't eat. She sat at the table then stood up again, not knowing what to do with herself. Her grandfather looked at her over his newspaper.

'Everything all right? You look a bit tired. What are your plans for today?'

'Oh, I don't know,' Ellie said. 'I've got a rehearsal this evening. Thought I might see Daisy beforehand,' she improvised.

He raised his bushy grey eyebrows. 'Your grandmother told me about your model theatre. D'you think I might take a look?'

'Yes, sure.' But she disliked this idea, wanting to keep it to herself. Why? What harm could it do to let him see it?

She led the way to her room. 'There it is.'

Her grandfather's eyes lit on the theatre and he hurried forward.

'My God, it is! My goodness, where did you find it? When your grandmother described it to me, I wondered . . . What a find!' He crouched down to stare at the front of the theatre, eyes eating up the details, peering into the interior.

'What is it?'

'Don't you see? No, I don't suppose you would. It's all very different now. They overhauled it in the late sixties – wanted to clear out the old. Covered it all up. Made it ugly.'

'What are you talking about, Grandpa?'

'Oh, it's a beautiful piece of work. I wonder who made it? I had no idea. It's a one-off, can you see? Handmade. Hand painted. Wait till I tell the museum!'

'What?' She felt a surge of protective anger. Her raised voice finally interrupted her grandfather's enthusing. 'What do you mean? It's mine!'

He blinked and stood back. 'I'm sorry, Ellie. I got carried away. It's . . . well, it's a remarkable find.'

'Why? What's so special about it?' Already she felt the pain of impending loss. She sensed greedy hands stretching out to take this away from her – this link with Harry.

'It's not any old theatre. It's a model of the old Marine Theatre. Don't you see? The original was built in the mid-nineteenth century, a glorious place by all accounts. We've got some photographs in the museum taken before the renovation. Then, in the sixties, there was this craze for making everything modern. It needed improvements by then, for sure, but they went for a complete facelift: ripped out the old seats, took off all the plaster mouldings and decorations, removed the old proscenium arch, the old doors, and covered everything in the horrible beige plastic-looking veneer you can see today. An act of cultural vandalism, that's what it was. I remember it all too well. I was a young man then, your mother was a baby. Everyone was so thrilled about their modern theatre but even then I thought it was ghastly.' He'd galloped on. Now he stopped to take a breath.

'This is the Marine Theatre?' Ellie said. 'Our theatre – how it used to look?' She thought of the little rooms down the stairs behind the stage, how she'd found a little cupboard behind the panel and, inside it, Harry's shirt.

'Yes. Yes! That's it! Where did you find it?'

Ellie told him about the bookshop and the manila folder. David expressed his surprise that the man in shop (Edward, he called him – they were friends apparently) hadn't himself spotted how precious a find this was. Ellie didn't answer because she remembered how the bookshop man had indeed noticed – until something distracted him. Were strange forces at work even then?

'I wonder who made it?' David mused. He picked up the theatre very carefully and peered at the bottom, the back and the sides, looking for information. 'It's beautifully made. Such attention to detail – and the painting is amazing.' He put the model back on the table and turned his attention to the papers – the play script, photograph and concert programme. 'This came in the folder too?'

'Yes,' said Ellie. It felt like a horrible invasion, having her grandfather's fingers paddling over the papers, though she knew how unreasonable she was being. These things had fallen to her by chance. They were part of the heritage of the town. She tried to rise above her feelings. How stupid to feel jealous.

'I'm sure we can find out who these people are. Perhaps we could have a special exhibition all about the theatre? What do you think? You could help me – do some research – sort out some exhibits. The Marine Theatre – past, present and future. What d'you reckon?'

She lost control then. Unwanted tears pricked her eyes. A choked sob escaped. The tears leaked out, spilling over her cheeks. Her grandfather stopped talking and looked at her, amazed. Ellie hurried out of the room, her hand covering her mouth, and ran down the stairs. As she slipped on her flip-flops, she heard her grandfather calling her, and then her grandmother opening her studio door to see what all the noise was about.

'Ellie, what's wrong?' she said. But Ellie didn't stop. She opened the front door and dashed into the street, down the hill and towards the sea.

12

Families crowded the beach. Sunlight poured, making sea and sky a brilliant mass of blue. The water shifted and glittered. A dozen little yachts with sails of lemon yellow, white and crimson travelled back and forth across the cove. Outside the seafront shops stood buckets of plastic windmills, multicoloured parasols and children's spades. Inflatable dolphins, sharks and bananas hung above them, bobbing in the faintest of breezes.

Ellie walked along the busy path, past happy children with ice creams and couples chatting to one another as they strolled. Sitting on a bench in the shade she saw an elderly man and woman holding hands and whispering to one another. At the water's edge children paddled and shrieked. Three boys in black pushed past on skateboards. A father and little daughter jumped from a low sea wall into the waves.

The whole spectacle – a noisy, colourful picture called Summer Holiday – was a scene from which she was excluded.

Ellie felt entirely cut off from them all. She envisaged herself as a piece of darkness – a body wrapped round a mass of hurt and isolation. She had no connection with these people, this scene. She was apart from them all, perhaps invisible to them, a witness from another, darker land.

Of course she'd been part of this once. She'd had her summer days with Mum and Dad, ice creams, games in the waves, sand sculptures – everything. But that time had ended. Her mother was dead. Her father had taken another woman to the other side of the world and Ellie was here alone, like a ghost herself. A ghost haunting a past life she would never again be part of.

She jumped from the promenade onto the beach and sat on the sand with her back against the sun-heated wall. The breeze carried the perfume of the sea and the faintest whiff of vinegary chips. She closed her eyes. An image of Harry rose up in her imagination. How hard it was to see his face. She could conjure up parts of it – his eyes, his nose, the colour of his skin – but not the totality. She remembered what he had said, and felt again that sensation of falling; a long, helpless plummet.

The noise of the beach receded. Ellie imagined what it would be like if Harry were sitting alongside her now, the two of them together, shoulders touching, him reaching for her hand, what it would feel like to have his fingers interlaced with hers, that most simple of pleasures. The fantasy was so powerful it made her dizzy. She created it again, this scene. It seemed to swallow her up.

Time passed. Distantly she could hear waves, voices, the tread of pedestrians on the path behind her, but the greater part of her mind was drifting in an ocean of imaginings, the same ones over and over, replaying the meeting with Harry in the night, and how it might feel if he were beside her now, reaching for her hand.

'Ellie? Ellie? Are you okay?' An irritating voice broke into her thoughts, bringing her back to an unwanted real world.

'Ellie, were you asleep?' A girl's voice. Daisy.

Ellie opened one eye and looked up. Daisy's face hung above her. She was standing on the promenade, bending over, hands resting on her knees.

'I wasn't asleep.'

Daisy jumped down, crunching on pebbles. She sat beside Ellie and scrutinised her face.

'Have you been crying?'

'No.' Ellie rubbed her face with the palm of her hand, removing any telltale traces. A look of kindly concern crossed Daisy's face, but she seemed to push it aside, perhaps picking up from Ellie's tone that she didn't want sympathy.

Ellie shifted position, conscious her spine was digging into the wall.

'What are you doing?' she said.

'Oh, I've just finished work. I'm on my way home. I thought it was you. D'you want a coffee? I'm buying.'

Ellie patted her pockets. 'If you don't mind. I haven't got any money on me.' Nor her phone, nor her keys. She'd rushed out without thinking.

Daisy guided her to a new place, tucked down an alley-way off the High Street. Ellie sat at an iron table outside while Daisy went in to order drinks. A little fountain sprinkled water over a bowl of pebbles in the middle of the narrow terrace.

'Rehearsal tonight,' Daisy said when she came back. 'You read your part through?'

'No. Not yet. I'll do it when I get home.'

Daisy chatted inconsequentially. Ellie found it hard to concentrate on what she was saying. All too easily her mind returned to Harry.

'What do you think of Alex?'

'What?' Ellie said.

'Alex. What do you think of Alex?'

Ellie blinked, bringing herself back to the present. Daisy blushed, evidently a bit nervous.

'He's lovely,' Ellie said. 'A really good guy.'

Daisy smiled and fluttered her lashes.

'You like him, don't you?' Ellie said. 'I mean, like him like him.'

'You won't say anything, will you?' This in a rush.

'Of course not.'

'I've liked him for ages and ages. It's hard though, isn't it, when you've been friends for a long time. We went to school together.'

'Do you think he likes you too?'

'I don't know. I really don't. I mean, he's lovely to me, but he's lovely to everyone.'

'That's true.'

'Would you do something for me?' Another rush of words. 'You're new. Would you watch him, tell me what you think? If he likes me?' She blushed more deeply, two scarlet roses blossoming in her cheeks.

'Sure,' Ellie said. 'I don't know how much use I'll be, but I'll do my best.'

Daisy picked up her cup and took a sip of coffee. Then she put it down and fanned her face with her hand. 'I'm sorry. You know, I've not told anyone else about this. I mean, it's not as though you and I know each other very well yet.'

'I'm honoured,' Ellie said. 'Thanks for trusting me.' And she was honoured. But she had a second motive. Could she tell Daisy something about Harry? How she would love an opportunity to talk about him. Almost telepathically, Daisy said, 'Is there someone special in your life, Ellie? Someone you like?'

It was Ellie's turn to blush. She pressed her hands together.

'Yes, actually, there is.'

'Who? Oh, tell me! What's his name? What's he like?'

'Harry. And he is totally the most gorgeous guy I've ever seen.'

The girls looked at each other – both broke into a storm of delighted laughter.

'Oh, tell me more! Does he live in your home town?'

'He's not from here,' Ellie said. 'He's nineteen. I haven't known him very long but he writes to me, and we talk sometimes.' Nimbly she wove truths with half-truths. How delicious it was to talk about him. Before, the encounters with Harry had existed only in her mind. Now this sharing with Daisy made him seem more real.

'Are you going out with him?'

Ellie shook her head. 'It's early days.'

'But he likes you?'

'I think so.' She fiddled with her coffee cup. 'He said I was beautiful.'

'Oh, did he? Oh! Oh!' Daisy bounced in her chair and clapped her hands, like a twelve-year-old.

They talked happily for a while, telling what it was they liked about the objects of their affection, delighting in the opportunity to share secret obsessions. Ellie told Daisy about her visit to Alex's house and their walk to the next bay, then enthused about his beautiful creations, the driftwood boxes and the strange fairy people.

'He is pretty amazing. I can understand why you like him,' Ellie said. 'I can see the two of you together someday, living here by the sea.'

Daisy smiled and blushed again, her eyes all dreamy. 'Wouldn't that be lovely?'

Ellie stayed out all afternoon. After the café, she and Daisy went to Daisy's house. This sharing of romantic confidences had cemented their friendship. They talked for a long time. Ellie found herself laughing till her tummy hurt and her body was weak and helpless. She couldn't remember the last time that had happened. She was lying beside Daisy on her pink double bed, among mounds of fluffy and embroidered cushions that looked very much like cupcakes.

Daisy caught Ellie's hand and they turned to face one another, faces only a few inches apart.

'You look much better now,' Daisy said. 'I'm glad we met up today, aren't you? I feel like we're proper friends now. I thought this would happen – well, I hoped it would. When we first met, I thought we'd be true friends.'

Ellie squeezed her hand.

'Can I take a picture?' Daisy took out her mobile and held it aloft. Ellie heard a click.

'There. What d'you think? Aren't we lovely?' Daisy showed her the photo, their two flushed faces, hair sprawled on the bed in a cloud around them. 'Would you mind if I put it on my Facebook page? You look so gorgeous.'

'Thank you. So do you. Sure, I don't mind.'

Ellie walked home in the early evening, when the crowds on the beach were dwindling. Families with tired, happy kids, carrying sandy towels and beach mats, crowded the promenade. Ellie remembered storming out of the house in tears. She'd felt so free laughing with Daisy – like an old self she'd forgotten. Even the obsessing about Harry had receded. She'd overreacted with her grandfather, been possessive and jealous, afraid he'd take the theatre.

Ellie knocked on the front door. A moment later, her grandmother opened the door.

'Sorry. Forgot my keys,' Ellie said, almost pushing past. 'I'm fine, honestly. Sorry about earlier.'

Jean was taken aback: 'What's going on, Ellie? Grandpa was really worried. What did he say? How did he upset you so much?'

Ellie went into the living room, where her grandfather was sitting. He said something, fumbling his words. He looked concerned, awkward and apologetic all at once.

'I'm sorry,' she said. 'I don't know what came over me. I just love that theatre – I was afraid you would try and take it away from me.'

'Of course I wouldn't. Oh golly, was I being insensitive? You know what I'm like, I didn't mean to be. My dear girl, I wouldn't take it away from you. I was excited, that's all. I thought you'd want to share it. But don't worry, it's entirely up to you.'

Ellie quickly tried to reassure him, then she went to her bedroom and pored over Harry's messages in her journal. The mood of freedom she'd enjoyed with Daisy disappeared and the earlier need for Harry replaced it. She felt empty. She had a huge void inside that only Harry could fill; a hunger that only his attention and appreciation would satisfy. Was she so lacking that now she only existed as an object in his eyes? She thought about her afternoon with Daisy and wished the happy feeling hadn't vanished so soon.

Later, as her grandparents prepared tea together in the kitchen, Ellie overheard them talking about her in low, worried voices. This had happened often over the last year or so – between parents, teachers, grandparents, friends – at first worrying about her grief and loss, and then concerned that she wasn't recovering, moving on. A grief counsellor had been suggested and refused.

Ellie didn't like it at all – this sense of her life being pawed over and examined – so she marched into the kitchen to interrupt them.

'When's tea ready? I've got a rehearsal tonight,' she said, in a bright don't-worry-about-me voice.

Her grandparents stopped talking. Jean smiled.

'It won't be long – half an hour?' She hesitated, then said, 'Ellie, may I give you a hug?'

Ellie nodded and stepped forward to embrace her grandmother.

'We want you to be happy, you know that, don't you? That's what your mum would have wanted too. More than anything.'

'You're worrying about me,' Ellie said.

'It's great you've made some friends but, I don't know . . . you look a bit . . . feverish. What's going on?'

'Nothing. Well, only good things! The play – you wanted me to try it. Please don't worry.'

They embraced again. Ellie wasn't sure her grandmother was convinced.

13

'We think the theatre's haunted,' one of the girls said, with a grin. 'There was another power cut this afternoon. And there's definitely a strange atmosphere here, don't you think?'

Ellie was sitting slightly apart from the others. She'd arrived early, wanting to get out of the house. Neither Daisy nor Alex had arrived. She turned her attention from the script on her lap to the conversation the other side of the table.

'Well, there've been lots of stories about ghosts here.' Mike had walked in and overheard the comment. 'Mind you, lots of theatres are supposed to be haunted.'

The girl's eyes widened. 'Do you believe it? D'you think it's true?'

Mike grinned. 'It'd take more than dodgy electrics to convince me.'

'Sorry we're late!' Daisy and Alex walked in. Daisy gave Ellie a big smile and plopped down in the seat beside her.

'We're talking about ghosts,' Mike said. 'Marie reckons the place is haunted. What d'you think? You've lived here the longest.'

Alex shoved his hands in his pockets and said, 'I think it might be, actually.'

Everyone laughed. Ellie studied him. Was he serious or making a joke? Mike shook his head and drew the meeting to order. They began to read through the first scene.

The rehearsal was slow, with a lot of hanging around. When Ellie wasn't needed, she slipped out of the practice room and took the opportunity to explore the theatre, thinking about her grandfather's revelation – that the model in her room was in fact the Marine Theatre before its twentieth-century makeover. The idea intrigued her – to think that once this place had looked so beautiful.

Layers of time and history. She tried to see beyond the modern façade to the theatre's hidden past. How deeply buried was it? The building's bones were intact – the walls, foundations, roof. Perhaps some of its interior had survived, cheaply covered up, like the panel covering the old cupboard where she'd found Harry's shirt.

'Ellie? You okay?' Alex had followed her. 'What are you up to?'

Ellie hesitated for a moment, then she said, 'I have a model theatre at home, and my grandfather told me it's how this place used to look before they covered it in beige in the sixties. I was just wondering if I could see anything of the old place. I did find something – those little rooms down the stairs at the back of the stage.'

Alex nodded. 'There are quite a few things. I've looked for them too. It's quite intriguing, isn't it? It's like, the old theatre's still there but it's wearing a mask. It was a pretty cheap makeover they did anyway. They took some stuff away but mostly it was just covered up. And lots they took away got salvaged. My dad told me – people were so angry about the revamp they collected things out of skips. My mum's got one and a half golden cherubs.'

'One and a half?' Ellie smiled.

'Yep. They're joined together, and the second one is missing from the waist up – just got its legs really.'

'I'd love to see it.'

'Come round again and I'll show you.'

They wandered about the place. Something had changed for her now she had learned the theatre's new identity. Small details she'd missed now jumped out. The office door was locked but they looked through the window and Alex pointed out the carved wooden scrolls, blurred with layers of paint, in the corners of the room. He led her upstairs to the circle, a balcony with more seats for the audience. It had the same ugly plastic chairs but Alex walked past them to the brown and ochre barrier at the front of the balcony.

'The original is underneath. All they did was cover it up with thin board. One of the pieces broke and had to be replaced – they had an article on it in the paper – and they found this carved, gold-painted barrier underneath. Apparently there's a lovely crest on the front.'

'I don't understand,' Ellie said. 'Why not simply restore it to how it was? Everyone seems to prefer it that way.'

'Not so simple. It would cost a hell of a lot of money and the theatre struggles to meet its running costs. Anyway, the sixties makeover was partly because of bigger problems with damp. If they start pulling it apart, who knows what problems they might find?'

Ellie stared over the barrier at the stage below, remembering the model theatre and trying to superimpose this image on the view. It wasn't so hard. Thoughts of Harry filled her mind. She imagined him standing on the stage, beneath the old proscenium arch with its fat gold cherubs holding a disc with the masks of comedy and tragedy. She imagined him making a speech from *Romeo and Juliet*, clad in black velvet, with old-fashioned gas footlights at the front of the stage. How handsome he would be. She closed her eyes, swallowed up in the fantasy.

Power drained from the theatre. The lights went out.

Far away, Ellie heard the voices of her fellow cast members – a comedy scream and some high-pitched giggles.

'Ellie? You okay?'

She opened her eyes. Without windows, the auditorium was very dark. She turned round. A little light from the summer evening spilled through the door at the back of the circle.

'Faulty electrics?' she said.

'Or the ghost.' Alex was now standing close to the door at the back of the balcony but the theatre's acoustics were good because she could hear him clearly.

'Maybe. It does feel strange.' She wanted to walk towards him but found she couldn't. Her body wouldn't respond. Something moved past – a cold presence, brushing against her. Ellie's body seemed to turn to water. She grabbed the barrier to steady herself. A moment later, Alex said, 'Did you feel that?'

'I felt something. What was it?' The words didn't come out right. Her voice wobbled.

Alex hesitated. Then he said, 'I don't know.'

Ellie felt a gallop of contradictory emotions – fear, excitement, sadness. A burst of laughter escaped her and she clapped her hand over her mouth. Alex hurried to her side.

'It's okay.' He touched her arm in reassurance. She couldn't see much of him, just a dark form. She could hear his breathing. 'Let's get out of here – into the light.'

'I don't think it has gone,' she whispered, reluctant to move.

'It's hot in here,' Alex said.

'I'm not hot – I'm cold.' She rubbed her arms.

'Let's get out of here.'

'No!'

She was thinking of Harry, sensing his presence in the theatre. 'You go,' she said. 'I want to stay.'

'I'm not leaving you alone.'

The lights snapped on.

The strange atmosphere dispersed in a moment. Now they were standing in harsh electric light in a tatty auditorium. They looked at one another, blinking.

14

'We're holding a séance in the theatre,' said Warren. He'd told them he was staying in the town all summer, his parents having found him a holiday job so he could save some money for college. Wiry and energetic, he was now bright-eyed and excited, almost jumping up and down.

They were standing at the bar of The Mermaid, half a dozen of them, including Daisy, Alex and Carly.

'Is that a good idea? That's dangerous stuff,' warned Alex.

'How would we get into the theatre anyway? It'll be locked up,' Carly said.

'I'm staying with my uncle. He's one of the trustees and he has keys. I'm sure I could, um, borrow them?'

They all stood in silence, wondering, looking at one another.

'How would it work? What would we do?' Ellie asked.

'A Ouija board,' Warren said.

'You have one of those too?' This from Alex.

'Actually, I do. I'm into all that stuff. Mediums, spiritualism. I want to try. Who's in?'

They looked at one another again, afraid and thrilled at the same time.

'I am,' Ellie said.

Daisy looked up, surprised. 'Well, if you are, so am I.'

The others nodded, more or less enthusiastically.

'Alex?' Daisy said.

'If you lot are set on this, I'll come along. I can't say I think it's a great idea though. I feel pretty uncomfortable about it.'

Drinks in hand, they took a table in the corner of the room and Warren talked more about his Ouija board and the various ambiguous experiments he'd conducted. The pub was fairly quiet but they kept their voices low. Alex didn't add much to the conversation. Neither did Ellie. Anticipation tingled. She knew who was haunting the theatre and longed to know if this proposed séance might bring Harry further into her world. At the same time, she felt possessive about him, and didn't want the others to make some kind of contact that she would miss out on.

'We'll meet outside the theatre at eleven forty-five,' Warren said. 'Don't wimp out on me. Make sure you're there.'

They finished their drinks, left the pub and dispersed. Ellie phoned her grandparents and told them she'd be late, then went to Daisy's house with Alex. They waited together, the three of them. Remembering Daisy's secret infatuation, she tried to suss out if Alex felt the same way about Daisy. It was hard to say. He was his usual self with both girls, and Ellie certainly didn't get the feeling she was a gooseberry.

They watched half of a film, a romantic comedy Daisy had on DVD. Her mum, a psychiatric nurse, had a night-shift so they had the place to themselves and Daisy said they should watch something light and cheerful. At eleven thirty they made their way back across town to the theatre.

It was a warm, clear night, the softest of breezes coming in from the still, inky sea. The lights on the promenade were on. Ellie didn't see a soul until they arrived at the theatre, where Warren was already waiting. Carly arrived ten minutes later, apologising profusely for being late.

'I had to pretend to go to bed,' she said. 'And when my parents had gone to bed, I snuck out.' She was a little more relaxed with the group now. They waited another minute for Warren's friend but a text arrived saying he couldn't make it. So – just the five of them.

'You have the keys, then?' Alex said.

Warren produced them from his pocket with a flourish. He had a jute bag over his arm too – presumably holding the Ouija board. Ellie felt a quiver of fear. The idea hadn't seemed quite real until now. As Warren fiddled with the door, she glanced at Alex. He seemed very still and contained. She knew he didn't totally approve of this adventure, but he was going to stick around for her and Daisy's sake. Did he believe in the ghost? He'd been with her in the auditorium – he'd felt something too. But ghost or no ghost, holding a séance clearly seemed to him a risky thing to try.

'Got it,' Warren said, as the door opened. They all slipped inside. 'Don't turn the lights on here, people might notice. Wait till we get into the auditorium. There're no windows, so if we close all the doors no one will see the lights from the outside.'

They crept through the entrance, one by one, and made their way into the heart of the theatre. The strange atmosphere of the early evening had gone. Now the place seemed empty and a little dingy, with its familiar odour of stale beer, damp and dust.

'We'll set up on the stage,' Warren said, taking charge.

They all sat on the bare boards. Warren rummaged in his bag and drew out the Ouija board, wrapped in appropriately ghostly layers of bubble-wrap. He removed this plastic coat and laid the board on the floor.

'It's beautiful,' Ellie said. 'Where did you find it?'

The board was evidently an antique, about half a metre square and made of smooth, dark wood. The letters of the alphabet circled the board, painted in an ornate style, the words 'yes' and 'no' in the middle, along with the numbers zero to nine. In the four corners she saw a moon, a sun, a cup and a sword, executed in a gothic style with flourishes of gold paint. Years and perhaps use had worn away some of the details, which added to its appeal.

'I found it in an antique shop a couple of years ago,' Warren said, dusting the surface reverently. 'I told you, I'm intrigued by this stuff.'

Ellie studied him more carefully. He was very slight and not very tall, with close-curling black hair and a narrow, pointed face: there was certainly something appealingly pixie-like about him. And he was slightly hyperactive, burning with energy.

'So, what do we do?' Daisy asked.

Warren took out a simple glass tumbler and placed it in the centre of the board, upside down. Next he handed out scraps of paper and pencils to the other members of the group.

'You have this all planned out,' Alex said.

Warren nodded quickly. 'I'll lead this session – don't speak. Just do what I say. When the session is over I'd like you to write down everything you remember on the paper I've given you.'

They were all suddenly quiet and subdued, facing the unknown.

'Is everyone sure they want to do this?' Alex said. 'It's not too late to change your mind.'

Warren gave him a quick, hostile look. No one else spoke.

'Right,' Warren said. 'Then we shall begin. First I want you to relax and clear your mind. Try not to be nervous. Instead, be open. I'll start off with words of protection for us, and a welcome for the spirits in this place. Then I'll ask some questions – simple ones at first. Keep your finger lightly on the glass – don't push it. And if anything strange happens around us, try not to freak out. Just stay focused on the board and don't move your finger from the glass. Then at the end I'll say goodbye to the spirit and close the session. Does everyone understand? Is everyone happy?'

Ellie glanced at the others. They already looked a little freaked out. Perhaps they were all wondering if this was a good idea, if they should back out. Ellie found it hard to gauge her own emotions. She wasn't afraid, as much as tense with anticipation. She also felt oddly distant and elevated, as though she were suspended in the air by a single glittering thread.

Was Harry here? Would he make a sign? She felt both longing and dread at the prospect. She wanted to see him. She wasn't so sure she wanted the other members of the group to see him too.

Warren placed his finger on the glass. The others followed suit. Ellie tried to clear her mind, letting unwanted thoughts pass through without holding on to them. Warren began to speak, addressing the unseen world, stating their good intentions, invoking a protective aura of golden light to protect them from any malicious influence. Ellie didn't listen very carefully. Instead her attention spread from the board and the gathering of friends to the greater space of the theatre, as though she were already tuning in to the place, prodding the fabric of the building for nooks and crannies where the spirits might reside; calling out with mind and body for the one particular compelling spirit who had come to haunt her life, heart and thoughts.

Warren was still talking. He invited the spirits to make themselves known, and offered respect and welcome. His voice filled the auditorium and suddenly Ellie had an image in her mind – that each of the two hundred empty seats was inhabited by a ghost, creating an entire, invisible phantom audience, all those people of a hundred years ago, or more, who had ever taken a place in the theatre to watch a performance.

'Is there anybody there?' Warren said

Surreptitiously Ellie glanced at the others. Sitting

shoulder to shoulder around the board, they all had their heads down, focusing on the board.

Nothing happened.

'Is there anybody there?' Warren repeated. Now Ellie caught Daisy's eye and realised her friend was about to burst into giggles. Ellie caught the current of hilarity and looked away quickly, before she succumbed.

Then the glass moved.

It slid abruptly across the board and came to rest on the word 'yes'. They all snatched their fingers away and stared, amazed. Ellie felt her hand tingle, from the tip of her finger through her palm and along the length of her arm.

'My God,' Daisy said. They were all afraid now. Ellie sensed it, the change of mood in the group.

'Put your fingers back,' Warren commanded. 'Don't worry. You'll be quite safe. It can't hurt us.'

They all obeyed. Warren pushed the glass back to the centre of the board.

'Who are you?' Warren said. Despite his reassurance, he couldn't keep a tremor from his voice. Nothing happened. He rephrased the question.

'Are you a man?'

The glass shot to the 'yes' again.

'Are you linked to the theatre?' Another yes.

'Who are you?' The energy in the board seemed to ebb away. Warren hurried in with another question.

'Do you have a message for us?'

Immediately the glass began to move, racing across the board. Ellie glanced at the others again, particularly Warren. Was he pushing it? Hard to tell. But she felt again the tingle in the finger resting on the glass as it slid from letter to letter, a tingle that began to feel perilously close to pain, as though pins were being pushed into her skin. A sensation of intense cold crept along her arm and down into her chest.

'What do the letters say?' Alex said. Ellie hadn't been keeping track but Carly piped up.

'E . . . L . . . L . . . I . . . E,' she read.

'Ellie?' Warren said indignantly. He took his finger off the glass, which skidded to a halt in the centre of the board. He glared at her. Daisy giggled.

'You did this. I suppose you think this is a laugh.' Warren said. 'Why can't you be serious? You want to make me look stupid?'

Daisy stifled her giggle, turning it into a cough. Tension drained away again. Everything seemed utterly, boringly normal. Carly rubbed her eyes and gave a huge yawn.

'You think *I* did that?' Ellie said.

'Obviously, yes! D'you think I'm an idiot?'

'It wasn't me,' Ellie said. The others were all looking at her, with a mixture of amusement and annoyance.

'She might not have done it on purpose,' Carly said. 'These things can be subconscious.'

Alex nodded. Warren shook his head moodily. Ellie wasn't defensive. She didn't think she'd moved the glass. She had a good idea who had.

'We'll try again,' Warren said. He gave Ellie a stern look. 'No fooling around this time.'

Ellie shrugged. She felt curiously calm; Warren wasn't going to upset her. They all put their fingers back on the glass. Warren took a deep breath, in and out. Then he said, 'Who's there? Please, tell us your name.'

Silence. The glass didn't move. They all stared at the board. Carly yawned again, and so did Daisy. Ellie glanced at Alex. It was hard to read his face. He wasn't giving much away.

'I'll try one more time,' Warren closed his eyes, seeming to gather his strength. 'Is there somebody there? Please, speak to us. Give us a sign.'

This time the glass bucked under their fingers and cracked through the middle, a sound like a gunshot.

They snatched their hands away and the glass fell neatly in two. The light switched off and on again. Nobody spoke or moved.

Ellie felt a wash of cold, then, just as swiftly, she was burning up and sweat erupted on her face and neck. The lights went out again.

'I'm really scared now,' Daisy whispered, invisible in the darkness. 'I didn't really believe anything would happen. Warren, I want this to stop.'

'Stay calm,' Alex said. 'Just hang on a moment. Nothing's going to hurt you.'

Something cold and wet brushed Ellie's face. She couldn't see what it was, in the dark. She jumped and rubbed her cheek. 'What was that?'

The lights came on again.

'It's snow. Oh my God, it's snow,' Warren said, jumping to his feet. Ellie looked up. Impossibly, snowflakes were falling onto the stage. They appeared on the air a few metres beneath the level of the ceiling. The snow settled on the boards, and on the hair and shoulders of the five people.

'This is very weird,' Alex said, standing up and holding out his hand to receive the snow. 'I think we should get out of here.'

Ellie didn't move, enjoying the feathery touch of the cold flakes on her face as she stared up at the ceiling. Harry was here. He'd spelled out her name on the board. Nothing else mattered. Nothing else in the world existed. The uncanny snowfall was no more strange than her previous encounters with Harry. She wasn't unsettled. Her connection with the ghost seemed more logical and real than anything else in her life right now.

The snowfall stopped as abruptly as it had started.

For a few seconds, the snow lingered on the floor before this too disappeared. The members of the seance were all standing up now, spread across the stage. Only Carly and Daisy stood huddled together.

'What's that?' Warren said.

Something else was falling from above – white, like the snow, though the pieces were larger.

'It's paper,' Alex said. 'Pieces of paper.' He tried to catch one. 'There's writing on it.' The paper flakes floated to the ground but didn't land. Each piece faded and disappeared just before touching the stage.

'It's something by Shakespeare.' Warren scrutinised the scrap in his hand.

'*Romeo and Juliet*,' Ellie said.

'How do you know?'

She wasn't looking at the pieces. 'Just a guess.'

Warren looked at her suspiciously, as though he suspected she'd set up the whole thing.

'I think we should leave,' Alex said again. 'Come on. Daisy? Carly?'

They both seemed frozen, unable to move. Alex shook his head and walked over to them. He took each by the hand, as though they were children, and led them from the stage.

'We can't just go,' Warren shouted. 'That's not the procedure. We have to close the session down! Don't you see? We have to send the spirit back!'

'You do what you like,' Alex said. 'I'm taking these two out of here. This was an incredibly stupid idea.' He glanced at Ellie. 'You coming?'

Ellie felt reluctant to move. 'I'll help Warren. You go on. I'm fine.'

Alex hesitated, the other girls to his left and right. Obviously he couldn't force Ellie to leave but he didn't look happy that she wanted to stay.

'I'll wait outside,' he said. 'Don't be long. Warren – do whatever it is you think you have to do, but get a move on.'

Warren straightened up, obviously bristling at Alex's commanding tone, but he didn't reply. Alex glanced once more at Ellie then turned away, taking Daisy and Carly out of the theatre. They both clutched his hands, saying nothing.

Paper was still falling. Ellie and Warren heard the main door shut.

'So, what do we do now?' Ellie said. Although she hadn't wanted to leave, alone with Warren and the spectral presence, she was afraid.

'Sit with me, at the board.' Warren was obviously nervous too. 'We have to send the spirit back, thank it, say goodbye. Otherwise – it might stay here. Like opening a door and not closing it again.'

Ellie did as she was told. Warren started his incantation. The falling paper disappeared. Although the lights were on, the rows of seats in the auditorium seemed to be in shadow. Ellie wondered again if all the seats were filled by ghosts, staring at her, watching them perform on the stage.

'Spirit, we thank you for your visit,' Warren said. He cleared his throat. 'Now it is time for you to return. We respectfully ask you to leave this theatre and go back to the place you came from.'

A loud clanking noise erupted from the bowels of the theatre, something from the antiquated heating system perhaps. Ellie and Warren exchanged nervous glances.

The crude metallic sound peaked and died away again. Warren repeated his request. The lights went out again. Silence.

'Warren? Are you okay?' Ellie couldn't see him in the dark, although he was only inches away from her.

Warren didn't answer.

'Ellie.' The voice came from behind her. Ellie recognised it instantly, went hot and cold. She wanted to say his name but couldn't speak. Did Warren hear this voice too?

Did she dare turn round? Slowly, slowly, she moved, still sitting, trying not to make a sound.

There. There he was.

Although it was dark, she could see Harry perfectly.

'Can you see him, Warren?' She forced herself to speak.

Warren didn't answer. She stood up, legs awkward, riddled with pins and needles. As were her hands and arms.

'What have you done to Warren? Is he okay?'

'Yes,' Harry said. He held out a hand, wanting her to move closer. Ellie took a step, and another, staring hungrily at Harry all the time, feeding on the sight of him, the face she could never entirely imagine. She was close to him now, her gaze wandering over him, never quite able to make eye contact.

'You look different,' she said. 'More real.'

'I am real. As real as I can be, for you.' His hand was still extended, solid-looking, tempting. Ellie reached out to touch it – but her fingers passed through. They both closed their fingers, as though they might be able to hold on.

'You're not real,' she said.

'What does real mean? You hear what I say. I'm here. Me.'

He was looking at her with the same intense hunger. It made her embarrassed, and pleased.

'Shall I show you the theatre?' he said softly. The darkness melted, replaced by a warm, yellow light. Ellie drew a breath, lost for words. She looked around, from the stage to the auditorium, at the balcony and the domed ceiling.

Red and cream and gold. Gas footlights burned in a line at the front of the stage. She turned to Warren, but he'd vanished, along with the Ouija board and everything else belonging to the Marine Theatre of the twenty-first century.

'Where's Warren? Is he okay?'

'He's fine,' Harry said. 'We won't be more than a moment. Take a look. Enjoy it.'

Ellie's gaze swept the place – the tiny provincial theatre seemed more like a miniature version of the Paris Opera. Rows of red velvet seats, a balcony framed in curlicues of gold, the ceiling painted with sun and moon, winged gods and cherubs. A huge chandelier hung from the ceiling, its multitude of glass drops glinting in the light.

'My God,' Ellie breathed. 'How did the town afford a place like this?'

'A wealthy benefactor,' Harry smiled. 'It's wonderful, isn't it?'

It was like standing inside a jewellery box, lined with scarlet, glittering with gold, a closed-off, precious place.

She turned to Harry again, a smile spreading across her face. Harry smiled too.

'I've been longing to see you smile,' he said. 'Do you have any idea how beautiful you look when you smile?'

This made her smile more, and the sight of Harry, his own face bright with delight, made her heart swell.

'You performed *Romeo and Juliet* here,' she said. 'As Mercutio.'

'I did.'

'What happened to you?' Ellie said. 'Why are you still here, in the theatre?'

'I'm waiting for someone.'

'For who?'

He frowned and shook his head. 'I waited a long time. I was angry and hurt. I remember – I was furious.' He paced across the theatre, thinking. 'Then everything began to fade. I was still here – still waiting – but I forgot why. Only the feeling remained. And gradually that grew thin too.

122

Until the day you found the model theatre. Till I found you. Now I am awake again. I think I was always waiting for you.'

Ellie shook her head. 'You can't have been waiting for me at the beginning. You didn't know me. And why would you be angry and hurt?'

'I don't know,' Harry said. He stopped pacing. 'But I was waiting for you. I know it. I feel it.' He touched his chest with his fist, not looking at her, caught up in his thoughts. 'There is so much I can't remember.' He scowled with the effort of it, trying to find his memories.

'You have to try,' Ellie said.

'Don't tell me what to do.'

She stopped short. Harry lifted himself from his thoughts and went to Ellie.

'I'm sorry,' he said. 'So – why are *you* sad?'

'I lost someone,' she said simply. 'Someone very precious. I lost my mother.'

'She died?' Harry said.

'Yes. Eighteen months ago now. She died, and everything fell apart. Everything – well, *my* everything. Obviously, life for everyone else went on pretty much as before.'

She shook her head. 'I don't want to talk about this now. I don't want to think about it.'

'No,' Harry said softly. 'Let's enjoy the moment.' He stretched out his hand. Ellie tried to reach out, but again her hand passed through his.

'Impossible,' she said. 'I can't touch you.'

Harry looked into her eyes, his arm still extended. The

gas light diminished and the scene of the old theatre was softly snuffed out.

'Ellie? Where are you?' Warren's voice, sounding plaintive.

Electric light flooded the auditorium, harsh and unforgiving. The place seemed dull and flat, all atmosphere drained away. Ellie frowned.

'What happened? How long were the lights off?' she said. Warren was still sitting in the same place.

'A couple of seconds, I think.' He looked tired and annoyed. 'Let's get on with this, shall we? Will you sit down again?'

Warren recited his closing and farewells to the world of the spirits. Ellie didn't pay much attention. She was too busy thinking about Harry. Warren was clearly unaware of the conversation she'd had with the ghost. He'd missed it all.

Warren shoved the board and glass back into his bag, and scooped up the pieces of paper he'd handed out for recording any visitation. No one had written anything.

'Let's get out of here,' he said. 'The others will be waiting.'

Ellie glanced at the stage. Snow and paper had vanished.

They turned off all the lights on their way out. Alex, Daisy and Carly were still standing outside.

'Everything okay?' Alex said.

Warren nodded. 'Sure. Fine.'

Carly and Daisy were huddled up, shivering in the chilly night air.

'Come to my house,' Alex said. 'Everyone. My parents

will be in bed – they won't mind, if we're not too noisy. I think we should have a coffee or something before everyone goes home. Calm us down.'

Ellie glanced at the other girls, who both nodded. Warren, however, had other plans.

'I've got to go,' he said. 'I'll be okay. But – thanks anyway.'

'Please come,' Daisy jumped in. 'I think you should. We need to come down from this – talk about it.' She looked to the others for back-up. Alex nodded.

'She's right. Just a quick coffee. We can talk about what happened.'

Warren looked from one face to the other.

'Please,' Ellie said. She touched his arm. 'You're shivering. Come with us.'

Warren glanced again at Daisy, then nodded. 'Okay.' He locked the theatre's main doors, and Alex led the way out of the courtyard and up the hill to his home.

15

A small light burned in the window of Alex's home.

As they approached the little house on the path through the overgrown garden, Ellie realised this light was a candle, flickering in an ornamental lantern on the windowsill. The sea sounded very loud. The garden, in the moonlight, was grey and silver – pockets of shadow, plains of glittering grass. Something rustled in a bush to their right. Daisy let out a squeak of alarm.

Alex opened the door and ushered them into the kitchen. He put the kettle on and took mugs from the draining board. The others sat around the big table as the cat came in and jumped onto Ellie's lap. She stroked its cool, fragrant fur.

Carly asked Alex about a picture on the wall. Daisy said something that made Warren laugh. Ellie stroked the cat as it kneaded her thighs with its paws. She felt very tired, and tremendously happy – high even – in the aftermath of her latest encounter with Harry. She'd seen him. They'd spoken. He'd tried to reach out to her. Ellie savoured the memory, playing over each moment in her imagination. Could she conjure up his face now, in her mind's eye? That was still difficult. But replaying her emotions, what she'd felt when he'd stood before her – that was easy and unspeakably delicious.

She watched the others – Alex making the coffee, Warren chatting with Carly and Daisy – and felt a million miles away. Her existence was bound up with Harry. When would she see him again?

Alex plonked a mug on the table in front of her.

'What are you thinking about?' he said. 'Are you okay? What happened after we went outside?'

Warren piped up from the other side of the table, 'Not a lot. Some noise, clanking pipes, that kind of thing. The lights went out for a couple of seconds, and then when they came on again everything was back to normal.' He looked at Ellie, seeking confirmation of his account. She nodded.

'Yeah. That's about it.' Why didn't she tell them about the ghost? Why didn't she share the story of Harry? Of course she had shared it with Daisy, a half-truth anyway, not mentioning her crush was a ghost, someone who'd died a hundred years ago. She didn't want them to know. Harry belonged to her. The relationship was too strange to be exposed. They wouldn't believe her. They'd think she was mad. (*Was* she mad?)

Alex, the perfect host, found a tin of chocolate biscuits and put it on the table. Finally, after the chat, Warren started talking about their experience in the theatre – what they had seen and felt. Ellie, too, told them what she could remember, up to the point when Harry had appeared. She felt uncomfortable about this deception – keeping the truth from them, her friends. But she was too afraid of what they might think if she told them everything.

The conversation took a curious turn. Once they'd all described what had happened, Alex, Warren, Carly and Daisy began to find rational explanations for everything. They all played down the fall of snow and paper, denying what had happened. The snow? Moisture from the damp roof. The paper? Some of the ceiling's dodgy lining. Imagination and group hysteria had made these incidents seem ghostly and uncanny, they rationalised. Ellie, sitting outside this process, observed how they colluded in smoothing over the supernatural events at the theatre. It was easier and safer to reframe these events so the world stayed safe and predictable. Perhaps people's minds were designed to work this way, a kind of mental immune system, to protect yourself.

'So, Ellie,' Warren said. 'You did move the glass to spell out your name. Admit it. I know you did. I won't be cross. Just tell me the truth.'

Ellie shook her head. 'I didn't move it.'

'She might have done it unconsciously,' Daisy said. 'Y'know. Without meaning to. Without knowing she was doing it.'

So the séance was explained away. Everyone began to relax. Warren's rather hectic, touchy manner changed. His face, which had become pinched and ratty, relaxed and opened again. How comforting it was to sit in a circle around the table nursing mugs of coffee and munching chocolate biscuits. At one thirty Warren stood up and said he had to go. He offered to escort Carly and Daisy, as they lived en route to his house. Alex glanced at Ellie.

'Then I'll take you home.'

'You don't need to – honestly. It's not far – and it's perfectly safe.'

'Nowhere's perfectly safe. There might be drunks around, all sorts, from out of town. It'll only take me ten minutes.'

They left the house and stood together on the road outside, a little huddle, hugging each other and saying goodbyes. Then the huddle divided into two. Alex offered Ellie his jacket to wear. Daisy glanced at them, then gave a little wave.

'You're shivering,' he said.

'I'm okay,' Ellie said.

'Please – take it. I've got a jumper and your arms are bare.'

So she took it, sliding her arms into sleeves already warmed by Alex's healthy, living body, grateful for the comfort.

'What's going on, Ellie?' Alex said as they walked.

'What d'you mean?'

'What aren't you telling me? I don't know, there's something about you tonight – like you're holding yourself back – y'know, apart from everyone else. I'm not stupid – something's going on.'

Ellie was nettled. She pushed her hair back from her face. Alex didn't sound cross so much as – hurt?

She thought quickly, wondering what to say.

'Is it about this boyfriend?'

'Boyfriend?!' Ellie panicked. How did he know?

'Daisy said something to me, about someone from home.'

'Did she?'

'Don't worry,' Alex hurried on. 'She didn't mean to betray any confidence. It's my fault – I asked her if you were seeing anyone, and she said she thought you had someone at home. That's all.'

Ellie relaxed. He'd given her a way out. 'Yeah, that's it. I was thinking about him. Harry – that's his name.'

Alex nodded. They walked in silence for another couple of minutes. Her house appeared at the top of a little hill. When they were outside the front door Ellie fished in her pocket for the key and handed back Alex's jacket.

'Thanks for the jacket,' she said. 'And for the walk home. I appreciate it.'

Alex hovered uncertainly for a moment. Then he said, 'Fancy another walk tomorrow? I'm at a bit of a loose end, and, well, I enjoyed your company last time.'

'What about Daisy? Can she come too?' She wondered what Daisy had thought when Alex had offered to walk Ellie home. Now she was fishing to find out what Alex felt about Daisy.

'She's working all day tomorrow.'

'Oh. Okay. That'd be cool.' Did he know Daisy liked him? Did he like Daisy too?

Alex was backing away. 'Come round in the morning,' he called out. 'Any time you like. And if you want to bring your script we can practise before the rehearsal.'

Ellie waved from the doorstep, watching Alex as he turned away and jogged back down the hill.

*   *   *

Bliss – to lie in bed and think about Harry. She tuned in again to the sensation of falling. That was how it felt, this letting go, reaching out for him. Nothing else mattered now. The rest of her life seemed faded, almost mono-chrome – a desert of time to be endured before she saw Harry again. When would that be? Would he come to her again tonight?

She lay on her back, staring at the ceiling, arms by her side. She replayed their meeting in the theatre, the giant jewellery box of red and gold, trying to remember his face, his gestures and expressions. How would she ever sleep?

But sleep she did, eventually, exhausted by the long day and the emotional turmoil. No dreams she could remember. When she woke ten hours later, she was still lying on her back and she could hear a gentle knocking on the door.

'Ellie?' Her grandmother, sounding worried. 'It's nearly lunchtime. Do you want something to eat?'

Ellie, groggy and disorientated, didn't answer right away.

'Ellie? Are you awake? I'm coming in.' The door latch lifted and Jean peered through the opening.

Ellie sat up in bed. 'Hey, Grandma, I'm okay. Tired, that's all. I didn't get in till late.' She rubbed her face and pushed her hair back. 'I'll just have a cup of tea, is that okay?'

Her grandmother retreated. Ellie jumped out of bed. She looked at her journal – nothing from Harry. She picked up her phone. Two texts from Alex. She'd agreed to see him this morning. Guiltily she read the messages. The first asked what time she was coming round. The second, sent twenty minutes ago, said he'd be at the Sea Point Café till 12.30 pm if she still wanted to meet up. Clearly he was fed up of waiting at home.

Ellie jumped out of bed and pulled on her clothes. She hurried downstairs, shouting out to her grandmother as she ran through the hall. 'Don't worry about the tea! I'm seeing Alex – sorry! Back later, okay? Love you!' She caught a glimpse of her standing with a mug in her hand and her mouth open in surprise.

At least, Ellie thought, as she jogged down the road, they can't complain that I'm spending all my time moping around the house.

16

She hurried through town to the café. Another hot day, another summer holiday scene. She pushed through meandering families along the seafront, kids sucking ice lollies and mums browsing racks of postcards on the pavements. The café stood at the far end of the promenade, with its row of tables on a terrace just above the level of the pavement. It was almost half past. Had Alex already given up and gone? She squinted at the tables. There he was.

'Alex? I'm so sorry I'm late! I overslept.'

He was sitting on his own, an untrendy orange cap on his head shading his face from the sun, a notebook open on the table. He looked up and gave a lazy smile. He didn't look upset.

'Ellie – hey. What d'you want to drink?' He signalled to the waitress as Ellie plonked herself in the seat opposite.

'So,' he said. 'You slept the morning away. Not surprised – it was quite a night.'

Ellie turned her thoughts to the séance in the theatre. Although the encounter with Harry still burned in her mind, the rest of the goings-on seemed a little hazy. She remembered the fall of snow, the tumbling paper, but these memories were fading. They didn't seem quite real. Her mind, too, seemed to be protecting her from the intrusion of the supernatural. Except for Harry, of course. Nothing could protect her from him.

The waitress brought a smoothie for Ellie. She peered surreptitiously at Alex's notebook. A sketch of some kind, and notes.

'What are you doing?'

'Oh, thinking of some stuff for the play. I'm supposed to be dreaming up a set. I told Mike I could make sort of puppets for some of the fairy characters. Might have been a bit rash of me. He was really keen, but it'll be a lot of work.'

'Can I see?'

Alex gave a goofy grin and pushed the notebook across the table. Ellie turned the book around. He'd sketched a stage set with twisted trees rising around an egg-shaped empty space in the centre of the stage, a magical heart of the forest. His drawing style had a light touch, pencil lines skimming the paper, very elegant and graceful.

'I like it,' she said. 'How would you make the trees?'

'Oh, simple enough. Two dimensional images painted on cut-out pieces of MDF. Time-consuming but not difficult. We can use lighting to change the colour and atmosphere.'

Ellie's hand hovered over the book.

'Can I look?' she said. 'Would you mind?'

'No, of course not.'

She flicked back through previous pages, studying his earlier drawings – observations of natural scenes – gateways and stiles; trees; rocks and driftwood on the beach – all drawn with precision, delicacy and a curious otherworldly atmosphere. Now and then she found a sketch of a fairy creature, like the ones she'd seen in his attic room; quirky, appealing creatures with elemental faces.

Alex studied her as she examined the drawings, waiting for her reactions.

'You're a curious mix,' she said, closing the book and sitting back in her chair.

'Why d'you say that?' He took off the orange cap and gave her a very direct look, his eyes vivid blue in the sunshine.

'Well,' she hesitated, 'you seem, you know, such a down-to-earth, rooted sort of person and yet you've got the kind of imagination that creates all this mystical fairy stuff.'

Alex grinned. 'I don't think that's odd. It makes perfect sense.' His strong, honey-brown hands played with the cap. 'But enough about me. I want to know more about you.'

'What d'you want to know?'

'I tell you what – I'll ask you questions, and if you don't want to answer, don't. How's that?'

'Okay.'

He hesitated a moment. 'I'm very curious about your mum,' he said. 'She and dad knew each other when they were young. He told me they were friends. What was she like? I mean, what sort of person?'

Ellie took a sip from her glass, giving herself time to think.

'People say I look like her,' Ellie said. 'Actually, that's

what your dad said. I suppose I do. She was very bright – brilliant at maths. Unlike me. She did some kind of university research, and after I was born, she gave that up for a while. When I started school she did some university teaching part-time. That was pretty cool because it meant she had the school holidays free.'

'But what sort of person was she?'

'Oh – quite quiet, actually. Sort of cool. Not a big extrovert. She didn't give much away, at least, not to people she didn't know. But she was strong – in some ways stronger than my dad, I think. And gentle, thoughtful, very kind.'

'Didn't give much away? That sounds like you too,' Alex said. 'And that quality of coolness.'

'Really? It's hard to know how you come across to other people. I don't feel calm. Inside I'm a mess.'

'Maybe your mum didn't feel cool or calm either.'

'She was always really organised. A bit *too* organised. She and Dad squabbled about it sometimes, he's so messy. She liked everything in its place. You should have seen her office – all white and uncluttered, not a scrap of paper lying around.' Now she'd started, Ellie found the words came easily. 'She made the house lovely. Clean and minimal, but not sterile, not at all. She liked art – maybe that's what she had in common with your dad. We had some great pictures. She chose odd, wonderful things. But she liked light and space so much, that's what I remember most about the house, when she was alive. Even in the winter, the place was full of sunshine. It was weird visiting other people's houses – they always seemed so dark.'

Alex listened attentively. His presence and focus were

exactly what she needed. She hadn't been able to speak like this to her grandparents or her father. They knew her mother too well. They had their own versions of her, their own memories. But Alex knew next to nothing about her mum and she could tell him all about her, the woman she knew, and he didn't interrupt or try to help, he simply gave his attention: a rare gift. She bathed in it.

'She gave me so much,' Ellie said. 'Of course I never appreciated it – well, not until she died. I keep thinking about what I've lost in the now – and all the things I won't have in the future. Isn't that stupid? I think, one day I'll graduate from university. One day maybe I'll get married. What if I have a child? And my mum won't be there to share it. I actually find myself grieving for something that hasn't even happened yet. I know it's crazy, but I can't help it.

'And it's only now, when she's gone, that I've started to appreciate everything she did and who she was. I wish I could tell her – but it's too late. I wish she could hear what I want to say.'

She stopped talking. Alex waited a moment then said, 'I don't think it's too late. It's never too late. You can still tell her.'

But Ellie only half heard him. Something had occurred to her. Something so stupendously obvious she couldn't believe she hadn't thought of it before. If Harry could speak to her from beyond the grave, couldn't her mother do the same? Would Harry be able to help her communicate with her mum again?

'Ellie?' Alex touched her arm. 'Are you okay?'

She was miles away, staring into space.

'What? Yeah, I'm okay.'

'I don't suppose you remembered your script.'

'No, I didn't. I rushed out. Sorry.'

'Rushed out? You rushed for me?' he teased. 'I hope I was worth it.' A big, sunny smile on his face. Ellie grinned back. No wonder Daisy likes you, she thought. You are a truly lovely guy.

17

Ellie stopped in the green lane. Huge hedges grew to left and right creating an arch above her head; a lush, leafy tunnel. Late dog roses dropped petals. Dusky blue harebells and tough nettles dotted the long grass.

She tried to see through the hedge. According to her map, North Hill House stood on the other side but the dense wall of foliage blocked her view. She walked on, map in one hand, a camera in the canvas bag on her back.

North Hill House was relatively isolated, being attached neither to the town nor the next village. She'd found it on the Ordnance Survey walkers' map, situated – of course – on a hill to the north, about two miles away. She decided to walk, taking a footpath past more old mills along the stream out of town, and then on the green lane. Harry's home . . . she wondered what she would find.

She walked on. A hundred metres further along, Ellie spied a thinning of the hedge. She waded through nettles and pushed her way through prickly hawthorn branches to a broken wooden fence in the middle of the hedge. Holding her arm in front of her face, bare skin snagged by thorns, she ducked and climbed through the bars, to emerge on a stony drive beside a tall, red brick wall.

She was cautious, not knowing what to expect. Some other family would live here now and wouldn't welcome intruders. She had no exact plan in mind, only a burning desire to learn more about Harry. If she could just see the place, she'd have another piece in the puzzle.

A cast-iron plaque on the wall declared 'North Hill House'. The drive opened up into a yard, where stables had been converted into garages and outhouses. The place was quiet, and tatty. Weeds sprang through the gravelled yard. Ellie peered through a wide iron gate, seeing a front garden with a long, rectangular pond. A chain looped around the bars of the gate, but it wasn't padlocked. Was nobody living here? She opened the gate and stepped inside. She imagined him, Harry, walking in the garden.

A red brick house, eight tall windows with white frames, and a door in the middle with a porch. Ellie looked into a window but saw nothing because pale wooden shutters were closed on the inside of the room. Was the place empty? It seemed so. No cars outside, all the windows obscured. She stood up straight, feeling more confident. She took out her camera and snapped a couple of pictures. She had an excuse lined up – some local history research – but it didn't seem as though she'd need it. She found an overgrown orchard and more gardens at the rear of the house, and a large conservatory, with green-stained glass. A solitary bird sang, spilling long, melancholy notes on the air. Ellie took another couple of pictures then sat on a low stone bench on the terrace behind the conservatory. It was a shady spot, occasionally pierced by bright sunlight. She took a deep breath, smelling roses and lavender.

'This is where you lived,' she said. 'This is your place, Harry. Are you here? Can you see me now?'

Again she imagined him walking in the garden, passing through light and shadow. She imagined him striding towards her through the long grass, sunshine and shade passing across his face, and him climbing the three steps to the terrace and sitting beside her on the bench, and his proximity, and the shape of his face.

Ellie opened her eyes. He wasn't here. Nothing indicated his presence. But the house was beautiful, and she loved it simply because he had lived here.

She looked properly at the conservatory. Something caught her eyes. Was the glass broken? Ellie stood up to investigate. Yes – on one side, close to the wall of the house, one of the panes had cracked and half the glass had fallen from the rotting wooden frame. Dared she climb inside?

Ellie glanced over her shoulder. Everything was quiet. It would be a squeeze, and she was wary of the glass, but this opportunity seemed such a gift, she couldn't resist it. She put her bag over the edge of the broken glass and clambered into the conservatory.

The light changed, filtered through the green-stained glass panes. Dry, dusty air. The conservatory was empty, except for a broken cane chair and a pile of paving stones. She opened the French doors into the main body of the house.

She stepped into a tall, well-proportioned room with white walls and bare floorboards. Her eyes adjusted to the low light as she wandered into the next room, a spacious kitchen with a window, without shutters, also overlooking the back garden. Judging by the style of the kitchen, she guessed it had last been updated in the 1980s but of course that didn't mean it had been empty since then. How would it have looked at the end of the nineteenth century when Harry had lived here? She stared out of the window. Maybe some of those apple trees had endured since that time. Harry might have seen a view similar to the one she was seeing now.

She took more photographs and then wandered into the other dim downstairs rooms before climbing the stairs to the first floor and exploring the bedrooms, which were all bare and empty. It was the shell of a home, though an elegant enough shell, well proportioned, with fireplaces and plaster mouldings on the ceilings. But she was a bit disappointed. Why was that? What had she expected? Of course, she'd nursed a quiet hope of seeing Harry.

'Oh, Harry,' she said aloud. 'Where *are* you?'

A fly buzzed in the fireplace. From beyond the window Ellie heard a bird clatter its wings. A moment of peace – and then – unmistakably – the sound of a car and the crunch of tyres on the gravelled drive.

Panic. Ellie bolted out of the room. She'd broken into someone's house. How was she going to get out? What if they caught her here and thought she was a burglar, or a vandal? Heart thundering, she galloped down the stairs. So many windows were covered she couldn't see out. Presumably whoever had come would enter through the front door? She careered along the corridor to the room with the French doors and out into the conservatory. Her bag lay where she'd left it, draped over the edge of the broken glass. Clumsy with haste, Ellie dived through the gap and fell onto the weed-broken terrace outside. Sweating, worried, she stood for a couple of seconds to catch her breath and listen out for the new arrival.

She couldn't hear a sound. Ellie skirted the edge of the house, senses alert. She glimpsed a small red car parked beyond the garden gates.

'Hello, can I help you?'

Ellie jumped back, in shock. As she'd peered at the car, she'd almost walked into a short, square woman with iron-grey hair: a smart, respectable-looking person, in a well-cut red skirt and jacket.

Ellie stared, open-mouthed like an idiot. The woman looked her up and down then eyed the camera in Ellie's hand. She had strong black eyebrows and perfect lipstick, reminding Ellie a little of the head teacher at her old school.

'Can I help you?' the woman repeated, a little louder. Ellie gathered her thoughts and noticed that she didn't actually sound unfriendly. 'Are you lost?'

'I . . . I . . .' Ellie began, thinking fast. 'I was looking for North Hill House. This is it, isn't it? I'm doing a research project on a family that lived here a century ago, it's in connection with plans for an exhibition about the Marine Theatre at the museum.'

'Oh. Oh I see,' the woman said. 'Well this is it, North Hill House. I'm Maddy Thurlow, the estate agent. The house is going on the market soon. It's been empty for several years – the owners live in London. Glorious place – would make a wonderful B&B. I just came to check it over.'

'So, do you think the owners know anything about its history? Do you know anyone round here who might be able to help?'

'I live in Axminster, so I can't help you. But I know someone's published a couple of local history books, and one of them has a lot of information about this parish. We've got it in the office. You should give him a try. Here.' The woman fished in her bag. 'Write down your email address and I'll send you his name.'

She was as good as her word. By the time Ellie had arrived home, an email had arrived, with a name and contact details. Ellie wrote an email to the suggested local historian right away, asking for any information on North Hill House and its previous owners. Then she sat on her bed and scribbled furiously in her journal until her grandmother called her downstairs for supper.

At seven thirty, the next rehearsal began. They had a punishing schedule, meeting four evenings a week, all day Saturday and, in smaller groups, on some weekday afternoons to practise individual scenes.

They were standing on the stage. Mike was cross. None of them had learned any lines and he harangued them to be serious. He told them what a challenge they faced, how hard they needed to work, how great the rewards would be.

No one seemed very enthusiastic. Warren looked tired,

yawning, hardly paying attention. Ellie gazed around the theatre. She was trying to see the auditorium as it had been the previous night, when Harry had shown her the theatre of his time, ripe with red and gold. With a little effort she could superimpose the image of the theatre-past on top of the tired modern version. Reality could fade away.

They rehearsed for three hours.

She had to admit, Mike was a good director. Ellie watched him focus, planning out the scenes. When her turn came, he was observant, constructive and encouraging. She tried to work out how to be Puck, otherwise known as Robin Goodfellow, the mischievous fairy. Gradually the obsessing about Harry faded away, and she lost herself in the flow of the work, paying attention to the text, her lines, the physical awareness she needed to forget she was Ellie, becoming Puck instead.

They had times of frustration and moments of triumph. By the end of the session they were all tired and happy. Everyone went to the pub, about twenty altogether, including Mike. Now the rehearsal was over, thoughts of Harry took over Ellie's mind again. Would he communicate with her tonight? Would he write in her book? Would she see him? At eleven she made her excuses and walked home, claiming, truthfully, to be tired. She turned on the computer and checked her mail.

Two messages: one from her father, and one from the local historian. She quickly scanned her father's email – telling her some details about his trip and asking how she was. He signed off with another plea for her to reply. Then she turned to the second email.

Dear Ellie

Many thanks for your email. I am always delighted to find young people interested in local history and I do indeed know your grandparents. Your family has deep roots in the town.

I am intrigued to learn about your research into the Marine Theatre and people connected with it, and your plans for an exhibition at the town museum. Your model theatre sounds quite a find – I do hope I see it for myself one day. I do know about North Hill House. At the turn of the twentieth-century it belonged to the Weatherstone family. I know little about them off the top of my head but I can certainly find out more. Give me a couple of days and I'll get back to you with anything I learn. In the meantime, you may find more in the archives at the museum. Many individuals and organisations have donated correspondence and various other documents to the museum. It's a long and sometimes arduous process trawling through dross to find the pearls, but your grandfather may be able to help.

Thanks again for your interest – and for giving me a little quest.

All best wishes
Roger Bishop

Weatherstone. Harry Weatherstone. Ellie turned off the computer and wrote the name in her journal, along with a description of North Hill House. Every ounce of information seemed to make him more real. She'd seen his home, she knew his name, and she had the promise of more to come.

The house was quiet, her grandparents already in bed.

Ellie wandered round her room, picking things up, putting them down. The longing to see Harry was so intense she didn't know what to do. She put on his shirt again, willing him to appear. She lay on her bed, hugging the shirt against her body, aching to know how it would feel to lie in his arms. She tried to read, but couldn't concentrate. She turned the computer on again and wasted time aimlessly surfing the net. Nothing held her interest. She turned it off again and crouched in front of the model theatre.

'Where are you, Harry?' she whispered. 'Why don't you come?'

Far away the church clock tolled once. Ellie paced her room. Why was time so slow now? How many minutes and hours did she have to endure before she could see him? She needed to move, to burn off this restlessness.

Still wearing Harry's shirt, Ellie slipped on her shoes, crept downstairs and out of the front door into a clear, cool night. The town was quiet, lights on in the pub at the end of the road, though she couldn't hear any noise from inside. A man stood at the door, smoking a cigarette. She strode past, down the winding road towards the seafront.

The tide was high, silvered waves unrolled on the pebbles. Ellie walked along the promenade, staring out at the sea. Behind the protective arm of the harbour wall floated dozens of boats. Street lights loomed at intervals, lighting the promenade and the edge of the sea. It was a relief to be moving. Ellie took long strides, eating up the pavement. She walked along the top of the harbour wall, a solitary figure, hands in pockets, until she stood right at the end. Then she turned back and stared at the town, the pebbled and sandy beaches, the lights shining like jewels. Waves crashed into the wall. The breeze picked at her hair.

She'd tried to stop thinking about Harry, but it was hopeless. Now, standing on the harbour wall, she longed for him to be with her. What would it be like, this moment, if his hand was holding hers? If his strong, warm body was beside her? If she could ask him a question, if she could share what she was thinking and feeling, the particular beauty of this moment? The endless sea beat on the massive stones in the wall. From far away came the low hoot of a distant ship. And Ellie was alone. No one knew where she was. Her father was on the other side of the world, her grandparents asleep.

She took out her mobile from her pocket and toyed with the idea of texting Daisy or Alex. They were probably asleep too. If only she could text Harry. He, more than anyone, was the person she wanted to connect with.

Outside the theatre, she stopped. Her feet had brought her here. The door was locked. She had no way to get inside. This place was her only real connection with Harry – the Marine Theatre and its replica at home. She tried the handle, hoping against hope it would open. Nothing. She was shut out.

Ellie walked home, spirits low. She crept through the house, not wanting to disturb her grandparents, and up to her bedroom.

She opened the door.

Her skin prickled, on her arms and the back of her neck. The subtle, spiced-woody scent, just a whisper of it, floated on the air in her room. Harry – was he here? She stepped inside. Her journal lay open on her bed. She picked it up.

Ellie – I want to see you again. Nothing exists for me, except you. I saw you leave the house. I looked through the window and watched you walking away and I wished I could be with you. What have you done to me?

I've never fallen in love before. How can I describe it? As though a hole has been torn in my heart and the only way I can stop my life bleeding away is to be close to you. You are the only one who can heal me.

I need you, Ellie.

Her hand lost all its strength and the book dropped back to the bed. Her heart seemed to clench like a fist inside her chest. He had described her own feelings about him.

I've never fallen in love before.

She heard him speaking the words in her mind. Slowly she took off her shoes, went to the bathroom, washed her face and brushed her teeth. Her body carried out these ordinary tasks like a robot, her mind detached, spinning with shock and delight.

Harry had fallen in love with her. Why her? What was it he'd seen that had so enchanted him? She raised her gaze from the sink and looked at herself in the mirror on the wall, seeing herself as a stranger would. A pale, unmade-up face, a mass of dark hair. Big eyes, the brows that slanted down to the top of her slightly crooked nose. A face like millions of other faces.

Ellie walked back up the stairs to her room, and lay in bed, in Harry's old shirt and unable to sleep. Every atom in her body was charged and tingling. She was strung out, tense, like a wire.

Did she love Harry? Was this what love felt like, every

fibre of her being focused on the one object, to be with him again? Could she fall in love with a ghost? How futile and insane was that? She was in love with someone she couldn't touch, whose body was made up of light, whose life ended a hundred years before. Except that it hadn't ended – because he could still see and speak and feel.

'I love you too, Harry,' she whispered into the room.

18

'May I come with you to the museum?' Ellie asked.

Her grandparents both looked at her, surprised.

'Why?' her grandfather said. 'I mean, of course, I'd be delighted. Just to look around, or do you have a particular goal in mind?'

They were sitting at the table. Ellie had a piece of buttered toast on her plate, but she wasn't hungry. She'd only taken a bite.

'I was thinking about what you said – about the theatre and the exhibition. I think it would be a great idea. I'd like to find out more about it.'

'But . . .' Jean began, frowning, obviously remembering how upset Ellie had been when David first came up with the idea. 'Are you sure that's what you'd like? Why the change of heart?'

'I'm sorry. I was just being stupid before. I would like to do this – honestly.'

David grinned, looking pleased and boyish.

They walked together, taking the footpath along the stream, past gorgeous gardens overflowing with flowers. Her grandfather chattered about various places and people in the town, while Ellie only partly paid attention. She felt gloriously happy this morning, on top of the world. Harry was in love with her, no matter how absurd the situation was.

The museum was tiny, an old square tower with a modern extension not far from the seafront. Ellie had visited it before, with her parents, when she was a little girl, but she didn't remember it very well. Museums were places adults seemed to find endlessly fascinating but she remembered them only as being static and dull. Her grandfather introduced her to the museum manager and another volunteer, a woman of about his own age. He was evidently proud of Ellie, showing her off like a new toy, telling his colleagues about her achievements. Ellie smiled shyly.

'I told you about the model theatre Ellie found – well, she wants to carry out some research,' he declared. The manager and the other volunteer expressed interest and enthusiasm and asked if she would bring the model down one day soon to show them. Again Ellie played along, smiled and agreed. When the chat had died down, she patted her grandfather's arm and asked him to show her the documents relating to the theatre. He led her through a room full of exhibits relating to the town's smuggling past, through the tower's ground floor, and unlocked a door onto a downward flight of stairs and series of three rooms without windows. She smelled the faintest hint of damp, similar to the underground rooms at the theatre.

David guided her to the third room. Metal racking lined the walls, piled high with folders, files, documents, boxes, and plastic bags full of paper: chaos. Ellie's heart sank.

'This is it?' She couldn't hide the dismay in her voice.

'Not what you were expecting? You're right, it is a mess. We have far too much stuff and not enough room. So many people and businesses and organisations bring documents in and we just don't have the manpower to sort and catalogue and file them properly. At least, not at the moment. We need extra space, but I'm not sure where we're going to find it.'

Ellie took a deep breath. 'So what shall I do? Where should I start?'

Her grandfather stepped over to a shelf on the right. 'This is where you'll find most of the theatre's archive. It isn't sorted. Why don't you start looking through this lot? I tell you what, it would be a great help if you started cataloguing it at the same time. I'll bring you some paper – you make a note of what you find, and its date. How about that?'

Ellie must have looked pained at this idea because David laughed. 'Okay, okay, don't bother if you don't want to. Just take a look for what you want.'

'No, no it's fine,' she said. 'I can do that – really, I'd like to help. There's just such a lot of it.'

Her grandfather left and Ellie stared at the haphazard wall of paper. She was daunted, not entirely sure what she was looking for and what she hoped to find. Something connecting the theatre to Harry, of course – but that might be a vain hope. Where to start?

She lifted piles of folders and papers onto the floor and started to sort them. Leather- bound ledgers full of accounts, letters to and from performers, theatre companies,

153

contractors offering lighting and heating. Most of the papers covered the second half of the twentieth-century – boring, mundane stuff – electricians' bills, documents to do with water rates or the price of gas. Ellie dutifully made a note of everything she found, writing a reference number on the document in pencil then recording its date and contents. Hours passed. Although the work was initially dull, she was surprised when her grandfather dropped by, telling her she'd worked for three hours and it was time for a break. The work had absorbed her attention.

They gathered in the manager's office for coffee and biscuits.

'I've found something that might interest you,' the manager said. 'It's a history of the theatre – locally published a few years ago. Mostly photographs, but still, it all helps.' He handed Ellie a cheaply published paperback book. She sipped her coffee and flicked through the pages. The manager's 'few years ago' was something of an under-statement. The book dated back to the early 1970s, when the theatre revamp was relatively new and fresh. The photo reproduction wasn't great but she was interested to see how the makeover had looked at the beginning.

'I think we have some of the original photographs in our collection,' the manager said. 'You could choose which ones we could use in an exhibition.'

She found a picture of the outside of the theatre at the turn of the century. It didn't look that much different. Only the clothes of the people standing outside flagged up the distance in time. The book also contained reproductions of theatre posters, old tickets and programmes.

'Who wrote the book?' she asked. 'It says Henry Tate. Who's he?'

'Used to work at the museum,' her grandfather said. 'I met him a few times. Henry was mad about the theatre. He took a whole load of pictures before it was renovated. He died in the late eighties, I think.'

Ellie turned another page. Yes, here they were, the pictures Tate had taken. No doubt about it, the theatre had looked pretty decrepit and in need of a facelift. Wallpaper was hanging from the walls. The proscenium arch had partly collapsed. Couldn't they have simply restored it though, rather than giving it that modernist mask? She flipped the page.

One last picture, covering two pages, was an old photograph, apparently taken in 1890, showing the stage and auditorium in all its glory. Ellie stared, transported back to the night of the séance when Harry had shown her the place: she'd stood on the stage and stared out across the sea of red velvet seats. It was exactly as she remembered. It hadn't been a fantasy – Harry had removed the veil of years and revealed the theatre as he'd known it. Ellie closed the book and placed it on her lap.

'Right, back to work,' her grandfather said. 'Will you be okay, Ellie?' She nodded, eager to continue now she'd found a link to Harry.

She spent another couple of hours looking through and cataloguing material. More bills, more correspondence with theatre companies, seventies rock bands, utility companies and councils. Statements of accounts, lists of income and expenditure. She was no expert, but clearly the theatre had always struggled to keep its head above financial water. Bills for building maintenance were constant and seemed to grow ever larger.

Ellie completed and closed another folder, and reached for a new one. Inside, she found treasure – a pile of elderly theatre posters. Yellowed and fragile, they slid into her hand like sheets of silk. Ellie laid them tenderly on the floor. She spread them out. About thirty all together – some creased, some bearing small tears, but all legible. Plays by Shakespeare, a production of *HMS Pinafore* by Gilbert and Sullivan, and many others she'd never heard of.

And at last, heart-stopping, there it was.

Romeo and Juliet.

The title written in an organic art nouveau font, the curls of flowers and leaves adorning the corners and borders. The date – August 1896.

Ellie's gaze ran all over it, absorbing everything the poster had to offer. The style reminded her of pictures she'd seen by other artists of the 1890s, like Aubrey Beardsley – the romantic figures of Romeo and Juliet in long, narrow panels to left and right drawn in pen and ink. Staged by the Lyme Theatre Company, and then, in smaller letters underneath, the names of the leading actors: Francois Lefevre, Violet Weatherstone.

The name jumped out. Weatherstone. Harry's sister? He'd told her he had a sister and she remembered the photograph she'd found with the model theatre. Had Harry's sister played Juliet? The name of her Romeo – Francois – was French. She picked up the poster and took it into the museum's public rooms – now busy with tourists and kids colouring line drawings of pirates and smugglers. Ellie's grandfather was standing behind the reception desk telling some new arrivals what there was to see. When they'd moved off, Ellie brandished the poster.

'Grandpa – I've found a lovely poster. I'd love to take a copy. Would that be okay? I think it would look great in an exhibition.'

More visitors were arriving so he waved her towards the office, where a photocopier waited. Ellie took three copies, in colour, and another of the photograph of the original auditorium, and slid them into a big brown envelope from the recycling box. Then she returned to the archive room and catalogued the remaining posters.

'Ellie – it's five o'clock. Time to go.' Her grandfather was standing in the doorway. Time had flown. Ellie tidied up, and they walked home together. David quizzed Ellie about her work and how she imagined an exhibition might look. When they got home, Ellie stuck her photocopies on the wall, close to the model theatre.

19

The rehearsal went well that evening. They all worked hard, more focused than before, seeing how much needed to be done and the effort required to make the play a success. No one talked about ghosts or hauntings. In fact, they all avoided talking about it and those of the cast who had attended the séance seemed particularly reluctant to even allude to the subject. When Ellie got home, she checked her email. Roger Bishop, the local historian, had sent another message.

Dear Ellie

Thanks for the quest – it has kept me busy all day – and I've made some interesting discoveries about North Hill House and the Weatherstone family. Rather than trying to write it all in an email, I am wondering if we might meet? I will be visiting the library tomorrow, and could drop by at about eleven if you and your grandparents agree. I haven't seen them for quite some time, so it would give me an opportunity to catch up with them too.

What had Roger Bishop discovered? She checked her grandparents were happy for him to call round in the morning, emailed a brief reply and then turned off the computer. She'd enjoyed the day, its busyness and the sense of accomplishment. This voyage of historical discovery had given her something to get her teeth into. She'd been working too hard to brood, and each nugget of information seemed to bring her closer to Harry.

The attic room was quiet. She didn't sense that Harry was near, but that didn't matter too much. She had the posters, she'd seen the photograph of the old theatre. Lying in bed that night, Ellie felt strangely calm. Harry had said he loved her. For now, in this moment, that was all she needed.

'Ellie? Are you awake?' Her grandmother knocked on the door and stepped into the room bearing a cup of tea.

'Sorry to wake you, but Roger will be here in an hour.'

Ellie blinked sleepily and rubbed her eyes.

'What's all this stuff?' Jean stepped carefully across the room. Ellie sat up to see. Papers from the table lay scattered over the floor – pages from the Shakespeare script. Ellie's heart jumped – but she tried to stay calm.

'Oh, research stuff,' she said. Her grandmother put the mug on the cabinet beside Ellie's bed, then squatted to look more closely at the pages, lifting one, and then another.

'Honestly, Grandma – please. Don't worry about it. I was sorting it out.'

'It's *Romeo and Juliet*, isn't it?' Jean stood up, her attention caught by the photocopies pinned to the wall. 'I remember the theatre looking like that – or something like it.' She peered at the photograph. 'It was rather splendid, wasn't it?'

Ellie fretted, longing for her grandmother to leave, but she took her time, examining the pictures and then the model theatre

'Wonderful. Fancy you finding something like that.' Jean sat on the side of the bed and smiled at her grand-daughter. 'I'm so glad you're getting involved, Ellie,' she said. 'Your mum would be proud of you. I know it's been hard for you – as hard as it can be.' She took Ellie's hand and studied her face.

'Your dad phoned last night – when you were out at the rehearsal,' she said. 'I told him what you were doing. He was delighted.'

Ellie felt a shrinking inside. So this is what the conversation had been leading to.

'He's longing to talk with you, Ellie. He said you hadn't answered his emails.'

'I couldn't think of anything to say,' Ellie said.

'He's a good man. No one could have loved Sophie more than he did.' She said Sophie – not 'your mum'. The name, charged with its own painful energy, hung on the air between them. Ellie felt the familiar surge of hurt.

'If he loved her so much, how come he's forgotten her so quickly?' She was belligerent.

'He hasn't forgotten her. Do you think she'd want him to spend the rest of his life being lonely and miserable? She's been gone a year and a half, Ellie. Life is short. She wouldn't want *you* to be miserable either.'

'How can you say that? You were her mother!' Another angry flash. 'I thought you'd understand more than anyone. Doesn't anyone really love anyone else, then? Is it

160

all words, all a pretence? Someone dies and they're forgotten so quickly, even by the people who're supposed to love them the most?'

Her grandmother flinched.

'I saw the way your dad took care of Sophie. I know how much he loved her. I could see it. All the days and weeks and months of her illness. He couldn't have done more. And now he deserves some happiness – just as you do.'

Ellie didn't answer. Her grandmother squeezed her hand. 'I know you don't deserve this – your mum dying. I didn't deserve it either – to lose my daughter,' she said bitterly. 'I watched them put my child in the ground. Not a single day goes by that I don't think of her. You're not the only one who's struggled with this, Ellie. But it's not right to blame your dad. He was amazing, and if he's managing to create new life for himself, then good for him. I know Sophie would have wanted that. You know what she was like. She wasn't selfish.'

This time Ellie flinched. Was her grandmother suggesting *she* was selfish? Ellie took her hand from Jean's and picked up the cup of tea. Her grandmother took a deep breath. She glanced back at the theatre, perhaps wondering if it was time to redirect the conversation.

'It's up to you, of course,' she said. 'But your dad would really appreciate it if you phoned him. I told him all the news but he really wants to talk with you.' Her pretty face crinkled into a smile, the negative emotion draining away.

'Would you like fried eggs for breakfast? I can have them ready for you in a few minutes.'

Ellie nodded. She put the cup down and held out her arms for a hug, which Jean reciprocated with her usual warmth. Ellie breathed in her grandmother's familiar perfume. She didn't want to see her as an enemy. She loved and needed her too much.

The conversation had distracted Ellie momentarily from the papers strewn on the floor – papers which had been tidily stacked on the table when she'd gone to sleep the previous evening. As soon as her grandmother left the room, Ellie jumped out of bed and began sifting through the script. Evidently Harry had visited again. Had he seen the posters on the wall? The scattering of the fragile, yellowed paper across the room suggested some fit of passion – anger? Frustration? She gathered the pages, finding her fountain pen lying amongst them, half obscured, top off. This discovery slowed her tidying. She picked up every page, examined it, turned it over, checking for any scribbled words, for a sign or message from Harry.

At last she found it. A page of the script, and on its reverse, the familiar bold, looping handwriting that seemed to leap from the page.

New words written on ancient paper. Ellie lowered it, looking away, delaying the pleasure of reading. She took three slow breaths, looked down again, and began to read.

I can't see you, the writing said. *I'm standing in the theatre but you're not here. Nothing else exists for me, except the longing to be with you. Those moments we share are like islands of light in a long, dark night in which I see, feel and hear absolutely nothing. I'm waiting for something – that's all I know. It is this waiting that keeps me – the strength of it. I'm waiting for you.*

Come to the theatre tonight. Let me see you, your face, your smile – let me hear your voice again.

Ellie read the text three times through, savouring every word, weighing every phrase. She pressed the page to her face and breathed the smell of it.

'Ellie! Your breakfast's ready!' Her grandfather's voice boomed up the stairs. She'd forgotten about both fried eggs and Roger Bishop. She jumped up, put the papers in the table, pulled her clothes on and ran her fingers through her hair.

The eggs, along with grilled tomatoes and a thick slice of buttered white toast, were waiting on a plate in the dining room. Ellie wolfed them down, finishing just as the doorbell rang. Roger Bishop had arrived.

Her grandfather answered the door. Ellie heard pleasantries exchanged in the hallway, exclamations of how long it had been, how they all were, the weather. Then he ushered their guest into the living room while Ellie mopped up her plate and took it into the kitchen. Her grandfather came to fetch her.

'You've got egg on your chin,' he said, wiping it off with the tip of his big, square finger. 'Come on. Let me introduce you to Roger, and I'll make some coffee. He's looking pretty well, I must say.'

He ushered her into the living room. Roger stood up and shook Ellie's hand, very formal. He looked a bit nervous and said something about Ellie's resemblance to her mother and then blushed, perhaps worrying whether this was an appropriate thing to say.

'Let's get down to business, shall we?' He opened an

old-fashioned leather bag with a buckle over the top and drew out a faded cardboard file stuffed full of papers.

'I was busy yesterday hunting this out,' he said. 'I knew I had some material on North Hill House. I hope you find this helpful.'

Now on task, his nervousness vanished. Ellie studied the man as he flicked through the documents. He was about seventy, she guessed, dressed in a tweed jacket and baggy corduroy trousers. He had a bald head, with wiry grey and reddish hair sprouting at the sides. Roger pulled over her grandparents' occasional table.

'This may be the most useful,' he said, opening the file. 'It's a list of all the residents who lived in the house. It was built in 1850.' He passed her a crudely typed piece of paper with a list of names. The first owners were Weatherstones, she saw, as were the second owners. She surmised it had been passed from father to son. In 1896, the year of Harry's death, it was owned by Nathaniel Weatherstone, who was married to Elizabeth and had three children, including Harry, the eldest (born 1876), and Violet, a year younger. After Nathaniel the house passed out of the Weatherstone family, changed hands half a dozen times, then was briefly a guest house in the thirties. The typed record ended in 1976.

'So what happened next?' Ellie asked. 'Do you remember who was living there after that?'

Roger shrugged. 'Various people came and went. Nice couple lived there in the eighties for about ten years. It's been empty for a while now. Not sure why – property like that. I don't know who owns it – a business, perhaps, maybe keeping it as some kind of investment.'

Ellie pondered. That didn't matter too much. What interested her most was Harry – and his family. Once again she had new pieces to fit into the puzzle – the names of his parents and siblings, including his sister Violet, the amateur actress who'd played Juliet opposite Francois Lefevre. She wondered why, after three generations of ownership, the Weatherstones had sold it out of the family to a stranger in 1919. Harry had been dead twenty three years by then. Had his parents died? Had none of the children wanted to live there?

Roger Bishop shuffled through the papers and picked out several photographs.

'You might find these of interest.' He handed them over: three pictures of North Hill House, reprints of photographs taken in 1900, 1910 and 1973. Too late for Harry – nonetheless Ellie stared at them avidly, studying the house and garden. The earliest picture showed a front view of the house, taken in summer, the garden full of lush foliage (except that the photo was black and white). This was how the place would have looked when Harry lived there.

'Anything else?' Ellie said brightly.

Roger Bishop looked a little disappointed. 'I thought I'd done pretty well – in a day,' he said.

'Oh, you did,' she said hurriedly. 'I mean, this is wonderful, thank you! I really appreciate it.'

Now he looked at her expectantly. She was supposed to reciprocate by sharing some research of her own.

'If you'll just wait a moment, I'll fetch the theatre. I expect you'd like to see it,' she said.

Ellie ran to her room and carefully carried the model theatre downstairs. She placed it on the floor in the sitting room, then scooted upstairs again for her photocopy of the poster. When she returned, Roger was on his hands and knees examining the model, evidently delighted with what he could see. Her grandfather arrived with a tray bearing cups of coffee and the two men traded excited comments about the theatre, the artistry and craftsmanship evident in its making, and its resemblance to the theatre they remembered from their youth.

Ellie sat down, poster in hand, feeling a little left out. The two men chatted together like happy boys. At last she said, loudly, 'Here, I've got the poster. See – it mentions the name Weatherstone. Violet. She was in the play.'

Roger got back into his chair, bright-eyed, and studied the poster. 'So it does,' he said. 'Well, the Weatherstones were rich. They may have supported the theatre, been patrons, taken out a subscription of some kind, you know – sponsorship.'

'How do you know they were wealthy? Have you got more information about them? I thought that was everything.'

'About the house – yes, that's all I have. About the family – well, I know a little more. There's a paragraph about them in my book.' He whipped a copy from his bag and handed it to Ellie. 'Here – this is for you. The first Weatherstones, the ones that built the house, made their money in coal mining. They made a fortune in Nottinghamshire, then escaped the industrial landscape and retired on the proceeds in lovely Dorset. They were industrialists, not aristocrats – at least, the first generation. Great-grandfather Weatherstone may have been a coal man, but his children and grandchildren were something else. You see, their name cropping up in all sorts of places in the town and the county – patrons of artists, galleries – and the theatre here.'

Harry, great-grandson of a Victorian mining magnate, whose family had taken on a new role as members of the rural gentry and supporters of the arts; Ellie smiled. Was this a story Harry would recognise?

Roger asked her some questions about the exhibition. Her ideas were vague because the research had begun as a cover for making discoveries about Harry. Once her answers had dried up, Roger turned his attention to her grandfather again and the two men began to talk about local history and politics.

Ellie jotted down names and dates connected to North Hill House, then, as the men's conversation continued, she felt justified in excusing herself. She took everything back to her room, pinned up her notes with the dates and names of the Weatherstone clan among her other resources, then lay on her bed holding Harry's latest message, written on the back of a page from *Romeo and Juliet*.

The romance of this thrilled her. She read some of Shakespeare's text, from the reverse of Harry's love letter:

My bounty is as boundless as the sea,
My love as deep; the more I give to thee,
The more I have, for both are infinite.

The words chimed clearly in her mind like bells. She'd studied the play at school – a tiresome, enforced boredom it had seemed then. Better, she'd watched the film with Leonardo di Caprio. Still, never till now had the words resonated, and with so much power. She knew what the words meant. She could *feel* what they meant. She read again:

O blessed, blessed night! I am afeard.
Being in night, all this is but a dream,
Too flattering-sweet to be substantial.
A dream? Flattering-sweet. Insubstantial.
Oh yes, all these things.

She folded the paper and slid it into her journal, to keep it safe. She yearned to see Harry again. He was waiting for her at the theatre – she had to get inside. No rehearsal was scheduled for the evening so the place would be locked up. How would she manage to rendezvous with Harry?

20

Ellie's phone bleeped. She was sitting in her room, a note-book in her hand, jotting down phrases and sentences, doodling, daydreaming about Harry. She picked up the mobile. Alex had sent her a message.

Want to come round? We can practise our lines. Daisy's at work – she'll join us later. Alex x

Ellie pondered. It was two o'clock. She had nothing in particular to do and the prospect of learning lines with Alex was more appealing than attempting the same job alone at home. She sent him a text back, saying she'd be over in ten minutes.

Another sunny day, with a cool blustery breeze blowing in from the sea and large fluffy clouds trawling across the sky. Ellie zipped up her thin, black jacket as she hurried down the road, clutching her *Midsummer Night's Dream* script. She glimpsed the sea through a gap in the houses, heard the gulls screech, as she turned uphill, along the road to Alex's house.

The wind chimes tinkled on the porch and the wind rushed through the lilac trees. She banged on the door, hugging her arms around herself, and peered through the kitchen window.

'Is Alex home?'

His father had opened the door and stood massively filling the space. He shook his head and its weight of blond-grey hair. She glanced down, taking in his thick, ripped jeans and bare feet.

'He isn't? He said he'd be here,' she said. Alex's dad continued to give her a curious look. Then he said, 'Just gone to the shop. He'll be back in a minute.' He moved out of the doorway, letting her pass. Ellie went into the kitchen and sat down at the table. Alex's dad put the kettle on and leaned his back against a cupboard. Neither of them spoke and Ellie began to feel a little nervous. For a moment she struggled to remember his name. Joe. Was that right? She wanted him to say something, to break the awkwardness of the silence, except she thought perhaps she was the only one feeling awkward.

'So, how are you?' she said brightly.

He turned his cool, blue eyes towards her.

'Very well. And you? You look a bit tired.'

'I'm fine, thanks,' she said. Though the truth was, now he'd said it, she did feel tired. Strung out, as though the obsession with Harry, the constant fever pitch of her emotions, was burning her away. She rubbed her face with the palms of her hands, wishing Alex would hurry up. Something about Joe's calm scrutiny made her uncomfortable.

'So did you know my mum well?' she asked, eager to divert the conversation away from herself.

'Yes,' Joe said. 'I was very fond of her.' The same level voice. Only his face moved, the strong mouth, the weathered, lined skin on his cheeks. His body, his hands, were still, though she sensed the energy and strength contained within him. This man – Alex's dad. Is this what Alex would become?

The front door burst open, fragrant summer air swirling into the kitchen, wind chimes tinkling.

'Hey, Alex!' Ellie jumped to her feet, relieved he'd arrived at last.

'Sorry I'm late,' he apologised, dumping a bag on the table. 'Got some food. Daisy's cooking for us later. I hope you can stay?'

Joe left them alone in the kitchen, closing the door behind him. Five minutes later Ellie watched him leaving the house, walking along the garden path and out of the garden.

'He's going to work,' Alex said. 'Got an extension to plaster.'

Ellie turned around again, watching Alex as he sorted out cups for coffee. His play script lay open, and crumpled, on the table.

'Your dad said he was very fond of my mum.' Ellie didn't know why she said this – hadn't thought it out in advance. Alex raised his eyebrows.

'What, you suggesting they had some kind of school romance?'

'No, no, I didn't mean that.' She felt her face burn, embarrassed – and something else. Upset? The idea of such a liaison seemed – what? Distasteful. And why was that?

'Well, who could blame him, I mean – if your mum looked like you.'

Ellie blushed again. Alex didn't seem to mean anything by it. He was busy spooning out instant coffee, not even looking at her. He'd made a light-hearted compliment. So why did she feel so unsettled? Quickly she changed the subject.

'I've been working on some research into the history of the theatre,' she said.

Alex placed a mug in front of her, sat down at the kitchen table with his hands together. 'Have you?' he said. 'What've you discovered? Anything exciting?'

In the end, the learning of lines went by the board. They talked for a long time about the theatre and the museum, then the conversation meandered into their own memories of the town and their growing up. Alex was a pleasure to talk to. Most of the boys Ellie had met seemed to think the way to impress girls was to talk about themselves at enormous length. Alex, on the other hand, while having plenty of interesting things to share, also had the rare ability to give his full attention, to listen and ask questions. That's because he isn't trying to impress me, Ellie reminded herself. He isn't putting on an act; he's simply being himself.

'So, if our parents were friends, why haven't we met before?' Alex wondered. 'I mean, if you were down here every summer with your mum. We're always having people round. It's a small place.'

Ellie shrugged. 'I don't know. People change, marry, move away. You know, lives drift apart.'

Again she felt a peculiar unease and she changed the subject.

'So, what's Daisy cooking for us?'

Alex grinned. 'I'm not entirely sure. Something with pork, apples and cider. Sounds promising. She's an excellent cook – not just cakes. I think she'll be a chef one day – you know, have her own restaurant.' His eyes gleamed with pride. They would be great together, Ellie thought. Doesn't he know she likes him? Surely he does.

Daisy arrived just after five, bringing a brown bag of vegetables and a party atmosphere.

'Ellie,' she said, surprised. 'You're here already?'

'Oh, I came over to practise my lines,' Ellie explained. She felt awkward as they had not, in fact, practised their lines at all. Was Daisy thinking she had designs on Alex? Perhaps she should remind her about her own obsession with Harry, to put Daisy's mind at rest. Ellie didn't miss the fleeting expression of hurt on Daisy's face, although Daisy hid it well, and within moments, noise and laughter filled the kitchen. Daisy gave them jobs to do. Alex peeled potatoes while Ellie wiped and sliced mushrooms, washed French beans, grated courgette and carrots. Steam from the saucepans and the aroma of grilled pork swirled in the room. Just after six Joe arrived, and then Sue, Alex's mum, a tall, slim woman in a dark suit, and soon they were all sitting around the table, Alex and his father drinking beer while Daisy panicked about the final preparations.

As they ate, Ellie studied Alex's mum. In some ways she was what Ellie had expected. She'd changed from her work clothes into a slightly hippyish dress with flowers embroidered around the collar and long silver earrings. She was probably in her late forties, silver strands streaking thick, black hair, still very slim with a beautiful, sculpted face. Ellie had always seen how much Alex looked like his dad. Now, meeting Sue, she could see the strong resemblance to his mother too, in the shape of his face, and perhaps, more than anything, in the way he smiled, and moved his hands.

Perhaps Sue sensed she was being studied. She looked up from her plate, catching Ellie's gaze, and gave her a lovely smile.

'I've heard a lot about you, Ellie,' she said. 'From Alex.' She picked up her wine glass, displaying a large amber gem on her silver ring. 'Are you enjoying your summer here? Must be great to get away from everything.'

'Yes, sure.'

Sue picked up on the ambivalent tone of Ellie's voice. 'Then again it's never entirely possible to get away from everything, at least for me. I mean, wherever you are, you're still yourself.'

'You're right,' Ellie said. 'I take myself wherever I go.' Now she took up her own wine glass and downed a generous swig of wine. She felt uncomfortable, to think they might analyse or judge. She imagined huge concrete shields descending around her mind, cutting out those who would try to see her thoughts. She didn't like to feel exposed.

The meal was delicious: the pork moist, the mashed potato flavoured with thyme, crispy vegetables, cider-sweetened gravy. They praised Daisy and toasted her culinary triumph, and Daisy, who was obviously welcome and at home here, blushed and grinned and blushed again. Ellie enjoyed the gathering – but not entirely. Something held her back, kept her apart from everyone else. Amid the pleasure of the meal and the company, she felt a stinging thread of regret and envy. She would never have this again with her own parents, a meal with friends. That whole precious part of her life was over and gone, broken, and she'd never have it back, no matter how much she wanted it. The dreadful Louise had taken her mother's place – the stranger her father had chosen, making a decision Ellie had no power to influence. Lucky Alex. He had no idea how fortunate he was, to have this secure place with the people who loved him most. And beyond these feelings, further taking away her enjoyment of the moment, was the yearning to see Harry again, knowing that all these pleasures – food, talk, company – were merely filling the time until she could find a way into the theatre (somehow) and encounter the ghost – talk to him, see his face, hear his voice.

O blessed, blessed night!

She took another gulp of wine, emptying her glass, and filled it again from the bottle in the middle of the table, savouring the rich, astringent taste. The plates were cleared away. Light ebbed from the room as the summer night drew on. Sue lit candles on the table, windowsill and dresser. The cat appeared, leaped onto the draining board and sat down, tail curled neatly around itself. They ate chocolate and vanilla ice cream then helped themselves to strawberries and raspberries from a wide wooden bowl Sue took out of the fridge.

Everything began to look unreal – the candlelight on the faces around the table, the fruit glowing on the bowl, even the taste of a strawberry popping sweet and cool on her tongue as she bit into it. The scene had the quality of an old oil painting, the light and the dark, the luminous glimmers of colour, the way her companions' expressions seemed to pause momentarily, as though they were representations of themselves.

I'm a little bit drunk, she thought to herself. She touched her cheek with the tips of her fingers, feeling how hot her face was.

Daisy was talking about Warren. Ellie had tuned out of the conversation, lost in her own thoughts, but the sound of Warren's name caught her attention, reminding her of the séance.

'He came into the shop this afternoon,' Daisy said. 'With his friend. You know, the one who's in the play. I've forgotten his name.' Her eyes sparkled.

I think you're a little bit tipsy too, Ellie thought, though she couldn't remember Warren's friend's name either.

'We chatted for a bit – the café wasn't very busy by then. He knows all sorts of stuff.'

For a moment Ellie worried Daisy would tell Alex's parents about the séance, Warren's Ouija board and occult interests. She glanced at Alex, wondering if he was afraid of the same thing (surely Alex's parents wouldn't approve of what they had done – even Alex hadn't approved; she knew he'd only gone along to make sure they were okay). But Alex's face revealed nothing of his feelings and Daisy rattled on to safer topics: Warren's interest in antique watches, pieces of surreal Victorian technology, graphic novels and steampunk fashion.

Ellie glanced at her watch. It was nine thirty. Some kind of olde-worlde music hall event was taking place in the theatre tonight. By eleven, surely, it would be over. Could she possibly sneak into the building before it was locked up? But then how would she get out again? She hadn't really given much thought to her plan, assuming that something would happen. It had to. Harry would help her – work something out.

'Ellie, are you okay?' Alex was looking at her across the table. The scene blurred. Ellie blinked.

'I think I'll go outside for a bit, if you don't mind. I need some fresh air,' she said.

Ellie, Daisy and Alex headed into the garden, ushered out by Sue and Joe who began to clear up after the meal. The night was cool and breezy, the sky blown clear of cloud. A half-moon leaped above the sea. Ellie shivered, but the fresh air was a welcome balm, taking the heat from her face. Alex led them through the long grass behind the house to a swinging chair overlooking the sea. Clumps of lavender and night stock smelling of sherbet grew around the random paving stones by the chair, which offered room enough for three. Daisy sat in the middle.

'What a wonderful view,' she said dreamily. 'I've had a brilliant time. Really. Your parents are so cool.'

'They are,' Alex said. 'But you cooked a great meal. Impressive. Loved it.' He was also a little affected by the wine too, Ellie realised. She agreed with his assessment of the meal, though. Daisy gave her arm an affectionate squeeze.

'You've been very quiet,' Daisy said. 'What are you thinking about?'

For one mad moment, Ellie was tempted to tell them everything – about the theatre, the ghost, her crazy passion for someone who'd died a century ago. The longing to share this impossible, inspiring, devastating happening raged inside her like a tiger. Ellie opened and closed her mouth. She took a breath, heart fluttering in her chest.

'Oh, nothing,' she said at last.

'Were you thinking about your mum?' Alex asked. He stretched out his legs, giving the chair a push so they swung very gently. From way down, Ellie could hear the sound of waves breaking on the rocks beneath the cliffs. High tide, she thought.

'Earlier I was, yes.'

'You must miss her.' This from Daisy: a trite, obvious observation and one that was also entirely, painfully, true.

'Yes I do. Every day. I don't think it will ever end, that missing. I'm going to miss her all my life.' Nobody answered. They stared at the sea and listened to the distant waves. Daisy took Ellie's cold hand. Her own was soft and warm. They were silent for a few minutes, until Daisy, probably emboldened by wine, said, 'So what's your dad's new girlfriend like? Is she really awful?'

'Yes, she is,' Ellie said.

'What's her name?'

'Louise. She's called Louise.' Loopy Louise, Ellie thought, revelling in her childish contempt for this woman, the very ordinary, boringly pleasant, odious new woman who her father had inexplicably fallen for. How could he like someone so dull when her mother had been so extraordinary? Was he that desperate? That lonely? Wasn't Ellie enough for him, that he'd brought this other woman, this dumpy, middle-aged English teacher into their house of mourning? Was it sex? Was that it? Did he need it so much, even at his age? The mere thought of this made her stomach turn.

They'd been so close, Rob, Ellie and Sophie, in the long months of Sophie's illness. Friends had receded into the distance. And, after the death, Ellie and her dad had been everything to each other – companions in mourning.

The months went by. A year. Ellie's life settled into a pattern of sadness, almost comforting in its regularity.

Then Louise appeared.

Her father had first introduced her to Ellie a year and a month after Sophie had died. Ellie knew, of course, to the day, exactly how long it had been. A few weeks before Christmas, he took Ellie to dinner at a Chinese restaurant, telling her he had someone he'd like her to meet. Ellie knew at once, with a plummeting fear, that he'd found another woman. Louise was waiting for them in the restaurant. She stood up when they walked in, smiling, holding out her hand. Ellie's dad was terribly nervous, Louise was nervous, both worried about what Ellie might think, wanting to make a good impression.

And Ellie wasn't happy. She was jealous.

What a horrible, visceral, painful emotion it was. Nobody wants to be jealous, she thought. It's an emotion you're embarrassed to have, an emotion to be ashamed of. She hadn't *chosen* to feel jealous – it afflicted her like an illness, cutting her feet from under her, almost as painful as grief – in some ways, more so because grief is allowed, at least for a time, while jealousy is something only weak, nasty people feel.

How could she be jealous of this plain, dull woman who obviously adored her father and tried so hard to be good to Ellie? At first Ellie thought her father would dump Louise, when he realised how hurt Ellie was. But he didn't. Even though he knew the situation made his daughter unhappy, he stuck to it, so Ellie felt betrayed and abandoned as well as jealous. She spent months suffering in a storm of emotion, unable to control her feelings.

So she behaved like a bitch: she took her revenge. Ellie refused to speak to Louise, or even mention her name. She stayed out all the time, or holed up in her bedroom, when Louise came to visit. Sometimes she shouted at her father, accusing him of not having loved her mother, of not loving her. Sometimes she inflicted subtle punishments on him. Just before Christmas, Ellie threw away the box of Christmas tree decorations she'd collected with her mother over the years. The old cardboard box, its cargo of handmade and shop-bought decorations accumulated over the years of her life, was a precious memory trove he didn't deserve to enjoy.

Ellie told him coolly she'd chucked them out and watched the pain blossom in his face, and then his attempt to hide it.

'It's old stuff, from our old life,' she told him. 'The life that's finished. I don't want *her* touching them. They don't belong to her. We need new stuff now.'

'If that's what you want,' her father said, his face white and strained.

Worst of all, Ellie *knew* her behaviour was appalling. She knew her father didn't deserve it, that Louise was okay, that she was making absolutely everyone miserable. But she couldn't help it. She couldn't. It hurt too much. She didn't want to accept this new situation. Every fibre, body and soul, rebelled against it.

Perhaps her father should have shouted at her, told her to grow up, announced that she was being selfish and unreasonable – but he didn't. Instead he pussyfooted around her, stricken with guilt, tried to keep her happy, accepting everything she did or said – bar one thing: he didn't give up Louise. He refused to end the relationship.

'I love her, Ellie,' he pleaded. 'I feel happy when we're together. I'd like you to like her too. That's what I want more than anything.'

'I'll *never* like her,' Ellie vowed, caught in a trough of pain. She wanted to get over of it – to break away from this place, these feelings – but she couldn't do it. She couldn't escape.

'Louise. She's called Louise.' A bird hooted from the end of the garden. An owl probably, though its call was strange. The sound drew Ellie back to the present. She lifted her head, focused on the sea. None of this could be shared with her friends. She was too angry, too sad, too ashamed of it all.

'Why don't you like her?' Daisy said. She was still holding Ellie's hand, which rested on Daisy's lap.

Ellie shrugged. 'There's nothing actually wrong with her – I mean, she's not evil or anything, I just don't think she's right for my dad, and I think it's way too soon for him to be seeing someone.'

Nobody spoke for a moment. Ellie could almost see them, thoughts and feelings caught in a log jam all around her. They didn't know what to say. Then Alex broke the silence. He said airily, 'Parents, eh? Think they know everything. Won't listen to a word you tell'em.'

And Ellie laughed. The terrible tension drained away. Daisy released her hand and stretched luxuriously. The bird, whatever it was, made the same peculiar sound and launched itself into the night air, hovering momentarily above a lilac tree before swooping down over the edge of the cliff.

They talked of inconsequential things – the recipe for Daisy's pork and cider, the shop where Alex thought his mother had bought her earrings, which Daisy coveted – while Ellie watched the hands on her watch inch their way towards eleven o'clock. The longing for Harry grew more acute. The passing of each minute grew ever more agonisingly slow. I'm wishing my life away, she thought. Here I am sitting above the sea with my friends on a beautiful night and I'm yearning for it to pass because nothing matters except being with him. With Harry.

I am afeard.

Being in night, all this is but a dream,

Too flattering-sweet to be substantial.

The words from *Romeo and Juliet*, printed on the back of the last note Harry had left for her . . . She loved a ghost – a dream. Flattering-sweet, yes, his yearning for her, the desire she could see in his face, the destiny that had kept

182

him waiting a century to be with her. To be wanted so much, to be truly seen, to be beautiful and desirable . . . How could she resist?

'I have to go now,' Ellie said abruptly. She stood up, the sudden change in weight causing the seat to lurch.

'Okay,' Alex said. 'Hang on a mo. I'll walk you back.'

'No, no, that's okay. You stay here with Daisy.' The words galloped out. She'd forgotten that gallant Alex would volunteer to take her home.

'It's fine,' Daisy said. 'I need to go anyway. Got to get up for work in the morning.'

'Really, I can walk home by myself. I'd prefer to. I mean, it's not exactly far, and I'd like a moment to myself, you know, to think.' She blundered on, aware she sounded weird and rude. Daisy and Alex stared at her, nonplussed.

'If that's what you want,' Alex said.

Ellie popped back inside the house to say goodbye and thanks to his parents. Daisy and Alex walked her to the garden gate, gave her hugs.

'Take care,' Alex said. 'Text me when you get home.'

Ellie walked along the road. The night air had cleared her head. Now she felt curiously bright and awake. Every step was taking her closer to Harry. The centre of the courtyard by the theatre was empty but flooded with bright electric light. She sat in the shadow on the wall for a few minutes then texted Alex to tell him she was safely home.

The moon had sunk towards the sea, creating a silver path on the restless black surface. Far out, a light flashed from an otherwise invisible boat. Ellie stood up. She felt entirely calm. Everything was perfect, just as it ought to be

– the wheel of stars, the *shush* of the waves below the wall, the black cut-out of roofs, walls and chimneys surrounding the courtyard. Harry was waiting; had waited a hundred years. This path was pre-ordained, utterly irresistible.

Ellie walked to the door and opened it. Not locked – of course it wasn't. She stepped into the silent lobby, walked along the corridor past the office, and turned into the auditorium. The place was dark, but she didn't need light to see. The form of the building, its old, pre-renovation interior, shone out for her to see – the plaster mouldings painted with gold, the deep red walls, the disc above the proscenium arch borne up by voluptuous cherubs. Had her imagination painted this, from the old photographs?

She didn't need to think. She knew where to go, every moment swelling with significance, taking her closer to him, to the moment of seeing him again. Her pulse beat through her body like a drum, in flesh and bones, in fingertips and toes. Gas footlights burned along the front of the stage, creating a pool of bright yellow light that shifted and shimmered on the deep red curtains, the ornaments of gold on the cherubs, balconies and columns.

Ellie climbed the steps at the side of the stage. The bare boards melted away, the empty space folding and reforming to create a scene. A stage backdrop revealed itself, a pale blue sky with delicate clouds coloured in before her eyes, and beneath it, misty hills, blue and sepia in the distance, and a river twining between them, and closer in uncanny perspective, idyllic meadows where peasants raked hay and fat cows grazed, and then, in the foreground, to left and right, two slender, leafy trees. This beautiful panorama, created on a huge piece of fabric, seemed so real Ellie could almost smell the trees, feel the movement of air from the far mountains. Were those birds, the specks moving across the sky?

A tiny classical temple stood on the stage in front of this artful vista, a folly of pale marble, steps and columns with a roof, open on three sides and at the back, a plaster statue of Cupid, the winged god of love, brandishing a bow and arrow.

There he was – Harry – sitting on the steps.

Ellie's heart leaped in her chest. Her throat tightened. Neither moved.

How beautiful he was – his strong, fierce face, the dark eyebrows, his thick, shadowy hair and blazing eyes. Ellie swallowed. She wanted to move towards him but her body refused to obey. Harry rose to his feet and stood on the stage, in front of the temple and the painted landscape. Ellie gazed at him hungrily – Harry dressed for the part in tight black breeches, long leather boots, a loose white shirt. A romantic hero, yes? And perfectly conscious of the spectacle he presented, the strong, slim body in its poet's costume. She could see his vanity too.

Harry took a step forward. 'Ellie?' His voice faltered. Some uncertainty after all? 'Do you like it, what I've done for you?' He gestured to the scenery and vaguely to his own costume.

Ellie swallowed, willing her voice to work.

'I love it,' she said. 'Was this the setting for the play? Your play, I mean, *Romeo and Juliet*.'

'Yes, I think it was,' Harry said. 'It's hard to remember clearly. The past – my life – seems closed off – locked away behind a hundred locked doors. And this one – this memory – I managed to open. I thought you'd like it. I wanted to share it with you.'

Ellie smiled. She relaxed, a little. 'I've seen it before, in miniature. In the model theatre.'

'Will you sit with me?' Again the air of authority, and confidence, in which she detected a tiny vein of hesitation. Harry gestured to a fake marble bench on the opposite side of the stage. Ellie nodded and allowed him to guide her to the place. They sat side by side, a space between them, not touching at all.

I can't touch him, she reminded herself. And yet he seemed more substantial tonight. Would it ever be possible, for him to take her in his arms? The simple imagining of this conjured a shocking desire. Better not to hope for that. It was too much.

'It's good for me to be with you,' Harry said. 'I woke up from the dark, and you were there. At the beginning, I could remember so little. Now I can open some of the doors. Because of you. You're like a light for me. A guide.'

His gaze ran over her face, as though he was looking for something.

'Tell me what you've remembered,' she said.

'Ask me a question. I'll try to answer it.'

Ellie took a deep breath and looked away from him. 'Have you ever fallen in love before?' It cost her to ask the question, but she wanted to know. Ellie glanced back at Harry, watching his reaction.

He thought for a moment, then his eyes flashed and a boyish grin filled his face. White, even teeth, except for the two at the front, which crossed slightly. This slight imperfection added a dash of roguishness to his appearance.

'I've known other girls,' he said. 'I can remember them, a little. Not their names, but their faces. I can even remember the dresses one of them used to wear.'

Ellie felt a fierce pang of jealousy. Why had she asked this question? Now he was sitting with her, but thinking of this other girl, and her no-doubt beautiful dresses. She'd asked it because she needed to know if his feelings for her matched the violent, unprecedented feeling she had for him. And he was so good-looking, surely he must have had countless admirers. Was he as attractive to others? He seemed so to her, indescribably so. It seemed as though she'd always carried a picture in her heart and Harry matched this image so perfectly she felt she'd always known him, always wanted him. If he'd been waiting for her, she too had been waiting for him. Was this how the story worked, of love at first sight?

Ellie shook her head, to clear her thoughts. Harry was studying her now, a wry smile on his face.

'I've hurt your feelings,' he said. 'But you asked the question.'

'Yes, I did,' she said.

'And you? Have you fallen in love before?'

Ellie shook her head. She'd gone out with a boy for a few months, when she was sixteen. It hadn't exactly been serious and it had petered out when her mother became very ill. Love? No, she'd felt nothing like this.

'Ellie, to answer you, I've never fallen in love before. I never imagined I could want something so much. It's hard to put in words how much I want to know you, to be with you, to protect you, to take your sadness way, to make you happy.'

Now Ellie smiled, feeling an intense rush of pleasure to hear what he said.

'Why me?' she said. 'I'm not very . . .' She ran out of words. What did she mean to say? Not so special. Not so beautiful. Not so remarkable. Of course she wanted him to deny this, to tell her why she was special and desirable. She wanted to see herself, the girl he saw, in the mirror of his regard.

'You are beautiful,' he said. 'You have no idea. And I don't mean, simply, the proportion of your face, your figure, though they are undoubtedly fine. It's much more than that. I think I can see who you are – it is that, the light of you, that shines out through each and every word and expression and movement you make. You have a quality – it's hard to describe – if you were a jewel you would be dark red, with a pure, intense shine.' He faltered. 'I sound stupid now. It's hard to answer the question – I mean, why you. Because you're you.'

Ellie smiled, shyly, his words branding themselves on her memory.

'Can I ask you another question?'

'Of course. Perhaps an easier one this time?'

Ellie laughed. 'Sure. Tell me about the play – this one. *Romeo and Juliet*. You played Mercutio, yes? And your sister Violet was Juliet?'

His eyes darkened, mind disappearing into his past.

'You must remember it. You created this from the play.' She gestured to the stage and its scenery. 'I have another name to help you. Francois Lefevre. He played Romeo.'

Something seemed to pass through Harry at the mention of this name. He gave a sudden shiver.

'I do remember him,' he said. 'Oh yes, I remember him.' Harry shook his head. 'I'll tell you about my sister,' he said, pushing this memory aside. 'She was beautiful – almost as lovely as you. And bright and vivacious. Always – even when she was a little girl.' His face softened, thinking about her.

'You were very fond of her,' Ellie said.

'I loved her dearly. Everyone did – especially my parents. She was a little wild, but charming and intelligent. She ran rings round us all. And she wanted to be an actress – always. We staged plays in the garden when we were children, and later, she wanted to be a professional – the next Sarah Bernhardt, her idol. Of course my parents wouldn't allow it.'

'But she joined the Lyme Players.'

'Yes, we both did. I joined because of her. I can assure you, I was only ever a moderate actor. She was the one with the gift.'

'She was good?'

'More than good.' He fell silent for a moment, remembering again, perhaps seeing her on the stage in his imagination. 'Of course it wasn't possible for her to be an actress, not as she wanted to be one, as a profession, travelling with a company, living away from home. My parents would never have allowed it. But they did yield to this, a compensation, acting with the Lyme Players, and I was part of the group, to take care of her.'

'Describe her,' Ellie asked. 'Violet – what did she look like?'

'Not tall, very slender – boyish even. With long, curled red hair, a great weight of it, and white skin with little freckles she tried to bleach with vinegar.' He smiled. 'Of course it didn't work. And anyway, her freckles were pretty, but she said an actress couldn't have freckles. She had an elfin face, big, round blue eyes . . . and a wild laugh. She read all the time, novels and absurd books about spiritualism. She drove our parents to distraction with her causes – votes for women, dress reform, raising money for orphans in Africa, all that sort of thing.' Harry shook his head. 'This place, the life here in the country-side, was never enough for Violet. She had too much spirit, too many dreams. I was always afraid for her. I knew she would never be satisfied with the life girls are supposed to lead, but it's a dangerous and unforgiving world for those women who dare step beyond the bounds, and for all her pluck, she was very sensitive. I didn't want her to be hurt.'

He looked into Ellie's eyes. 'I adored her,' he said. 'I'd have done anything for her.'

He leaned forward, head drooped, arms resting on thighs, hands clasped. His posture expressed his sadness and Ellie didn't want him to be sad.

'You've told me you can see I'm sad,' she said. 'But you're sad too. Is it something to do with Violet?'

Harry sat up straight. 'Is that why you woke me, I wonder? We're mirrors, each for the other.'

Ellie had another question to ask. It was the hardest, the most important – and the most frightening.

She cleared her throat. 'Harry? Where you were – in the dark. Are there others there? I mean – if I wanted to contact someone on the other side, could you do that? I mean, if you endure, that means . . .'

'That you might be able to speak to your mother again?'

'Yes.' This thought filled her at once with dread and terrible longing.

'I'm sorry Ellie. I'm all alone. I've been alone, caught in this one place, for a very long time. In Violet's books, they talked about crossing over. It wasn't like that for me. If I died, as you think, then all I did was to back myself into a small black box. Where I waited.'

'Waited for me?'

'You've set me free, Ellie.'

Was he truly free? She felt a first tremor of fear. If he were free, wouldn't she lose him?

'Do you know how you died, Harry?' She didn't work up to the question, or worry about it. Now it hung on the air between them.

Harry brushed it aside and stood up. 'I don't want to talk anymore. I want to be happy. I want to enjoy this time we have together.'

Ellie rose to her feet. 'What do you want to do?'

'Shall we walk? It's a lovely day and a beautiful place.' He gestured to the landscape on the backdrop. Ellie giggled.

'Take my hand.' He held it out.

'Harry, I can't.'

'Pretend,' he said. So she closed her eyes and imagined how it would feel if she could indeed take his hand – the strength and heat of it, the smoothness of his skin, the grip of his fingers around her own. She opened her eyes again.

'I am pretending,' she said.

'So am I. It's very nice.' They both laughed then, out of childish delight, sharing the game.

'Beautiful weather we're having,' Ellie said.

'Be careful you don't burn. Your complexion is very fair. Perhaps we should walk in the shade.'

'Look at the birds.' Ellie pointed to the sky. 'I wish I could fly, don't you? Can you imagine it, being so high, having that mass of space beneath you as well as above you?'

Harry began to speak but a cataclysm struck.

Blinding light, an explosion of white, obliterating everything. Landscape, temple, footlights – and Harry. They were all wiped out, blown away. Light lanced Ellie's eyes. She clapped her hands to her face, bereft, her fantasy world ripped away.

'What are you doing here?'

Ellie blinked, her eyes adjusting to the electric light filling the auditorium. Bare stage, stink of beer and damp and old carpet.

The crone's voice repeated, with increased hostility, 'What are you doing here?'

Ellie shaded her eyes and peered ahead of her. An old woman stood close to one of the main doors. She'd seen this woman before – yes, that time she was hunting for the keys in the office.

'It's nearly midnight,' the woman said. 'I need to lock up. What on earth are you up to?'

Ellie's mind worked fast. 'I'm a member of the youth theatre group – you know, doing *Midsummer Night's Dream*? I wanted to practise – rehearse some of my lines on my own. I mean, I'm not much good, to be honest. I need extra work.'

'What, in the dark? You were practising in the dark? Can't you do that at home? Is anyone else here? Weren't you talking to someone?'

Ellie didn't try to answer these questions. She climbed from the stage while the woman looked around suspiciously.

'How did you get in here?' the woman said. This question, at least, Ellie could answer honestly.

'Through the main doors. They weren't locked.'

The woman scowled. 'I'll have to talk to the cleaner,' she said. 'The door needs to be locked – even when they're working. We can't have random people just walking in.' She gave Ellie another hostile glance but since Ellie had neither broken in nor caused any visible damage, she could do nothing more than disapprove. The woman escorted Ellie to the exit and ushered her out. Then she locked the door behind them. For a moment they both stood where they were, in the pool of light, itself contained within the greater pool of night. The old woman raised her querulous, beaky face and looked at Ellie properly.

'Are you ill?' Her voice had softened. She was seeing

Ellie properly now, having dispensed with her fear of intruders, thieves and vandals in the theatre.

Ellie shook her head. 'I'm fine, thanks. And – I'm sorry I frightened you.'

The woman smiled. 'Yes, you did a bit. The place is supposed to be haunted, you know. Weren't you afraid, on your own?'

'No, not at all,' Ellie said.

'You look very pale.' The woman sighed. 'I think you should go home. Go to bed.' She turned away, shoulders hunched, and walked slowly across the courtyard, under the archway and into the darkness. Ellie watched her go.

She took a long, deep breath. Yes, she was tired. Utterly, deeply tired. But happy too. The glow of the time with Harry was still upon her. She replayed the memories in her mind, their conversation, the glimpses he had given her of his life and the people in it, the playfulness of their imaginary walk, hand in pretend hand. A smile spread across her face. It was enough, for now, just to remember it, to bathe in the feeling of love and happiness.

Harry loved her, and she loved him.

She walked home through the midnight town, past the houses full of sleeping people, the dark shop fronts, the closed pubs, and up the hill to her grandparents' house. Moments of perfection – the glimmering stream, the forms of the houses, the glitter of faraway stars. The path shone in front of her feet; the night air caressed her face.

Ten minutes later, lying on her back in bed, Ellie was still smiling. She spread out her arms, enjoying the sensation of the cool sheets against her skin. She gazed into the darkness, seeing Harry's face in her mind's eye, hearing his voice.

Then sleep crept over her, obliterating thought.

And, despite her happiness when she fell asleep, she dreamed of loss. She dreamed Harry's head lay upon the pillow beside hers, but when she tried to touch him, Harry turned to ash. The grief was so profound that an hour before dawn she woke up crying, tears soaking her pillow.

She hadn't cried like that, in her sleep, for months.

21

Ellie stood outside the office, shifting nervously from foot to foot. The place looked decidedly Dickensian, despite the bright colour photographs in the window – pictures of kids in party hats, an old couple grinning over an anniversary, suited people brandishing an oversized cheque. The gloomy interior did not invite.

A sign above the big window announced this was the local office of the *South Dorset Echo* but still Ellie wondered if it were the right place, tucked away in one of the winding alleys leading from the High Street. Precious little holiday sunshine here.

At last, summoning her courage, she pushed the door open. A bell jangled as she stepped inside, and a smart little woman in her fifties stepped forward to the old-fashioned counter.

'May I help you?'

'Yes, I, uh, I've been told you have an archive of old newspapers here. I wondered if I might see them.'

One of the women at the town museum had suggested this to Ellie. She'd spent the morning continuing her research into the history of the Marine Theatre, and now, in her lunch hour, she was taking the opportunity to find out more.

'We do indeed. You can find articles from the last ten years on our website. In the back room we've got papers going back fifty years. Is that any help to you?'

Ellie frowned. 'Actually, I was hoping to go back further than that. The 1890s.'

'Ah – well, you'd need to go to the library headquarters in Dorchester for that. They've got the newspapers stored on microfiche. Everything's there – right back to 1820.'

The woman looked very pleased about this wealth of newspaper archives but Ellie's heart sank. She'd been hoping for a quick and easy answer. No such luck.

'What are you researching?'

'Oh, I'm working on a project for the museum about the Marine Theatre.'

'Really? Oh, that sounds marvellous! Do you have a minute? I'm sure our reporter would like to talk to you about it. Hold on a minute, will you?' She made a call, relaying this information to the unseen reporter, then she said to Ellie, 'He'll be down in a minute. Take a seat, please.'

Some five minutes later the reporter appeared. Ellie saw him, through the doorway behind the counter, emerging from the bottom of a stairway. He was very young and looked decidedly bored. His expression lifted, however, when his eyes lit on Ellie.

'Oh,' he said, his voice surprised. 'You're the one researching the theatre?'

'I'm not what you were expecting?' Ellie said drily.

'No, I mean, not at all.'

The receptionist glanced over, lifting her eyebrows. The reporter held out his hand.

'I'm Nick Valler,' he said. 'How about a coffee? I could do with getting out of here for a bit.' He glanced back at the receptionist, who gave him another wry look. 'Back in ten,' he said. Then, with a grin at Ellie, 'Let's go, shall we?'

They were sitting outside a café-gallery, in a courtyard where fuchsias grew in wooden tubs. Nick's notebook and pen waited on the table. Ellie guessed he was about twenty-two, not so much older than herself. Evidently life as a cub reporter in a small seaside town hadn't proved quite as exciting as he'd hoped. Nick talked about himself for ten minutes, before switching to the topic in hand.

'So, tell me about this exhibition. How come you're researching the theatre?' he said. Nick was short and chirpy, with curly brown hair and a cheap suit. He was also very restless, unable to sit still for a moment, shifting on his seat, twitching his foot.

'You're not what I was imagining,' he said, before she had time to answer. 'To be honest, well, I thought you'd be about seventy. You know – interested in history and all that.'

Again she opened her mouth to answer, but Nick jumped in, 'Everyone's old round here – except the holi-daymakers. Not much going on, really.' Then, hopefully, 'D'you live here? I moved from South London. Big change, I can tell you.' He shook his head. Ellie closed her mouth again, waiting for a chance to speak.

'Well then, tell me all about it. The old theatre, yeah? I visited the place. Saw some God-awful local play. Had to write a review.' He clapped his hand to his forehead. 'Ah – now you're going to tell me your mum had the lead role, and I've offended you dreadfully. All the locals are related to each other, aren't they?'

Ellie barely flinched when he mentioned her mother. She managed a smile instead. 'No worries. No relatives in the play.'

Nick the reporter managed to rein in his enthusiastic talk about himself and picked up his notebook and pen.

'Go on, then. Tell me everything. The theatre – your research.'

So Ellie told him about the model theatre, her research at the museum, her desire to find out more from newspaper archives, the plans for an exhibition on the history of the Marine Theatre. She also talked about the youth production of *A Midsummer Night's Dream*. Nick listened attentively, jotted down notes in shorthand, and occasionally interjected a comment or question. Apparently he'd written a story a few weeks ago announcing the youth theatre production was taking place.

'This is great,' he said, at the end. 'A few things I can use here. First of all, I'd like to send a photographer to the dress rehearsal and write a play preview. Afterwards I can write a review – I'll be kind, honest. I'd also like to write something about your research, and we'll need a photo of you and the model theatre – maybe we could ask people to contribute – memories, artefacts and stuff? I can write something else when the exhibition actually opens too.'

Ellie raised her eyebrows. 'You short of news around here?'

'You wouldn't believe,' he said, raising his hands, sighing theatrically. 'The lead story this week is the drama surrounding the choice of town clock.'

Ellie laughed. Nick put the notebook down again.

'I do have some information that will interest you,' he said, more serious now.

'What?'

'About the theatre. The county council owns it, but it's managed by a board of trustees. They were talking about it at a council meeting a couple of weeks ago. The place is falling apart, apparently. It needs hundreds of thousands spent on it, which the council can't afford. They're talking about selling it for redevelopment.'

'Redevelopment?'

'Yeah, pulling it down, building flats. Retirement flats probably. Big demand for those round here.'

Ellie felt a chill. 'My God. Who knows about this?'

Nick shrugged. 'Everyone should know. I wrote a story about it. The trustees certainly know. I was wondering, maybe that's why you were doing this exhibition. A retrospective kind of thing. Or a protest. But you didn't know.'

She shook her head. 'I'm not a local,' she said. 'Just here for the summer.'

Nick looked disappointed. 'Pity,' he said. 'Never mind. I'm surprised the folks at the museum didn't tell you. Keep in touch, yes?'

He took her number and made arrangements for the photograph of Ellie and the model theatre, made a note in his diary about the dress rehearsal and the play's opening night, checked his phone then bade Ellie a brisk farewell, with what he thought, perhaps, was a rakish grin.

Ellie remained at the table for a while longer, thinking. During the entirety of the long conversation, she hadn't, of course, mentioned Harry. He was the true reason for her interest in the theatre and her desire to see the newspapers of the 1890s. Harry was the sun around which all these matters revolved, and no one knew about him, except her. Ellie felt a curious pang of guilt, as though she was deceiving all these people (the local historian, the museum, her grandparents, and now Nick) – but that wasn't true, was it? She was genuinely interested in the theatre and now she'd embarked on the project, she was enjoying the work and challenge of the research. At the same time, it was as though she was creating an elaborate cover for an illicit affair. She shook her head, to banish these thoughts.

Would the council really sell the place? Allow it to be pulled down? The thought filled her with horror. The theatre was a significant piece of history – a key element of the old town architecture. And it was Harry's place. If they destroyed it, what would happen to him?

Ellie went back to the museum and told her grandfather she needed to go to Dorchester to see the older newspaper archives. Then she checked out the bus times on the internet. Half an hour later, she was sitting at the back of the bus, staring through the window at the unwinding summer landscape, the old villages, patches of lush woodland, the smooth, swooping hills, some crowned with pagan-looking circles of trees.

The journey lasted a tedious hour, and then she was

disgorged, with the other passengers, in the centre of town. The library was only ten minutes' walk away, a modern building with a tall, glass front. An assistant guided her to a microfiche viewer, informed her with an air of complaint that all this would all be transferred to an electronic retrieval system before too long, then left Ellie to it.

Ellie took a deep, slow breath, in and out. Here, at last, she might find out what happened to Harry. If he had died in the second half of 1896, the son of a prominent local family, surely some account of it would be found in the local newspaper. A funeral report, an obituary, a news story? She would find something.

Ellie began with the August papers. *The Echo* was published weekly. Columns and columns of dense, old-fashioned print appeared on the screen. Slowly Ellie got the hang of scanning through it, up and down, left and right, straining her eyes to see. She jotted down anything she could find about the theatre (adverts for shows, reviews) all the while impatient to know more about Harry's fate. It took a long time. On the wall above ranks of local history books, the clock hands moved towards four thirty. The place closed in an hour. Ellie continued to plough through the pages.

She found a review of the production, *Romeo and Juliet,* written in precise, antiquated prose, politely praising the performances of the leads and enthusing about the quality of local theatre. No mention of Harry (well, he'd admitted he was no actor). Then – two weeks later – the report of the death. The headline read: Local Man Dies in Tragic Accident.

The name jumped out.

Harry Weatherstone.

Ellie's gaze locked onto the screen, hungry to know, and afraid of what she might find. On 14th September, 1896, Harry had died in a riding accident. He'd been galloping along the cliff path when his horse tumbled over the edge of the cliff, and fell a hundred feet to the rocky beach below. The report mentioned details about his life – his surviving siblings, parents, the schools he'd attended, and the time and date of an inquest, the following week, when the circumstances surrounding this accident would be investigated.

Ellie scooted forward to the paper published just after the inquest. This furnished further details. Harry had died late at night. Just after eleven, according to a groom's testimony, he'd ordered his horse to be saddled. The groom was surprised, because a storm had blown up outside. Torrents of rain were falling, the wind was high. Harry seemed angry, the groom said, bellowing, stamping up and down while he waited for his horse.

Another witness had seen Harry galloping through the town, the horse skidding on the wet streets. He'd taken a track along the cliff path, a short cut to the main road but a dangerous one to ride at speed, certainly reckless to attempt at night, when visibility was poor and rain sluiced the ground.

Harry didn't return. His frantic parents sent out a search party. At midday, according to the police officer, the storm having blown out by the early hours of the morning, the bodies of horse and man were discovered on the beach, broken on rocks, two miles out of town. Although the hoofprints on the path had been washed away, marks on the cliff indicated where the horse had fallen. Perhaps it had shied, or lost its footing, or simply not seen the cliff edge.

The coroner recorded a verdict of death by misadventure.

Something was missing though. The report, and perhaps the inquest itself, had faithfully examined the facts surrounding the death but hadn't touched on the reason for Harry's crazy night-time ride. Where was he going? What had made him so angry? Why had he ridden so recklessly?

'We're closing now.' The same library assistant stood at Ellie's shoulder. 'Please finish off your work. The doors will be locked in ten minutes.'

Ellie had to wait half an hour for the bus, which was crowded with people travelling home from work. She was hardly aware of the journey, lost in thought, seeing in her mind's eye the young man galloping through the night and the rain, imagining the terrifying scrabble of the horse's hooves, the plunge into space and darkness, the impact of flesh and bone on the unforgiving rocks thirty-metres beneath. How sudden and violent an end, caught in a moment of rage. But why? Why had he done it?

22

Ellie barely had time to eat before rushing out to the theatre. Her mind reeled with so much new information. The
rehearsal was already underway when she arrived. Carly
and some of the others were standing on the stage, Mike
barking out instructions as to who should be where. Daisy
and Warren were sitting side by side in the front row of the
auditorium, whispering about something. Ellie plopped
down in the seat next to them.

'Where's Alex?' she said.

'Not here yet. He texted me – he'll be along later.'

Mike turned round and hissed at them to be quiet, but
Daisy caught the giggles and had to press her hand to her
face to stifle the noise.

The rehearsal went well, for the most part. Mike kept
them at it till nearly eleven, by which time they were all
exhausted. Ellie, after her busy day and trip to Dorchester,
could barely keep her eyes open by the end. She could
remember her lines better though and, after several poor
efforts, Mike finally seemed pleased with her performance.

Alex didn't turn up till nearly nine. Mike looked angry
when he first appeared, probably preparing to tell him off,

but Alex was carrying something very peculiar, an articulated structure of sticks and streamers of gauzy fabric. As he drew closer to the stage, everyone stared, trying to make out what he had. Alex leaped up the steps on to the stage, looking pleased with himself.

'What is it?' Mike said, warily. Alex moved the object, lifting it a little, altering the balance, so the rods shifted (a broomstick? Some bamboo canes?) and resolved themselves into arms and legs. All of a sudden, Alex was holding a human figure, something graceful and oddly unearthly: wings of draped fabric, a narrow, flat wooden face. But it was less the shape that suggested a figure, and more the way it moved, poised in Alex's hand.

They all stared, lost for words.

'Meet Cobweb,' Alex said, shy about and happy with the reaction to his creation. 'There's still some work to do – I want to embellish her a little you know, add to the costume. Some silver paint maybe. And decorations. But in essence – here she is.' He manipulated the figure, nearly as tall as himself, so she gave a low, elegant bow. Everyone burst into a round of applause. Someone cheered and whooped. Mike grinned and shook his head, clapping Alex on the shoulder.

'That is the most remarkable piece of work,' he said. 'Truly. I mean, one moment it looked like a bunch of sticks, and then – this.'

They all looked at each other, grinning, terribly pleased with themselves.

'Dead simple,' Alex said modestly. 'I'll make a couple more for the other fairies, it's no big deal.' But his face was pink, which Ellie noticed, feeling warmth for him, his talent, and also his modesty.

After the rehearsal they gathered for a swift drink in the pub. Ellie finally had a chance to tell them what she had learned about the threat to the theatre, the plans for sale and redevelopment.

'I do remember something about it,' Alex said. 'It's been on the cards for years and years. I suppose I just ignored it, because the council's been threatening to close it for so long, and the theatre has always struggled on.'

'Aren't you upset about it?' Ellie was nettled by his small concern.

'Sure,' he said. 'But *something*'s got to happen. The place is a dive. It's in a terrible state. They've either got to seriously smarten it up or pull it down.'

He was thinking about something else, she could see. And she was right. Alex reached inside his jacket and pulled out a photograph.

'What d'you think of this?' he said. 'I found it.'

Ellie took the photograph. A young couple: a tall blond man with his arm around a woman with lots of crimped, scarlet hair. Taken in the eighties, judging by the clothes and hairstyles.

'My mum,' she said. 'My God. How about that? My mum and your dad.' She stared at the picture and into her mum's face, seeing the big grin, how young she looked, and how happy. Ellie found herself feeding on the picture, wanting to absorb every detail, committing it to memory. A moment from the life her mum had enjoyed before Ellie was born – such a strange idea. She had been a little plumper then, with round cheeks, a lot of eye make-up, a belt cinching her waist over the top of a baggy white shirt. And Joe, Alex's dad. Ellie turned her attention to him – long black coat, tight black jeans. Less like Alex than she might have expected. Good-looking, certainly. He had a smouldering, intense look – the sort of look a girl might fall for.

Alex was looking at her expectantly.

'What do you think?' he said.

'What do you mean?'

'You know – the two of them. Together.'

Ellie was taken aback. Although Joe had his arm around her mum, she hadn't thought it signified anything more than friendship. Now she noticed just how close they were.

'You think . . . they were an item?' She could hardly say the words. Of course she knew her parents must have had other partners and love affairs before they'd met and married each other. That didn't make the idea exactly palatable. She tried to be offhand about it.

'Well, it was a long time ago and it's a small town. What if they were? Anyway, where did you get this?'

'In a drawer in my dad's desk. He had a couple of pictures of your mum in an envelope. Now look at the back,' Alex said.

Ellie turned the picture over. A note on the back, in blue biro. She recognised her mother's handwriting. It said: 'I love you, Joe. I'll love you forever.' This inscribed inside a big, biro heart with lots of kisses.

Ellie handed back the photo. 'Why are you showing me this?'

'It's your mum. I thought you'd be interested.'

She heard something in the tone of his voice, and glanced into his face.

'You're upset about it?' she said softly.

'I . . . I don't know. I mean, obviously my dad had other girlfriends. But I wonder why he never said anything about your mum. I mean, he's talked about her from time to time, especially with you here this summer. But he never mentioned she was an ex.'

'Maybe it wasn't a big deal? You know – a fling.'

'Doesn't look like that to me.'

Ellie looked at the picture again, now in Alex's hand. He was right. Something about it – the smile on her mother's face. It didn't look like a fling to her, either.

23

A chilly wind whipped up from the sea to the graveyard. The square Norman church perched on a mound not far from the cliffs, giving views over the wide bay. The grey and blue sea was turbulent. A lone seagull perched on a stone cross in the graveyard, the breeze ruffling its feathers. Atop the church tower, a weathervane shaped like a sailing ship gave a golden glint in a flash of sunshine.

Ellie pushed the black gate open and stepped inside. She shivered and rubbed her bare arms. The wind blew hair into her face, and tied it in knots. Ellie walked along the little gravel path to the west of the church, then stepped on to the short, dense grass to wander among the headstones and sarcophagi. Her mother's grave, a simple grey headstone with a name and the dates of her birth and death, stood in the sunny side of the churchyard. Of course it still looked very new. Ellie had only visited it once since the funeral: the stone, for her, had little connection with the mother she remembered. The name, engraved in the stone, was too stark and final a reminder. She knew her grandparents tended it, sometimes left flowers. She only glanced at the grave. Now she was looking for another particular name.

The seagull fixed her with its beady yellow eyes, white breast shining in another burst of sunshine. Here the headstones dated mostly to the nineteenth century, decorated with ochre lichen and moss, draped with occasional picturesque strands of ivy. A few older, eighteenth-century graves stood behind the church, weathered and sinking into the ground. Others, close to her mother's – all clean, scrubbed marble – were only a few years old. Flowers, fresh and plastic, decorated some, and on one, a collection of children's toys. Ellie walked on.

Wasn't it here? The funeral had taken place in this church, according to the report in the newspaper. An interment had followed. Someone of Harry's wealth and status would have a memorial here, surely? He'd been so young when he'd died, his devoted parents would have wanted one – a place of remembrance, a focus for their grief? She mooched around the churchyard, scrutinising each and every piece of stone. On some, the names had been obliterated by coastal weather and time. Others leaned precariously, as, over the centuries, the ground slid slowly and inexorably towards the sea.

Ellie stopped short. There it was. The name jumped out. A plinth of white marble, woven over by ivy, beneath an angel with long, curved wings. The angel's head was bowed, its hands covering its face. Slender, androgynous and purely graceful, its attitude communicated picturesque grief. A stone scroll at its feet announced the name – Harry James Weatherstone – the dates of his birth and death, and the inscription: *Always loved*.

Ellie's vision blurred, with a rush of tears. She thought

of Harry, and then she thought of her mother. She wiped her eyes and gazed at the angel. How utterly lovely it seemed to her, with its naked feet and long hair, the sculptor inspired by the Pre-Raphaelite artists perhaps. Harry's parents had commissioned this. For the first time, she thought about them, how they must have felt, losing a son. She imagined them now, standing beside the memorial, the mother and father, who'd lost him at only nineteen years of age – lost his beauty and intelligence and all the promise of his life to come: lost the unique, irreplaceable person he was and all they might have shared with him in the future. Ellie's eyes filled with tears again, which now spilled over onto her cheeks. She imagined Harry's mother returning here week after week, tending the grave, leaving flowers as the more recently bereaved had left flowers on the new graves.

Ellie sniffed. She had a piece of old, grey tissue in her jeans pocket which she fished out to mop her eyes and blow her nose. Then she took her phone from her bag and snapped half a dozen pictures of Harry's grave, from various angles, with close-up shots of the angel and the scroll with its inscription.

The wind billowed up from the sea, rustling the leaves on the weather-bent hawthorn trees. High on the tower, the weathervane swung to the north. Ellie shivered, dropped her phone back into her bag and walked from the graveyard. She glanced back once, seeing Harry's angel silhouetted, the cloudy sky on its shoulders, articulating in stone an eternal sense of loss and sorrow.

It was nine o'clock, the town shops and cafés opening

up, the streets and pavements washed clean by showers of rain in the night. Ellie wandered down the road to the Marine Theatre and waited outside. Within ten minutes, two enthusiastic people, a little older than Ellie, arrived and unlocked the door. They were running a kids' holiday workshop and didn't bat an eyelid when Ellie told them she needed to rehearse for the youth theatre play. Ellie had the script in her bag to brandish, for extra effect.

The workshop leaders were setting up in one of the rehearsal rooms so Ellie made her way into the auditorium. The place seemed flat and dreary today. Odd how much the mood of the place altered. She noticed how jaded the interior of the building looked in the light of day, and remembered the threat to its future. Alex didn't seem worried – he'd said closure had always been on the cards and, so far, had never happened. But what if the threat was serious this time? What would happen to Harry?

Harry.

The thought of him conjured up a diffuse feeling of happiness and longing.

Another letter had appeared in the night.

This time, written on the back of another page from *Romeo and Juliet*, it was neatly folded on the table, in front of the model theatre, waiting for her when she woke up.

Dearest Ellie

I cannot express how I feel about you. You have an intensity, a radiance I find hard to put into words. I've spent so long waiting, sinking into the shadows, trapped, fading away. You've brought me back – channelled colour and life and feeling into

my existence. You are my path, Ellie.I never imagined it was
possible to want something so much. Every long minute I spend
without you is hard to endure. Come to the theatre as soon as
you can. I'm waiting for you there. I love you.

She sat on one of the plastic seats in the auditorium then
looked around, taking in its tattiness, and remembering
how beautiful it had once looked. Where was Harry? She
was keyed up, fired with adrenalin, aching for him to
appear.

'Harry?' she said softly. 'Where are you? I'm here.
Waiting for you.'

She drummed her heels against the stage. Five slow
minutes passed. Ellie stood up, paced from side to side of
the stage, then jumped to the ground and wandered among
the aisles, impatient for something to happen. From
beyond the auditorium she heard the voices of children,
no doubt arriving for their workshop. She remembered
coming here herself for one such event, years before, being
dropped off by her parents. A lifetime ago – she'd been a
different person then.

Ellie sat down at the end of a row of seats. She closed her
eyes and took a long, deep breath, trying to calm herself.
She could feel her pulse beating inside her head and
rubbed her arms, feeling the goosebumps. *Harry, where are*
you?

'I'm here, Ellie.'

Her eyes flicked open. She stared straight ahead. He
was sitting beside her, but for a moment, she resisted the
urge to look at him. Her heart seemed to gallop inside her

chest. The moment stretched, delicious and terrifying at once, because she wanted it so much.

She swallowed. 'Harry,' she said softly, looking at her lap. 'Thank you for your letter.' Ellie still hadn't looked at his face. She saw his strong, narrow thighs next to hers, where his hands moved restlessly, clenching and unclenching. Was he as nervous and keyed up as she was?

Ellie cleared her throat nervously.

'Harry, I . . .' She stopped.

'What? What is it, Ellie?'

'Do you remember anything more? About what happened to you?'

'You've found something,' he said.

Ellie nodded. She raised her head and looked directly into his face.

'I visited your grave,' she said. 'I know how you died.'

A shadow seemed to cross his face. He blinked, looked away, then back into her eyes.

'Tell me,' he said softly. 'I need to know. I have to remember.'

Ellie summoned her courage and plunged into the story. She described the journey she had taken to find out the truth, the newspaper archive, the grave in the churchyard. She tried to be cool and objective, recounting this tale, keeping her focus on the facts because she didn't know how Harry would respond and she was afraid of hurting him. He stayed very still and didn't interrupt. He absorbed all the details, and gave nothing away.

At last Ellie stopped. For several moments they were both silent. Then Ellie said, 'What are you thinking?'

Quiet again: Ellie could hear the sea. Except now the sound seemed to come from inside the auditorium.

'Your hands are shaking,' Harry said. 'Please – don't be afraid.'

'The sea . . . What's happening? I *am* afraid.'

'You want to be with me, don't you?'

'Yes. Yes, of course I do.'

'The more you give me, the more I remember. And the more I remember the stronger I become.'

'Stronger? You mean, you can come further into my world, the living world?' Ellie looked into his eyes. His face – so perfectly itself, so known to her: a face she hadn't learned, but remembered.

'No,' he said. 'I think I can take *you* deeper into *my* world.'

Ellie lifted her hands in front of her face. They were shaking harder now. She felt very cold and the sound of the sea was louder, as though waves were crashing into the building, spreading water inside.

'Your world? The land of the dead?'

Harry shook his head. 'The land of my past,' he said. 'That's all I have. All I am.'

'Okay,' Ellie rallied. '*A* land of the dead, if not *the* land of the dead.'

Harry inclined his head, with a smile. 'That I will concede.' He stood up. 'Will you come?'

Ellie hesitated. He was asking her to cross a boundary now – to move into his world. He stood before her, faintly phosphorescent. Perhaps the lights in the auditorium had dimmed. She glanced around – the entire theatre had receded. Only Harry truly existed now. Harry and herself.

'Yes,' she said. He held out his hand and Ellie moved her own cold hand towards his. She felt the warmth of his skin before they touched and, when finally the moment of contact came, she felt an extraordinary jolt – as though an electric circuit lying dormant in her body had leaped to life for the first time. His fingers closed over hers. They stared at each other, amazed.

'I can touch you,' she said. 'I can't believe it. I've longed to do this.'

Harry grinned: something rakish in his expression. He tugged Ellie to her feet.

'Let's not waste time,' he said. Ellie felt dizzy. The theatre unravelled, its details and colours swirling away. She closed her eyes, still clinging to Harry's hand, nauseous and disorientated.

'Ellie? Open your eyes.'

A summer garden. The wind had dropped. Bright sunshine, the scent of roses – lemon, honey and incense. Those roses clambered and clawed over an iron archway, blooms dangling, fat with red, velvety petals.

Ellie and Harry were standing underneath this arch. She looked around.

'Your home,' she said. 'North Hill House.'

Harry lifted his hand, the one still holding hers, and turned to face her. He straightened his fingers so they were palm to palm. Then he raised his other hand, inviting her to do the same. And so they stood, faces only inches apart, hands pressed together. Ellie could feel the heat of him, the smoothness of his skin. For the first time, she breathed the smell of him – warm, male, quite distinct – and, more strongly, a perfume, something masculine and exotic – a perfume she recognised immediately, with a physical sense of shock.

'What is it? You're wearing something,' she said. 'I've smelled it before – that first night – coming from the model theatre. It filled my room.'

'It's sandalwood,' he said. 'Do you like it?'

Ellie watched his mouth as he spoke, the soft lips, his strong teeth.

'Yes, I like it.' She couldn't explain to him how it affected her – like the current that had leaped into life when her hand touched his, and now continued to flow. She felt it pass between them, through the connection of their hands.

Too much. She drew away. Harry smiled again. They both relaxed, a little.

'Let me show you around,' he said.

The garden was lush and beautiful, full of flowers and butterflies. On the lawn at the back of the house a girl was lying on a blanket, reading a novel. She looked up as Harry and Ellie approached. Could Violet see Ellie? Perhaps not, because she grinned at her brother. She sat up, cross-legged, and dropped her novel on the blanket. She was about the same age as Ellie, though her manner made her seem a little younger.

'Hello, Harry,' she said.

'What are you reading?' he asked.

'*Wuthering Heights*. Don't you approve?'

Harry smiled. 'If I disapproved, would that make any difference?'

'No,' Violet said. 'No difference at all.'

'Shouldn't you be learning your lines?' he said.

'I've learned them already.'

'And your Romeo, has he learned his too?'

Light suffused Violet's face. Ellie saw it, the emotion rising to the surface.

'Oh yes, of course he has. Francois is very committed, you know that,' Violet said. She wasn't looking at Harry. Her eyes were focused elsewhere, beyond the limits of the garden.

She's in love with him, Ellie thought. This French actor – what was his name? Francois Lefevre. Ellie kept her gaze on Violet. The girl came back to the present, glanced at Harry and masked her feelings again. She gave her head a contemptuous little shake, perhaps realising she'd given herself away.

Did Harry know Violet was in love with her Romeo? Of course he did. These were his memories. He'd created this scene from the past. Somewhere, on some level, he'd understood that Violet loved Francois.

Harry turned to Ellie.

'I'll show you around the house,' he said.

He led the way, into the conservatory. Ellie remembered the state of the house as she'd seen it before. Now it was elegant, beautifully furnished, with paintings on the wall. In the kitchen a cook was making cakes. Ellie absorbed it all, every detail, wanting to remember it. After the tour Ellie and Harry sat in the drawing room. A screen of embroidered peacocks stood in front of the empty fireplace.

Then Ellie and Harry were standing in the garden again,

beside the long, rectangular pond where koi carp fish shone like huge, living jewels in the sunshine.

'Are you happy?' Harry said. 'Do you like being here, with me?'

Ellie nodded. 'Very happy.' They were holding hands again. Harry moved closer. He lowered his face towards hers. He filled her mind, his nearness, the shape and smell of him, the sandalwood and his own personal perfume, the heat of his body. He was going to kiss her. She raised her face towards his.

'Excuse me. Are you okay? Excuse me.' A querulous, worried voice.

Someone was shaking her arm. Harry's world dissolved: sunshine, garden, kiss. Ellie opened her eyes. A woman – one of the people from the kids' workshop – was leaning over her, peering into her face.

'Oh thank God,' the woman said, putting her hand to her chest. 'You gave me a terrible shock. You looked – well, I don't like to say it, but I thought you were dead you were so still and cold. Oh I'm sorry, you scared me.' She gave a nervous laugh, evidently relieved.

Ellie tried to move. Her body was numb, her limbs heavy and cold.

'Were you asleep? You were so still, I wasn't sure you were breathing. Are you feeling okay? Shall I get you something to drink?' The woman wittered on, still agitated. Ellie slowly sat up straight. She rubbed her face. Her skin was chilly, and felt, oddly, as though it didn't belong to her.

'Yeah. Yeah, I dozed off. I'm fine, really. Don't worry.'

'Can I get someone for you? Perhaps you were out drinking last night, is that it?' Another anxious laugh. 'These holidays – sometimes they're more tiring than being at work. Though I am working, of course, well, today I am. All these kids. Well, they're exhausting I can tell you.' The woman went on and on. Ellie was grateful for her concern but, more than anything, she wanted to get away before the memory of her encounter (dream?) with Harry had faded into nothing. She stood up awkwardly, gripping the back of the chair to steady herself.

'I just need some fresh air. I'm fine, honest. But thanks anyway.' She started to walk away, the woman behind her still talking.

Outside, alone, Ellie was caught in a swirl of intoxicating cool air, carrying the smell of sea and seaweed, and the sound of waves and screeching seagulls. She ran down to the beach, crunching on pebbles, to the water's edge, where the pebbles gave way to stone. She began to walk, away from the town and around the cove.

Harry and Violet, at North Hill House. She replayed the scene in her mind, the memory so fresh and vivid she could almost smell the roses, hear Violet's voice, feel again the rush of anticipation as Harry bent forward to kiss her.

'Ellie! Hey, Ellie!' A girl's voice, carried on the wind. Ellie was snatched back to the present. She shaded her eyes. There – further along the beach – were two familiar figures. Warren was sitting on a slab of ash-grey rock. Daisy was jumping up and down waving her arms, feet bare, shoes perched on a hunk of black stone. Ellie grinned and strode across the strip of smooth, wet sand to her friends.

Daisy whooped and ran towards her, arms out, and gave her a theatrical, consuming hug. Her little flower-print dress fluttered in the breeze.

Ellie glanced at Warren, who gave her a sheepish wave. Daisy and Warren? What was happening here? Didn't Daisy fancy Alex anymore? Perhaps divining her thoughts, Daisy blushed very prettily.

'What are you up to?' Daisy said. 'I was shouting for ages. You were miles away.'

'Oh, I was thinking about Harry,' Ellie said, blushing too.

'Her boyfriend,' Daisy explained, for Warren's benefit. 'You missing him? When are we going to meet him?'

Ellie shrugged. 'Don't know.'

Warren stood up. 'I've got to go,' he said. 'D'you mind?'

Daisy shook her head. 'No worries. I can talk with Ellie.'

Warren sloped off towards the town. Ellie took off her shoes, following Daisy's example, and the two girls strolled along the sea's edge, letting the chilly water wash over their feet.

'So, you and Warren?' Ellie said. 'Something going on?'

'Oh, I don't know,' Daisy said, suddenly shy. 'Not yet. Maybe.'

'What about Alex? I thought you liked him?'

'I do like him, Ellie. I mean, I'll always like him. He's my best friend.'

'But?'

Daisy stopped walking and turned to face Ellie. They stood, the two of them, in the blustery sunshine. A succession of shallow waves lapped around their ankles.

'A couple of days ago he told me he'd fallen for someone,' Daisy said. A succession of emotions revealed themselves in her face: hurt, pride, determination. 'I mean, I didn't say anything about me and him, he just came out with it. You know, this being on his mind and me being his friend. It was horrible. I felt so hurt. I didn't tell you before because – well, I just didn't want to talk about it.'

'Oh, Daisy – I'm so sorry.' Ellie reached out and touched Daisy's arm, a gesture of comfort. 'Did he say who she was, this someone?'

Daisy shook her head. 'He wouldn't say.' She gave Ellie a peculiar, piercing look.

'So – Warren?' Ellie said brightly.

'I don't know. He's an interesting guy and, to be honest, it's a good way to distract myself. We'll see how it goes.'

A larger wave tumbled into their legs, wetting them up to their knees. Daisy shrieked. The mood altered, tension draining away with the seawater. The girls started to walk again.

24

A wide expanse of shimmering golden sand. Still air, a haze of heat over a motionless sea. Nobody existed, except the two of them, walking slowly, side by side. Ellie carried a parasol, wore an elaborate long dress and white lace gloves. A tight corset encased her body. Pale silk flowers decorated the tiny hat pinned onto her hair.

She had her arm through Harry's. He was tall beside her, dressed in a black suit, a white shirt underneath. He was perfect, as the scene was perfect, and just as unreal. Ellie couldn't make out the horizon, which was caught in a blur. She and Harry walked in a bubble, beside a painted sea.

'I have to leave you now, Ellie,' Harry said. He stepped away from her.

'You love me, don't you?' She felt a terrifying pang of pain, anticipating the separation, the loss.

'Yes I love you,' he said. 'But I have to go.'

Something opened inside of her, like a trap door into which she would fall and fall indefinitely, into darkness.

'I can't live without you,' she said. 'You're part of me – inside me.' The prospect of losing him revealed vistas of

224

hurt and grief. He couldn't go. She wouldn't survive it. He'd become a part of her. His image was imprinted on her psyche, her heart. She couldn't lose him. She'd spend the rest of her life trying to find him again.

Harry took a further step away. Ellie's pain intensified. He was losing definition, blurring, as though the painted picture had smeared. Then he was gone altogether. He left a dark space, which then filled up with sand and sea, so she was alone on the beach.

Ellie sat up, her body aching, gasping for breath.

A dream, only a dream. She was sitting in bed, in her dark bedroom. She looked at her phone – it was just gone four in the morning. Her heart was pounding. She was too hot, covered in sweat, so she climbed out of bed and opened the window.

Two days had passed since the visitation in the theatre. Two busy days; research at the museum, making notes, picking out interesting information; another rehearsal for the play; an afternoon hanging out, baking and cake-testing with Daisy; a solitary walk inland past the old mills. She was hardly home at all. Her grandparents seemed happy Ellie was occupied. She wasn't thinking so much about her mother and father. She thought, a lot of the time, about Harry. Each day she'd dropped in at the theatre but he hadn't appeared. And now this dream. Was it a sign? Had he gone for good? She didn't think so. Something had to happen. She knew how he had died – but she didn't know *why*.

Ellie returned to bed, but sleep eluded her. She turned on her laptop and checked her email. Another message from her father, with a picture of him standing in front of an enormous redwood tree, in a forest. He had a huge, happy grin on his face, and looked decidedly, unnervingly boyish. Louise, presumably, had taken the photograph. She scanned the email swiftly, the news of his travels, questions about her own summer, the affectionate sign-off with another plea for her to contact him and a wish for her happiness. Half a dozen kisses. She looked at the photograph again. Despite herself, the picture of him touched her heart.

She saved it to the photograph folder on her laptop, then browsed through the other pictures. She had a small collection of photos from her childhood – snaps taken on holiday and at Christmas, one of her playing the piano. Some of the three of them together, a few with just her mother.

She stared at her mum's face. She'd looked so old and scrawny by the time she died. Ellie didn't want that memory. She hung on to recollection of those earlier times, when her mother had been healthy and pretty. And she thought again about the picture Alex had shown her – of her mum and Joe. Something about it niggled at her.

At last Ellie fell asleep. She woke up at nine, the laptop beside her on the pillow. She could hear her grandmother singing downstairs, and then the irritating noise of the vacuum cleaner. She glanced at her bedroom wall. She'd printed out the photos of Harry's grave and stuck them to the wall with the rest of her collection.

'Grandma, did you know Mum used to go out with Joe, Alex's dad?' Ellie was spooning up breakfast cereal while her grandmother fussed in the kitchen. She stopped whatever it was she was doing and stood in the doorway.

'Yes. Yes of course. How did you hear about that?' Her grandmother looked disconcerted.

'Oh, Alex had an old picture of them together.'

'It was a long time ago,' Jean said, pushing the matter aside and disappearing back into the kitchen. Ellie stared at the doorway, her curiosity aroused. Her grandmother was never usually evasive. So what if Joe had once been her mother's boyfriend? Was there more to the story than that? Ellie finished her breakfast and took the bowl to the kitchen.

'Did they go out for long?' she said.

'Oh, quite a while, yes,' Her grandmother dunked the dish in the washing-up bowl. She didn't look at Ellie.

'So what happened?'

'It ended, I suppose. Like these things do.'

Ellie waited a few moments more, studying Jean. What was she keeping to herself?

'I'm off out,' Ellie said finally. 'See you later.'

Half an hour later, she was sitting in the auditorium in the theatre, waiting. Why hadn't Harry written again? Why wasn't he here? Another kids' workshop was underway in the rehearsal room. She could hear their voices. No doubt the workshop leaders thought she was strange, sitting here alone for an hour at a time. She told them it was necessary for her role in the youth theatre production, but all she did was sit and wait and lose herself in elaborate daydreams about Harry, daydreams so increasingly detailed and lifelike that sometimes it was hard to snap back into reality. Waiting. That seemed to be her life now. The other activities – play rehearsals, friends, research – seemed colourless in comparison to this passion for Harry. They filled the empty space of his absence.

Nothing happened. At eleven she left the theatre and went to the museum. Her grandfather dumped a lidded cardboard box in front of her.

'This might be of some use,' he said. 'A new donation. Your friend the reporter published his story, and we've been spreading the word about the theatre project, and one of the volunteer wardens brought this in. Stuff from her neighbour, apparently.'

Ellie opened the box. Papers, letters, photographs. A real mishmash of personal documents, all belonging (or once belonging) to one Edith Marsh, who'd lived in the town. What was the connection with the theatre? Not much. Ellie found some old concert programmes which she put to one side, and reviews clipped from the local newspaper. The rest she returned to the box. As she did this, a name written on one of the envelopes caught her eye. She almost missed it. The envelope was addressed to Edith Marsh, and the name was small, part of the return address on the back. A return address in Paris.

Ellie stared. *Violet Lefevre.*

She pulled the letter out. The date – July 1913. The letter was written in a bold hand, with flourishes and curls.

Dear Edith,

Sorry it has taken me so long to write. We've been very busy! . . .

Ellie glanced at the bottom of the letter to the signature – Violet written with a large 'V'. She remembered the girl she'd seen in the garden of North Hill House, with her red hair and freckles. The girl who'd wanted to be an actress.

She read through the rest of the letter. It didn't say much – some observations of life in Paris, a little about a new role she had in a production of a play by Moliere, questions for Edith about her own family.

Ellie stared at the letter. Violet had written this. The material artefact, nearly a hundred years old, connected her dreams and visions to the real world. So Violet had married Francois and moved to Paris. She had achieved her ambition to be an actress, despite the opposition of her family.

Letter in hand, Ellie went to find her grandfather.

'Who brought this in?' she said.

'Something useful? It was Mary – she's over there,' he said, waving towards a tall, grey-haired woman talking to a family of visitors. 'I'm sure she'd be happy to tell you more. Wait till she's free.'

The box had come from Mary's neighbour, Maud Avery, a very elderly woman of ninety-five, who had just sold her house and moved into Whitewood House, a residential home on the edge of the town. Ellie asked if she could visit her, to ask about the documents. Mary, perhaps seeing how excited Ellie was, phoned the home at once.

'You can drop by any time between two and six this afternoon,' Mary said. 'They're going to tell her to expect you. She's a bright old bird. A little deaf and not very mobile, but her mind's quicker than mine.'

* * *

The home was right on the edge of town, a twenty-minute uphill walk along the main road then off through a very new housing development. Whitewood itself was a large old farmhouse, once surrounded by fields and now engulfed by the modern estate.

Ellie carried photocopies of Violet's letter and envelope in her bag. She pressed the buzzer and waited to be let in. She felt hot and cold with shyness. How should she speak to such an elderly woman? What would she say?

A young woman in a blue uniform opened the door, signed her in then escorted her along a corridor to Maud's room. It seemed a friendly place, very bright if rather hot. Several very decrepit old people were hobbling around the place on Zimmer frames. The young woman knocked on the door and opened it.

'Maud? Your visitor's here.'

Ellie took a deep breath, gripped her bag and stepped inside. Maud was sitting in a chair by the window. It was a small, tidy room with a bed, table and a couple of cupboards. A huge bunch of roses in a vase, several photographs of family members on the wall.

Ellie introduced herself. Maud was very tiny, with snow-white hair and brown eyes, and thin, veiny hands. Ellie didn't think she'd ever spoken to someone so old, and she was shy and awkward at first. But Maud had a strong, clear voice and as soon as she started speaking Ellie forgot about her nerves and the old woman's daunting fragility. They exchanged some pleasantries about the weather, the town, Ellie's family and her theatre project, and then Ellie drew out the photocopy of the letter.

'This was amongst the stuff you donated to the museum archives. It was sent by Violet Lefevre to Edith Marsh. I've been researching Violet – she performed in the theatre and evidently went on to be a professional in France. I wonder – do you know anything about her? And Edith Marsh, who's she?'

'Edith was my mother. And Violet – I never met Violet, but oh, I heard all about her from my mother. A very romantic story. No wonder you want to know about *her*.' A mischievous, rather flirty smile crossed Maud's pleated face. Ellie laughed.

'Really? How wonderful! Please do tell me.'

Maud patted the end of her bed. 'Do sit down and I'll tell you everything I know.' Then she leaned forward confidentially, as though sharing a secret. 'Violet was my mother's best friend. They were both members of the Lyme Theatre Company, and I gather they had a rare old time. My mother told me she was invited to some marvellous parties at Violet's house – a big place just out of town.'

'North Hill House,' Ellie reminded her. 'I've been to see it.'

Maud nodded. 'That's the one. Well, Violet wanted to be a professional actress, but in those days, and coming from a family like hers, it simply wasn't allowed. One summer they put on a performance of *Romeo and Juliet* – how perfectly romantic – and Violet, who was playing Juliet, fell in love with her Romeo – a handsome French actor who was staying in the town. I forget his name, but my mother tells me he was the most beautiful man she'd ever seen. They were *such* a glamorous couple, everyone talked about them, but it was quite a scandal too. I mean, she was a Weatherstone, and he was a poor French nobody without a penny to his name, and an actor to boot.' Maud had a glint in her eye, enjoying the telling of the story, keeping Ellie on the edge of her seat.

'Apparently Violet outraged her family. Once the play was over, nothing could restrain her. She and her Frenchman rode like demons all over the local country-side. They went down to the beach to swim at midnight, and all sorts of exciting and romantic things – really like something from a novel. Violet's parents tried to keep her locked up at home, forbade her to see her beau, but she was so in love with him, nothing could hold her back. So can you guess what happened?'

'She ran away with him – to Paris.' Ellie remembered the name on the envelope – Violet LeFevre. Violet and Francois had married.

'Yes, she did,' Maud said, with considerable satisfaction. 'My mother told me all about it. Violet bribed her servants to take letters to Francois. The couple eloped to Paris. The Weatherstone family cut her off without a penny and never spoke of her again. She became an actress, and had some degree of success I think. Violet didn't write often, but she and my mother exchanged a few letters over the years. When Mother died, I kept that one you have. It was such a wonderful story, I never forgot it and the letter was my little souvenir of the romance. But when I moved into here – well. I had to clear my house and I wanted to make sure that letter was never lost. I thought it would be safe forever in the museum archives – even when I'm gone. That's why I donated it.'

Ellie smiled. 'I'm so glad you did. It is a great story – a real love story,' she said. 'Apparently Violet had a brother, Harry. Do you know anything about him?'

Maud frowned. 'I did know about her brothers, yes. Sad stories. One died in a riding accident. The other died in the Great War. The Weatherstones sold the house soon afterwards. They'd lost so much by then. So many people had.' The old woman sighed, lost in thought. Then she looked at Ellie. 'I'm sorry. I hope I haven't bored you. Would you like a cup of tea?'

'No, you've not bored me at all. It's just what I wanted to know,' Ellie said. 'And yes please to the cup of tea.'

She left the home an hour later, mind bulging with stories of the past. Maud had given her some more reminiscences about the Marine Theatre which would be useful for the exhibition.

Best of all, Maud had confirmed what Ellie had suspected. Violet had run away with her French actor, married him in Paris and become an actress. Did Harry remember this? Should she remind him? She was afraid to. Harry adored his sister. Ellie wondered if this cataclysmic event had some connection with the accident that killed him.

What would happen if she opened the door on this terrible memory?

25

Ellie Googled Violet LeFevre. What chance of finding anything about a minor actor in Paris from a hundred years ago? But Wikipedia turned up trumps: two paragraphs and a link to another website. The Wikipedia site gave brief details about Violet's life, and mentioned one particularly famous performance. Violet had played Salome, in Oscar Wilde's play of the same name, at the Le Petit Theatre in 1899. Apparently the play had been an enormous success, much talked about at the time. She had one son and died, still in Paris, in 1966. Ellie checked out the link. It took her to a website about Le Petit Theatre, now closed. The famous production of *Salome* merited a paragraph on the history page. Ellie also found a picture of a poster for the performance and a tiny head and shoulders shot of Violet in costume. She saved both, and printed them out.

She Googled Francois' name. She found only one relevant link, taking her back to the Le Petit Theatre website where she discovered he'd become manager, a position he maintained for thirty years. No pictures of him.

Ellie picked up the pages from the printer tray. The

Salome poster was beautiful, in the art nouveau style with exotic twining stems, lotus flowers and lilies. She stared at Violet. Was this the girl she'd seen in the garden with Harry, at North Hill House? Hard to say for sure. In the picture she looked older, and she wore heavy make-up and an elaborate headdress. Ellie pinned up the pictures on her bedroom wall with the other documents.

Her computer chimed. Another email. She glanced at the screen: a message from her father. She opened it.

Dearest Ellie,

I hope you are well and happy. I receive some news about your various activities from your grandparents but I am very sad you never take my calls or respond to my messages. I know too well you are angry with me for my relationship with Louise. I have asked you to give her a chance, and I ask you again.

You are eighteen now – officially an adult. You could get married, sign up for the army, vote, take out a loan, or simply decide never to see me again, and I couldn't stop you. You can make your own choices.

But I think about you every single day. I wish you were here with us. I miss you so much. I love you, have always loved you and will always love you.

These last years have been so hard for all of us. Don't let the past destroy your life, Ellie. Mum's gone – but she wanted us to celebrate the life we still have, to care for each other and be there for each other. I'm here for you. I want you to enjoy every day. Appreciate what you have. Be happy, please. It's what she'd want. That's what I want most of all.

I won't keep chasing and pleading and placating. I won't keep badgering you. The door is open. When you want me, I'll be here. Always.

Dad xxx

Ellie blinked. She'd been staring at the screen, not seeing, not thinking, hardly conscious. Zoned out. She'd been holding her breath too. She closed the message and turned off the computer, then lay down on her bed, curled up on her side. Gradually she allowed herself to think about her father's message. She felt such a tumult of emotions – rage, guilt, fear, loneliness. These plaited over each other inside her, creating a hard, painful lump in her belly, making her feel sick. Yes, her mother had asked them to take care of each other – but her father had swanned off with this new woman. Yes, Mum had asked them to be happy and make the most of their lives, but Dad had made Ellie miserable with his selfish choices. He said he was 'there' for her – but in truth he was thousands of miles away, on the other side of the world, romancing, God forbid, with loopy Louise. In some cool part of her mind, a quiet voice told Ellie she was being unreasonable, but the tiger of fear and fury in her belly chased it out. She sensed the new tone in her father's email. He wouldn't chase her any longer. Now he would wait for her. An uncomfortable development: Ellie had to acknowledge she'd wanted him to chase her.

Ellie lay on the bed for a long time, thoughts running in circles inside her head. Finally she must have fallen asleep because when she opened her eyes the light had changed.

Evening was drawing on. She glanced at her mobile: six o'clock. She had a rehearsal at seven thirty – and she didn't want to go. Could she make an excuse? Thoughts of Harry filled her mind. She wanted him. She pushed all thought of her father out of her mind and instead let the light and warmth of her feelings for Harry fill her, body and soul. Harry was the only one who truly saw her and cared for her. He needed her, and she needed him. She closed her eyes and remembered the afternoon in the summer garden at North Hill House, the warmth of the sun and the smell of the roses. She imagined his face bending over hers, and the astonishing feelings of desire and happiness that had filled that one, perfect moment.

'Ellie? Dinner's ready!' Her grandfather's voice bellowed from the ground floor. Ellie sighed and climbed reluctantly from her bed. She went downstairs and poked her head into the kitchen.

'Actually, I'm not hungry. I don't think I'll have anything, thanks. I'm feeling a bit off colour. I'll go out for a bit of fresh air. I won't be long.'

Her grandmother raised her eyebrows. 'You're sick? What's the matter? Can I get you anything?' She stepped towards Ellie, ready to check the temperature of her forehead or give her a concerned hug, but Ellie retreated.

'I'm okay. Please, don't worry. I'll just pop out. See you later. Sorry about dinner.' She dived out of the front door and into the street.

Where were all the holidaymakers? At home, perhaps, after a long day of seawater, ice cream and sunburn. Uncanny though. The street and the air were sun-baked after a long, hot day. Ellie hurried to the Marine Theatre. The rest of the *Midsummer Night's Dream* cast would be there in an hour or so. The main doors were open, a volunteer sitting in the box office doing some kind of administration. Ellie said she'd come for a rehearsal and the woman nodded without concern.

Ellie went to the little room where she'd found Harry's shirt, and shut the door behind her. The desire to see him was intense. Just now it seemed nothing else mattered – not the play, not her friends, not her father. Only this – the consuming, burning wish to be with Harry. He had to come: he *had* to.

She sat on the floor, back to the wall, knees bent up to her chest.

'Harry,' Ellie said aloud. Her voice echoed strangely in the room. 'Please be here. I need you so much.'

A beam of sunlight poked through the odd little window, making a slanting geometric shape on the carpet. Motes of dust spun in the light. Ellie waited. Her mind, her thoughts, were fixed on only one thing, the need to see Harry.

Half an hour passed. The others would soon arrive for the rehearsal. She didn't have long.

Another ten minutes. The light on the floor shifted slightly.

'Ellie.' Harry's voice.

She scrambled to her feet. 'Where are you?'

'Here.'

She saw him standing on the other side of the room. He was ghostly and insubstantial. She could see through him, to the wall. When he stepped towards her, he passed through the sunbeam, into which he momentarily disappeared.

'You're hardly here,' Ellie said. 'What's happened?'

Harry shook his head. 'I don't know. I feel weak. I heard you call me, but it's hard for me to be here.'

Ellie reached out for him, hopelessly, but her arms flailed through the place where he stood. Harry gazed at her. Pain filled his face. She could hardly bear to look into his eyes, seeing the intensity of his misery.

'What's happened?' she said softly.

'I want you. I want to hold you,' he said.

Ellie reached out her arms again, through him.

'I can't,' she said, tears filling her eyes.

'Will you come with me? I am so alone. Without you I'm nothing.'

Ellie closed her eyes and dropped her arms by her side, stretching out her fingers. She sensed him step towards her, into her, like a cool tingling shower that passed through her skin and into her heart, blood and bones. He filled her mind.

A ride on horses through a forest, under towers of cloud, then across moors golden with flowering gorse to a pinnacle of black rocks. Harry was always in front of her. She watched the way he managed his horse, steering it through the trees and then along narrow moorland paths, jumping over ditches and streams. She was a helpless passenger, allowing her mount to follow, holding tight. When they reached the pinnacle of rocks, Harry jumped off his horse and started to climb to the summit. He didn't wait for her, seemingly oblivious to her presence, so Ellie dismounted and hurried after him, scrambling up the huge, dark slabs.

At the top – a small stone plateau, green and golden moorland spreading below them. A small, twisted hawthorn tree had contrived to grow in a crack in the rock. Harry was waiting for her, the sun behind him, his face in shadow. He held out his arms.

Ellie stepped towards him, warm sunlight touching her face, and then his arms were around her, and she was pressing herself against his warm, strong body, breathing sandalwood. He held her in a fierce grip. Her face rested against his chest, feeling his heat, hearing the thunder of his heart. The wind tugged her hair. Ellie closed her eyes and for a moment she was soaring above the rocks, looking down at Harry and Ellie embracing on the peak of stone, the wind whipping about them, pressed together. And then they were kissing, Harry's face bent over Ellie's, and Ellie shot back into her body, feeling the shocking, intoxicating sensation of his mouth against hers. A storm of feeling broke out inside her – delight, and desire, in extraordinary measures. She would remember this forever. No moment of her life would be more intense, more perfect.

Ellie opened her eyes. Darkness, and discomfort. Her body ached. She was shivering. Nothing made sense. Where was she? What had happened? She was lying on the hard floor in a cold, dark room. Slowly she moved, shifting stiff, painful limbs, until she was sitting up.

Gradually her mind made sense of things. She was in the little room at the Marine Theatre. She took out her mobile. Midnight: and she had two text messages and a voicemail. *Midnight?* She'd been so long with Harry? The rehearsal had come and gone, while she lay hidden away in the storage room. Now her head ached.

She had concerned messages from Alex and Daisy, asking why she wasn't at the rehearsal, hoping she was okay. The voicemail came from her grandparents, with a similar worried enquiry about where and how she was. The phone started to ring – another call from her grandparents.

'Hello?' Ellie didn't know what to say. She couldn't tell them she'd gone to the rehearsal as either Daisy or Alex may have phoned and told them she hadn't turned up.

'Sorry I'm late, I went for a walk,' she lied. 'I'm on the beach. Please don't worry. I've been thinking about stuff, that's all. I needed to get away – and yes – I'm feeling fine now. I'll be back soon.'

Her grandfather didn't sound convinced. As soon as the call ended Ellie realised her assurance had been rash. How would she get out of the theatre? The place would be locked up. Would she have to spend the night here? How would she explain that?

The main doors were indeed locked. Ellie prowled round the place looking for a window. She found one in the office, a tiny square window she could just squeeze through by climbing onto the windowsill and twisting her body. She emerged head first, and plunged dangerously onto the tarmac of the courtyard outside. She wrenched her shoulder and bruised her upper arm, but at least she was out. Ellie pulled the window to, hoping no potential thief or vandal would notice it was open, then hurried through the town, and home.

They were both standing in the hallway when she arrived, staring at her anxiously.

'Are you okay, Ellie? Alex called us, wondering where you were. You missed a rehearsal, did you know?' her grandmother said. 'Where did you go, all this time? We were so worried.'

'I'm sorry. Sorry, sorry, sorry,' she said. 'Wanted to walk, that was all. You know – time to think.'

Ellie's grandparents both hugged her. Ellie surprised herself by bursting into tears in her grandmother's embrace. Jean was taken aback too. Ellie clung to her like a little girl, and soon her grandmother's shoulder was damp with tears. She stroked the back of Ellie's head and made soothing sounds. Her grandfather stood beside the two of them, in the hall's twilight, till Ellie stopped crying, when he offered her a handkerchief and then volunteered to make them all a cup of tea.

'It's okay,' Ellie said. 'I don't want one. I need to go to bed. I just want to sleep.' She felt empty now, all worn out. She blew her nose, wiped her eyes, then trudged up the stairs to her room.

She hadn't told Harry what she'd found out about Violet's running away with Francois. Perhaps she should have done, but she was too afraid of his reaction: afraid, most of all, that this knowledge would lead to his departure. She wanted and needed him too much. The moment of their kiss flashed into her mind, all vivid colour and passion in the monochrome of everyday life. She lived for their time together. Without him, what would she have left? Nothing mattered, really, except him. Not any more.

26

In the morning, Ellie texted Daisy and Alex with the excuse she'd given her grandparents. Both texted her back, sorry to have missed her and hoping she was okay. Daisy suggested they meet up in the afternoon, but Ellie made an excuse. She wasn't in the mood to leave the house or see anyone. She wanted to hide away.

Ellie had breakfast with her grandparents, forcing herself to eat. They asked how she was, and if she felt better after a good night's sleep. Ellie reassured them as they fussed, explaining she'd been tired the night before, that was all, and yes, now she was fine. Later they left for Bridport to do some shopping. Ellie made herself some coffee and went back to bed. She studied the model theatre and all the information she'd collected on her quest to unravel the mystery of the Weatherstone family. The trouble was, now she didn't want to know more. She didn't want the situation to change.

Ellie took out her journal and described the time with Harry in as much detail as she could. She didn't ever want to lose it, the memory, so she pinned it down in words. The account took several pages. When she'd finished, Ellie showered and dressed. She drank another coffee in the shady garden, still daydreaming about Harry, then wandered around the silent house, remembering the long summers she'd spent here as a child with her mother. Strange, how far away her mum seemed now. So much had happened since Ellie had arrived at her grandparents' house.

But thinking about her mother gave Ellie an idea. She took out the stepladder from the cupboard under the stairs and carried it to her grandmother's writing room. This room had a tiny loft hatch in the ceiling, leading to a small attic space where various bits of family junk were stored. Ellie had peered inside it once or twice, when her grandfather was retrieving the Christmas decorations.

She positioned the ladder, climbed up and pushed the hatch open. A torch waited just inside, to the left of the opening. Ellie climbed inside, turned on the torch and looked around. It was a low-ceilinged, dusty, tiny place covering the west end of the building, which had been added on to the older mill house. The air smelled hot and stale, trapped in a pocket under the tiled roof. Ellie wondered about mice or bats: the place also possessed a faintly animal, musty smell.

Layers of fluffy yellow insulation lay between the rafters to her left. On the other side, several pieces of chipboard, on which stood the old collection of Christmas decorations, and half a dozen lidded plastic boxes. Ellie edged her way towards these, wary of hitting her head on the roof, cobwebs and dust tickling her nose. She examined the boxes. One contained old bank accounts and business papers, another held a collection of winter coats and jumpers. The third – yes – what she'd hoped she might find: a collection of her mother's stuff – old school exercise books, reports and letters. Ellie lifted it to the hatch, lowered herself carefully onto the stepladder, took out the box, turned off the torch and closed the hatch.

She put the stepladder back under the stairs and carried the plastic box, still closed, to her bedroom.

Long ago her mother had mentioned something about the old exercise books and school reports Grandma still kept in the attic. Her grandmother had wanted her mum to sort them out or take them away but Ellie wasn't sure she'd ever got round to it. Evidently not.

From her bedside table the mobile bleeped. Another message had arrived – this time from Alex, asking if she was okay, and did she want to meet? Ellie didn't reply. She put the phone down and opened the plastic box instead. First she emptied the contents onto the floor. School books, folders of photographs, a file of school reports, a large, old shoebox stuffed full of letters.

Where to start? The exercise books didn't look exciting so Ellie put them all back into the box. Next the school reports: she skimmed through them. Her mum had been a talented and diligent pupil, by all accounts. *Sophie excels in art and maths* – no surprises there. They went back into the box too. Next the photographs – which were contained in old Truprint packets from the days when you had to send your films off to a developer. These were taken in the eighties, when her mum had been in her late teens and early twenties. Some of the pictures looked familiar. They had a photograph album at home dating back to this time, in which her mum had displayed her favourite pictures.

Dates were written on the back. How strange, to see her mother at the same age as Ellie was now. Despite the make-up and big eighties hair (or because of it?) she and her friends seemed so young and naïve. The photos had been taken around the town, in pubs, on the beach: her mum and a couple of other girls; some of a big gang, boys and girls. Ellie felt an oddly maternal feeling for her, the girl of eighteen who'd become her mother. She looked so bright and open. Little did she know what lay in store for her. Ellie thought of the long illness, how it had stolen all the youth and flesh and life from her mother, leaving behind the wasted body and a self eaten up by suffering.

'Poor Mum,' Ellie said, touching the girl's face with her fingertip. Little had her mother known . . . And what did Ellie know? What secrets lay in her own future? What was waiting for her? Ellie shivered. No way of knowing. It would come to her, day by day, this hidden future, with all its pleasures and pain.

She spread the photographs over the floor. Then she found him – the one she was looking for – Joe Sullivan, Alex's dad. He appeared in the photographic chronicle when her mother was about twenty. In most of the photographs he wore the same intense, moody expression. This was, perhaps, the face he pulled when someone pointed a camera at him. Always wearing black clothes, the longish blond hair. In one of the pictures he had a huge rose pinned to his lapel. In another, smudged black eyeliner and crimped, back-combed hair, like several of the others in the photos. Ellie smiled at their assumed seriousness. Well, she could see why her mother had liked him, despite the dire fashions. Joe had evidently joined the gang, and at some point he and her mum had become an item. Photos of groups gave way to portraits of Joe on his own, or snaps of him with her mother, arms around each other, holding hands, laughing, even kissing. One, a photo of Joe sitting up in a double bed, duvet over his legs, bare-chested, hair hanging over his face.

Ellie took a deep breath. She felt very peculiar and uncomfortable – as though she was a peeping Tom peering through a keyhole at her mother's intimate past. Wasn't that exactly what she *was* doing? Perhaps you gave up your right to secrets when you were dead. She put the photo down and turned her attention to the shoebox instead.

Lots of letters to 'Sophie' – fifty or sixty probably. Judging by the address on the envelope, most had been written to her by friends when she was at university. Pre-email and Facebook – how archaic, Ellie thought. Still, there was something nice about these real, crumpled, handwritten letters. She searched through them, glancing at the contents, putting them back into the shoebox – until she found one from Joe. This she kept to one side. It didn't seem he'd been a great letter writer. By the end of the process she had just three letters, covering a period of two and a half years, by the end of which time her mum had been twenty-three.

Ellie again felt reluctant to invade her mother's private life. But didn't these letters belong to her now, by right of inheritance? Sophie and Joe. The Sophie who'd existed before her dad and marriage and baby Ellie. What had happened to her? Ellie wanted to know, yet didn't want to know.

She opened the first letter. A love letter from Joe – intense, passionate, wordy, a little juvenile – or so it seemed to Ellie. Still, it made her smile, to think her mother had inspired such devotion. Clearly he'd been head over heels in love with her when he wrote this – and nearly as much in love with himself. Hard to think that this kid had grown up into the strong, level man she'd met at Alex's house. How time changed people. What would Joe (Alex's dad!) think if he knew she was reading these letters, written by his former self? The second letter, composed six months later, seemed less gauche. He wrote of his plans for art and life, enquired about Sophie's studies, expressed his desire to be with her again. A year and a half had passed before he wrote the third and final letter in her mother's box. Ellie opened it with trembling hands.

. . . I don't know how to write this, what words to choose, how to excuse myself or help you understand . . .

Ellie felt a plummeting inside. What had her mother felt, reading these words at the letter's opening?

. . . break off our engagement . . . I think it would be a huge mistake . . . impossible to explain . . . too many differences . . . met someone else . . . never felt this way before . . . hope we might one day be friends . . . you will always be in my heart . . .

Ellie lowered the letter. Engagement? They'd been *engaged*? Her mother had never told her this. Had her father known? She felt a multitude of emotions – shock, hurt, disillusion. Her mother had been serious about this man. She'd wanted to marry him. If he hadn't dumped her, she wouldn't have married Ellie's dad and Ellie wouldn't have been born at all: a strange, unsettling thought. Life was so random. In some peculiar, unexpressed, egotistical way Ellie had always assumed she was meant to be here – that the universe had conspired to create her for a purpose. Perhaps everyone thought that way. Now she felt unimportant and insignificant. Joe had broken up with Sophie. Two years later, Sophie had married Rob, and Ellie was born. Had Sophie loved Rob as fervently as she'd loved Joe? Had Rob turned out to be the 'real thing'? Or had her mum always harboured a secret regret? Ellie remembered Alex expressing his surprise that her mother hadn't seen Joe and his wife during their childhood holidays here. Now that didn't seem so surprising.

Ellie sat up straight, surveying the collage of photos strewn over the floor. She felt . . . confused. She felt something, but she wasn't sure what it was. What did it mean for her that her mum had, long ago, loved someone else? If she hadn't died, Ellie might never have found out. Perhaps Ellie shouldn't have nosed around now – what did she gain by knowing?

Ellie put her hands to her face. She had tears on her cheeks. She'd been crying without even noticing. She wanted her mother. Inside her, the never-ending, empty mother-shaped space ached. She stared at the smiling face of the young Sophie, the girl who would one day cradle infant Ellie, love her, nurture her and take care of her when she was ill, soothe her worries, cuddle her and be there for her, and once again the sensation of loss and loneliness crashed over her, like a wave. Ellie wanted her mum, but her mum had gone. She would never see her again.

'Oh, Ellie! What are you doing? What's wrong? What's happened?'

Her grandmother was standing in the doorway, surveying the scene – Ellie crying, the old pictures and letters scattered over the floor. Ellie hadn't heard her grandparents come home. She'd no time to hide what she was doing. Jean hesitated for a moment, dismayed, then she stepped over the photos to Ellie's side. She knelt down, close beside her granddaughter. She picked up one of the pictures, and studied the young, smiling face of the child she had lost.

'I hated the hair dye,' she said. 'That awful crimson colour! She had such beautiful golden-brown hair. And all the make-up and stuff she liked. Seems silly now, the fuss I made about it. We had some rows . . . I didn't know what to do with her. Of course it didn't really matter. She was a lovely, lovely girl. So clever and creative and quirky. So special.'

'It's not fair, what happened,' Ellie said, wiping her nose on her sleeve.

'No, not fair at all.'

'I miss her all the time.'

'Yes. So do I.' Jean put the picture down and picked up another. She gave a small smile. 'Still, I think I was lucky to have her, even if it wasn't for long enough.'

They were both quiet for a minute or two, looking at the photos. Then Ellie said, 'She was engaged to Joe Sullivan. I didn't know that. Why didn't you tell me?'

Her grandmother glanced at the letters but didn't

reprimand Ellie for snooping. She hesitated for a moment, evidently thinking, then said, 'No, I didn't tell you. It wasn't anything to do with you and it was a long time ago. Your mum didn't tell you either, did she?'

'No.' Ellie shook her head.

'She had a life before you were born. That belonged to her, not you.'

'They were engaged! That's serious. And he dumped her for someone else. Was that someone Sue? Alex's mum?'

Jean nodded.

'How did Mum take it?'

Her grandmother sighed. 'Very badly. She had some-thing close to a nervous breakdown.' She rubbed her cheek with the palm of her hand, her eyes unfocused, evidently remembering. 'Your mother was more fragile than you may think. She changed once you were born – I mean, she grew stronger and more resilient. But underneath – well, maybe we're all more fragile than we let on.

'Anyway, after the break-up she dropped out of college for six months. She hardly went out, and she was taking medication, though I don't know if it helped. And she did get over it, bit by bit.'

'Weren't you angry with him? With Joe?'

'At first, yes. Furious. I could have killed him. But it wasn't really his fault. They were young. Relationships end. They weren't right together. And I know he did care about her. And anyway, when she went back to college she met your dad. I was worried at first, in case it all went wrong again, but she was very happy with him.' Jean raised her head and looked straight at Ellie.

'To be honest, at the beginning I thought your dad wasn't really good enough for her. I hope you don't mind me saying this. Everyone thinks that of course – I mean, no one is worthy of your precious child. He seemed – well – a little ordinary compared with her. But I came to see what a special man he was, and how right for her. He supported everything she did and he never let her down. Never. And he was – is – a brilliant dad. She was lucky to find him, Ellie.'

Ellie felt the sting of this, the assertion that her father was a brilliant dad. Her grandmother was criticising her, wasn't she? She was wrong, Ellie bridled: her dad *had* let her down. He'd behaved selfishly.

Did Jean see these thoughts written in Ellie's face? Perhaps she guessed them.

'You'll be going to university soon,' she said. 'You'll have a new life. There'll be loads of friends, and romance, all sorts of discoveries. Do you want your dad to be sitting on his own at home waiting for you, while you forget about him and have lots of adventures?'

Ellie sighed. She couldn't respond to the question because her answer was yes. That *was* what she would like. This was the childish, selfish answer, she knew, but deep down that's what she wanted. She took a big breath, sat up straight, looked her grandmother in the eyes and said, 'Okay. I hate to admit it, I know it's wrong and I shouldn't feel this way, but yes. That is exactly what I'd like. I want to fall in love, go to university, begin a new life, change, have all those new adventures – and I'd like Dad to stay the same, and my old home to stay the same, and none of that to change at all, so I can always go back, and always feel safe.'

Her grandmother smiled. And Ellie smiled back, and then they both started to laugh. Jean put her arms around Ellie and they hugged each other hard, and Ellie felt her spirits lift, simply to have acknowledged and admitted what it was she was feeling.

27

Ellie walked along the beach. She was barely conscious of the view – the hazy sky, the sea a still, milky blue.

None of it mattered much, this outside world. She was thinking about Harry. He filled her thoughts, pushing everything else out. She saw his lovely face in her mind's eye. She saw the darkness of his hair in the colour of the cliffs, heard his whisper in the *shush* of the long, tiny waves on the plateau of grey rock at the water's edge. She'd read about it before, this being so in love that the whole world seemed to be a symbol of the beloved. It had sounded ridiculous – cheesy, over the top. Only now she was here, and Harry had become the prism through which she viewed everything else. *This pebble is the brown of your eyes . . . In this shell's underside, I see the smooth ivory of your skin . . . .*

She recalled their last encounter, the kiss on the pinnacle of rock, and played it over and over in her mind. The vivid memory conjured up a symphony of emotions. How addictive it was, this intoxicating reminiscence.

Ellie texted Mike and told him she couldn't attend the rehearsal scheduled for that afternoon. She couldn't think about anything but Harry. She didn't want to extricate herself from this web of daydreams and memories. And more than anything else, she wanted to see him again. Could she manage it, to sneak inside to the little room, beneath the auditorium? Surely Harry would be waiting. Ellie realised how stupid she would look if she were discovered in the little room, having told them she wasn't able to attend the rehearsal – but it was worth the risk. She had to see Harry. She had to.

The rehearsal was due to start at two, so she sneaked into the theatre at half past one, just as the kids' summer workshop session was ending. Ellie pushed past the kids and parents, hurried through the auditorium, down the stairs and into the odd little room. She closed the door.

'Harry?' Almost immediately she felt him all around her. Although she couldn't see him, something engulfed her, wolfed her down. She felt the hunger of it, as though the air in the room had wrapped itself around her. Her mind whirled.

'Careful – please . . . Harry.' She tottered to the side of the room, dazed, leaning against the wall. The presence drew away, contracting, creating itself into something she could see – the ghost, the familiar face and form of the man she loved.

'Ellie, I've been waiting. I've been longing to see you.' His gaze ran over her face, as though reassuring himself she hadn't changed since the last time they'd been together. He held out his arms and without a word she stepped into his embrace.

* * *

They stood on a cliff top, above the bay. The town flowed through the valley to the west, spreading to meet the sea. The land to the east fell away, downhill, to the next town then rose again in a smooth curve of green fields to another summit.

Ellie and Harry stood close together, holding each other, kissing from time to time. She felt the current again, running through their clasped hands, between their bodies, the energy that flowed between them.

After an indeterminate time, Harry drew away, still holding her hand. He led her through a gap in a drystone wall, into a field where a wild apple tree grew. They sat down together in the shade. Side by side, their bodies touching, he touched her face very gently with the tips of his fingers. He kissed her neck, breathing in the scent of her.

'You have to tell me, Ellie.'

'Tell me what?'

'You're hiding something. What do you know?'

'I don't know what you mean,' she lied.

'Don't you think I know you? Last time you were keeping something from me. Today it's still there. The hidden thing.'

Ellie's heart clenched in her chest.

'I'm afraid to tell you.'

'It's about me.'

'Yes.'

'Then I have to know.'

She swallowed. 'Harry. I don't want to lose you.'

'You'll never lose me.'

Ellie shook her head. She didn't believe him.

'Tell me. You have to tell me. I've been waiting.'

'Waiting for what? I thought you were waiting for me.'

Harry's grip loosened. He looked away, across the field. 'It's true. I was waiting for you. But you have to tell me.'

Ellie sighed. 'It's Violet. Your sister. I found out what happened to her.'

'Violet? What happened?' Urgency in his voice.

'She was in the play, *Romeo and Juliet*, with the French actor, Francois Lefevre. They fell in love, Harry. She ran away with him – to Paris. They married. Don't you know? What happened to you – I think it was because of this. Can you remember now?'

Harry was silent. He stared ahead of him, lost in thought, as though Ellie no longer existed.

'Violet,' Harry said. The summer scene trembled all around them, losing substance. 'She ran away? She fell in love with that actor – with Francois . . .'

Ellie sensed the boiling inside him. Harry's eyes went black. His face blurred. She tried to reach out for him but his body seemed to melt on the air. He was coming apart – breaking in pieces.

'Harry, what's happening? Please! Don't leave me! What are you thinking? What's going on?'

She sensed the cataclysm inside him – the storm of rage and helplessness and thwarted love. The passion he'd felt for her seemed to unravel into this furious brew. Fear overcame her. What had Harry done? What was he capable of?

'Harry, please!' she shouted out. 'Where are you? Don't leave me here!'

The summer scene winked out of existence. Ellie whirled

257

through an ocean of darkness, drawn by currents of memory, buffeted by waves of anger. The darkness divided, into a night sky and the glittering inky black of the sea.

Harry was standing outside the Marine Theatre, pacing up and down. Everything about him suggested rage – his movements, the aggressive stance. He was waiting for Violet. Harry had intercepted her letter and knew the couple intended to meet here, before their running away.

He had to stop her. He *had* to. Harry was furious. He loved his sister. She was so young – a child. And this man, this useless, selfish, unworthy man wanted to take her away, to ruin her life, destroy her reputation and the honour of her family. Violet was a fool, she didn't know what she was doing – the harm that would be done to them all. Harry had to stop her. He was seething with rage. He wanted to get hold of Francois, to hurt him – to destroy him for this threat to his sister.

These violent thoughts went through Harry's mind, over and over again as he paced back and forth in the courtyard outside the theatre. Ellie, sucked into his memory, could see his thoughts, share his feelings. He was out of control, overcome by emotion. It frightened her – what was he capable of?

Beyond the wall, the sea crashed onto the rocks. The wind was rising. Clouds marched across the sky.

Still Harry waited, caught in the circle of his thoughts.

At last, a horse clattered under the archway and into the courtyard, hooves sending up sparks. The rider, cloaked and hatted like a character from a melodrama, leaped from its back.

'Harry! Harry!' A man's voice, shouting above the wind. 'They've gone already! She must have discovered the letter was intercepted. We're too late! They were seen heading out of town. They'll be making their way to the station.' The man shook his head. 'We've lost her, Harry. My daughter . . . He's taken Violet. What am I going to do without her? I failed her. I've failed you all.'

Harry swore. 'It's not too late,' he said. 'It's not finished yet.' He climbed onto his own horse. 'I'll ride across country,' he said. 'I'll catch them up. I'll get her back, Pa. I'll teach him a lesson.'

He drummed his heels against the side of his horse and they were off, thundering through the town, then out along the narrow rocky path along the cliff top.

Ellie followed him, caught in Harry's memory. He recollected the scene in dramatic fragments – the horse slithering on the stony path, the flash of the moon when the cloud momentarily parted, the deep crash of waves on the rocks below. She felt his burning rage, the spikes of adrenalin, moments of fear when the horse veered or stumbled, the terrifying exhilaration of their speed. Fields spread to one side. The cliff plunged away on the other. The path fell down, precipitous, to a stream which the horse leaped over, then climbed again on the other side, weaving between boulders. And in Harry's mind, all the time, the thought of his sister and his desire to save her from Francois, and the ruining of her life. He wouldn't let her go.

The horse's breathing was laboured. Once, in stumbling, it wrenched its leg and afterwards galloped unevenly.

Another flash of moonlight and then a spatter of rain,

259

making the path more slippery. Harry took a hand from the reins to wipe his eyes. Waves boomed below them. A spear of lightning, apt and uncanny, dived into the sea on the far horizon. Harry saw it, momentarily distracted. Something dived from the undergrowth – a bird probably – and the tired, struggling horse shied – snatching the bit, losing its footing.

For one long, terrible moment they hung in space – horse and rider – then the horse's hooves scrabbled for purchase, a wild, hopeless struggle.

Then they were falling, Harry still in the saddle, bound to his horse by stirrups, hands gripping reins, rain and wind all about them, down and down, till they hit the rocks at the bottom.

Then Ellie could see nothing. Strangely, she heard the beat of the horse's heart. Three times it pumped, with a sound like a drum – and then it stopped. Only the sound of the sea remained, the ceaseless rolling of the waves, but this too faded, moment by moment. The sea seemed to draw everything away, soaking up life and memories . . . until everything was still, and silent.

Everything was over.

All was done.

Except that it wasn't. Something about the sudden, violent death kept Harry from passing over. He continued to wait at the theatre, to rescue Violet, caught in the moment of rage and anguish. He waited for years, till he could no longer remember why he was waiting. He waited till waiting wore him thin: till Ellie picked up the model theatre he had made with his sister, and jolted him into consciousness again.

28

Ellie's eyes opened. Noise around her: people talking in low, urgent voices. She couldn't hear what they were saying. She was moving – no, being moved. Someone was carrying her. The room – what had happened to the room? The carpet was rucked up and torn. Strips of wallpaper hung from the walls. Wide cracks wormed across the plaster ceiling and dust hung on the air. The pane in the little window had smashed. Fragments of glass lay over the floor.

'Take her out, into the fresh air!'

'What happened? My God! The building isn't safe.'

'Should we call an ambulance?'

'Is she okay? Look, she's coming round.'

The voices assaulted her ears. Ellie's mind was empty, her head heavy. She could barely remember who she was, why she was here – as though a huge electric current had passed through her brain, obliterating everything, leaving only a cold, white light.

A familiar face looked down into hers. She closed and opened her eyes again, trying to work out who it was. This person was carrying her out of the room.

'Alex?'

'Don't worry. Keep still. We'll get you out of here.' His face was calm but she could see he was worried. What had happened?

He carried her into the office. One of the others shoved piles of papers and files from the old sofa in the corner so that Ellie could lie down. Daisy appeared with a glass of water. They all talked amongst themselves, as though Ellie wasn't present.

'Did something fall on her? What was she doing down there?'

'I think the whole place's falling down. They want to build flats here, did you know?'

'What about Ellie? Should we take her to hospital?'

Mike appeared by her side, taking on an air of authority.

'Ellie, are you okay? Are you hurt? Can you tell us what happened?'

She shook her head. 'I'm not hurt. Really, I'm fine. Just – I don't know. I think I fainted.'

'You look very pale. What were you doing down there?'

'Oh, I don't know. I got here early – I was exploring . . . and then . . .' she shook her head. 'What happened?' She sipped the water Daisy had offered and sat up. Already she was feeling better but her hands and feet were still numb, blood circulation sluggish.

'We were all in the auditorium,' Daisy said, her eyes wide. 'And then there was this tremendous noise! A great crash, and a crack, and a kind of rushing. Warren says he thought he heard someone shouting. Anyway, this horrible racket went on for several seconds. We thought the building was collapsing or something.'

'Then everything went quiet,' Warren interrupted, appearing beside her. 'So we tried to find out what'd happened. The noise came from beneath us, so we went downstairs. The door into that room you were in wouldn't open. We thought it was locked, but Alex heard something from inside. He said he thought someone was in there. The door just wouldn't budge, but Alex and Mike kicked it down, and there you were.'

'You had plaster dust and glass all over you,' Daisy said, dramatising the information with her hands. 'We thought the ceiling had fallen in or something. You were so out of it. I was scared you were dead!'

'Thanks for rescuing me,' Ellie said. She drank some more water, clearing dust from her mouth and throat. Everything was coming back to her now, the memory she'd shared with Harry, reliving the wild ride along the cliffs and the terrible moment of his death. She felt again the vertigo of his fall, the long plummet into darkness. Her vision blurred.

'Catch her!' The world slid out of focus.

A moment later she opened her eyes again, seeing the ring of faces looking down at hers.

'I should take her to the hospital,' Mike said.

'No, please,' Ellie said. 'I don't want to.'

'Then I'll take you home. You're in no fit state to walk. I'll fetch my car. Daisy – keep an eye on her.' Mike hurried off. Daisy and Alex stayed by her side. Warren, Carly and the others huddled by the door, talking among themselves.

Five minutes later Mike reappeared. He helped Ellie into his car.

'I'll come with you,' Alex said, jumping into a back seat. Mike got into the car for the short drive through the winding streets, to Ellie's home.

Her arrival prompted fuss and alarm from her grandparents. Mike explained what had happened. Jean ushered Ellie into the living room, David asked a dozen questions. Mike drove away, back to the rehearsal, but Alex stayed on. Ellie heard him in the next room talking to her grandmother – discussing her, no doubt. Oh, but she didn't care. She felt so weary now, all energy gone. Mind, body, heart – drained of everything. She was empty. Let them talk. What did it matter? What did anything matter?

She struggled to her feet and went to the door.

'Grandma? I want to go to bed. I'm really tired.'

They helped her up the stairs. Alex opened her bedroom door. She heard him gasp as he stepped inside. He scanned the room, alarm all over his face.

Ellie slipped into bed, still dressed. Her grandmother plumped up the pillows behind her.

'I think I should get the doctor. And I have to call your father. My goodness, what's happening to you? You fainted, Ellie. That's not right.'

'No, please – I don't need the doctor. And don't call Dad. Really – I don't want you to! Promise me you won't. I'm fine, honest. Just tired. It's nothing serious.' Ellie glanced at Alex. He was still staring at the wall, taking in the collection of pictures and documents she'd pinned up.

Jean pursed her lips. 'I don't know, Ellie. Really I should.'

'Please! At least, wait till tomorrow. I'll be okay then, you'll see,' she pleaded. Ellie had always been able to talk her grandmother round. She was, after all, the beloved only grandchild.

'Well, I'll wait till tomorrow then,' her grandmother said. She didn't seem convinced this was the right thing to do. She hesitated in the doorway, dithering.

'Could I have a cup of tea, Grandma?'

'Of course. What am I thinking? Alex?' He nodded, and Jean hurried off, glad to have something to do.

When she'd gone, Alex sat on the side of the bed. He stayed very still, studying the model theatre and the bedroom wall. Ellie couldn't work out what he was thinking.

The room was quiet. From the street below, she heard the voices of children.

'What's going on, Ellie?'

'What d'you mean?'

Alex didn't answer. He stayed very still.

'What d'you mean, what's going on?' Her voice had a shrill edge.

Alex sighed. He gestured to the wall. 'What's this?'

Ellie looked again. She saw, as though for the first time, what she had done. She saw what Alex saw. Pictures, cuttings, photos, posters: covering the wall from top to bottom. The material she'd collected, her own photographs – North Hill House, Harry's grave, the theatre – the picture of the old theatre, from the local history book, her newspaper research, the photo of Violet, copies of the letter Violet had written to Maud, the posters for *Romeo and Juliet* and the Paris production of *Salome*, the photo of Harry, pages from the play script that had accompanied the model theatre. Not a square inch of the wall remained empty. Some of the pictures and posters she'd copied several times. The photo of Harry and the one of his grave she'd enlarged and copied half a dozen times, pinning them in rows.

'Okay. A stalker wall,' Ellie said. 'It makes me look like a stalker. Like I'm mad.'

'So what's going on? What's it about? Your grandmother was telling me about this – she's worried about you too.'

Ellie sighed. 'I'm okay. She doesn't need to worry.'

'Ellie, you're not okay. Just look at yourself – how you've been behaving. Wandering off in the night, fainting, obsessing about – something. And you've got so thin. Even in the weeks I've known you, I've seen you change. Aren't you eating? Your face – it's like you're burning yourself away. I thought maybe it was about your mum, or your dad. Or that you were really ill – physically, I mean. Or mentally. But seeing your wall – something's going on, isn't it? Something else.'

Alex stopped talking. He wasn't looking at Ellie, but down at his lap, where his hands were clasped. A seagull flew past the window, casting a quick shadow in the room.

'We haven't known each other long, but I care about you, Ellie. The times we've spent together – I feel like I know you – that we made a connection. Please tell me what's happening to you. Whatever it is, I won't judge you. I'd like to help.'

Ellie took a tense breath and swallowed. She wanted to tell him, and she was afraid to.

'It sounds totally crazy,' she said. 'You won't believe me. I hardly believe it myself.'

She was about to say more when her grandmother burst into the room, carrying a tray with mugs and a plate of biscuits. She looked from Alex to Ellie, perhaps sensing she'd interrupted a significant conversation. She balanced the tray on the bedside cabinet.

'Give me a shout if you need anything else,' she said, glancing at Alex. 'I'll be downstairs.'

When she'd gone, Alex said, 'Go on. Whatever it is, tell me.'

'You remember the séance?'

'Ah yes. The séance. A bad idea.'

'There's a ghost – in the theatre.' She said it in a rush, needing momentum. 'A ghost boy. He's called Harry. He used to live at North Hill House, and he was killed in a horrible riding accident when his horse fell from a cliff, and he was trying to stop his sister running away with an actor, and his grave is in the churchyard.' She paused for breath and then went on. 'I've been researching him, and the theatre – but I've seen him, spoken to him. He's haunting me – through the model theatre at first, and then in the real theatre because I can move into his world, I mean, his memories. At the beginning he was haunting me, stepping into our living world, but afterwards he was taking me into his world. That's what happened this afternoon in the theatre.' She stopped again – then said, more slowly, 'The maddest thing of all is that I've fallen in love with him, Alex. I mean, deeply, crazily in love with him. I find it hard to think about anything else. How about that? I've fallen in love with a ghost!' Ellie gave an absurd, painful little laugh and tears started to spill from her eyes. She hiccupped, trying to rein in her feelings, but it was too late. Deep, agonising sobs racked her body. She felt as though her heart was tearing itself to pieces. Alex turned and put his arms around her and she held him tight, pressing her face against his strong, warm shoulder.

Ellie cried for a long time. Then she blew her nose and wiped her face. She felt very tired, but lighter inside, relieved to have shared her secret obsession.

'Now tell me properly,' Alex said. 'Tell me everything.'

At the end of the story, he asked half a dozen questions. Then he said, 'I'm going to run something past you now – and I don't want you to get upset or think I don't believe you. Please – just consider this, okay?' He touched her shoulder very lightly, a gesture of reassurance.

'Sure. Ask away. I think I know what you're going to suggest – that I've conjured all this from my imagination.'

Alex inclined his head. 'I'd just like you to entertain the idea. Obviously this Harry Weatherstone existed – you have plenty of evidence for that.' He gestured at the wall. 'But seeing him – meeting him . . . The times in the theatre – is it possible you entered some altered state of conscious-ness and created those episodes? Are you able to see, from my point of view, why that might seem likely? I mean, you've been under considerable emotional pressure.' He spoke very kindly, not wanting to upset her.

Ellie hesitated. 'It's possible. But I don't think it's true. What about the notes and letters he wrote me?' She reached for her journal, flicked through the pages to find something Harry had written and then showed it to Alex. He studied the note.

'There is a possible explanation for that.'

'You think I wrote it myself?' Her voice was a little sharp.

'Please, Ellie.' He raised his hand. 'I don't think anything. I'd just like us to consider the possibilities. You've heard about automatic writing. Or maybe writing in your sleep. Is it possible you could have written it yourself?'

Ellie sighed. 'It is possible, but truly, I don't think I did. And what about the theatre? You saw the state of the room this afternoon. The broken window, the plaster, all the mess. I certainly didn't do that!'

'No, you didn't,' Alex admitted. 'But that doesn't mean it was a poltergeist or a ghost. The theatre is very old, badly built and chronically unstable. It's built by the sea. The land subsides. That's one of the reasons the council wants to pull it down. The place needs a huge amount of work just to shore it up. Maybe your vision just happened to coincide with a movement in the building.'

Ellie didn't answer.

Alex glanced at her, sensing the change in her mood. 'Please, I'm not saying it's not true, that you didn't see a ghost. What do I know? It may well be true. All I'm asking is for you to consider all the possibilities. I want you to be happy, Ellie. I want you to be well, and ghost or no ghost, you're not happy or well at the moment.'

'I love him, Alex. I love Harry. I can't tell you how much I love him. I had no idea it was possible to love someone like this.' Her voice trembled, tears threatening again. A peculiar look crossed Alex's face, a moment of hurt he swiftly covered.

'I know you do, Ellie,' he said softly. 'We have to sort this out somehow, whoever or whatever the ghost might be. You can't go on like this.'

29

Ellie slept from eight that evening till nine the following morning. She had no dreams she remembered. When she woke, three messages waited on her mobile, from Mike, Daisy and Alex, asking how she was. Mike sent good wishes. Daisy and Alex sent lots of love. Daisy added a cargo of kisses and half a dozen smileys.

Her grandmother brought her breakfast in bed, and stayed with her while she ate, talking about inconsequential things – the garden, events in the town. Ellie lazed and read. She didn't get out of bed till eleven, when she had a shower and dressed. Then she strolled down to the beach, bought a rich chocolate ice cream and spent a long time sitting on a little wall, watching the multitude of families on a stretch of sandy beach: kids paddling, shouting, swimming, digging in the sand; parents reading and sunbathing or playing with their kids. Bright colours everywhere – towels and windbreaks, garish inflatables, plastic buckets and spades – candy pink, scarlet, acid yellow, royal blue.

Ellie didn't think about much. Instead she observed, watching people enjoying themselves. An old lady in a long coat, despite the heat, walked along the promenade with a little white dog on a lead. A couple of overweight bikers with lush, long hair, sunglasses and leather jackets were sitting on a bench eating ice lollies. A girl of about fourteen, sitting further along the wall, alternately shouted at and fervently kissed a cute, smiling boy of about the same age. All these lives going on.

What was she going to do? Ellie tested her feelings for Harry. The burning obsession had subsided for the moment – cauterised by the experience of his death. She considered Alex's suggestion that she had created the entire experience with the ghost. An invented boyfriend? Someone to adore and need her? Ellie shook her head. No, that wasn't true.

Her mobile bleeped. Another message from Alex.

I'm at your grandparents' house. They said you went out. Can we meet? I have an idea / information.

Ten minutes later Ellie was sitting on the terrace of a seafront café. She saw Alex walking towards her. He grinned and waved, hard to miss in a stripy white and yellow T-shirt. Ellie studied Alex as he drew near, noting how much more burly he was than Harry, broad-shouldered, his muscled, golden-brown arms revealed by the slightly girly T-shirt. He could get away with it though, these quirky clothes and his liking for bright colours. He was far too masculine for them to make him seem effeminate.

'Can I get you another drink?' He seemed more himself today, cheerful and resilient. Ellie was sipping orange juice. She agreed to have another.

'Guess what?' he said, in a theatrical whisper.

'What?'

Alex leaned over the table. 'Daisy's going out with Warren.'

'Really?'

'Really and truly.'

'That's brilliant. Is she happy? I hope she is.'

Alex pondered. 'I think so,' he said. 'But I won't tell you anymore. I'm sure she'll want to share all this herself. You know – girly chat. Don't let her know I've already told you, okay?'

'Okay,' Ellie said. They smiled at each other. Then Ellie said, 'So is that the information you had for me?'

Alex shook his head. 'No. Something else.' His expression became serious.

'About Harry. It's something to do with him, isn't it?'

Alex fished in his pocket. 'Last night I continued your research,' he said. 'I went to the website on the Le Petit Theatre and I checked up on what you'd found out about Violet and Francois LeFevre. I followed up all the links from the site. Lots of time wasting really, but I did discover that they're both buried in Pere Lachaise cemetery. And much more importantly, I found out they have a grand-daughter, still living in Paris.'

'A granddaughter? How d'you know that?'

Alex smiled, pleased with himself, and with Ellie's reaction.

'She's called Violette,' he said. 'A French version of the name Violet. It wasn't that difficult – it just took a long time. I typed *Violet and Francois Lefevre* into Google and then I checked out every single link. Eventually I found an online article in a French magazine about Le Petit Theatre, which mentioned Monsieur and Madame Lefevre, so I emailed the journalist, using some very ropey French. She emailed me right back and told me she'd gathered lots of her information about the Lefevres from this granddaughter, Violette Lefevre. I was pretty stoked to think I'd found a granddaughter, but the journalist said she couldn't give out any contact details, that would be unethical etc., but confirmed this woman did live in Paris, so I took another tack and looked up Violette on Facebook. And guess what? She does indeed have a Facebook page. Well, I found someone with that name, from Paris, so I sent a friend request with a message in more ropey French about where I lived and 'our' (I hope you don't mind) research into local girl Violet Weatherstone and the Marine Theatre.

'It was about two in the morning by then, so I went to bed, and this morning, about an hour ago, when I checked my email, Violette had accepted my friend request and sent me a long message. She sounded so excited! She said she'd always wanted to come here and see Lyme-on-Sea, the town where her grandmother was born – and – guess what – she's invited us to go and visit her so she can talk to us about her grandparents!'

Ellie's mouth dropped open.

'She wants us to visit? You mean, to go to Paris?'

Alex nodded, a huge grin across his face. 'Yep, Paris.'

'What, now?'

'As soon as possible. I think you need to. So you can . . .'

'Sort this out? Lay the ghost to rest?'

'Yes. Exactly that.'

Ellie hesitated. 'We can't go to Paris.'

'Why not?' Alex said. 'We could take the Eurostar. We'd be there in a matter of hours. It's not difficult.'

'You and me? You'd come with me?'

Ellie looked at Alex. He looked at her. 'Yes,' he said. 'I'd love to go with you. It'll be an adventure whatever happens. Let's go.'

30

Ellie and Alex were sitting side by side in the train to London, watching the panorama of late summer countryside through the window. Wide, sun-bleached meadows, sheep lying in the shade beneath leafy horse chestnut trees, fields of ripe wheat and golden stubble, some punctuated by the huge snails of round bales of straw.

How strange it was to travel inland, after weeks on the coast. Ellie found herself missing the almost constant sound of the sea and the cry of the seagulls. A real mix of travellers on the train: they were sharing the carriage with business people in smart suits, families on day trips to the capital with excited, noisy kids, and a few other young people like themselves, carrying backpacks and looking for adventure.

Ellie glanced at Alex and smiled. 'I can't believe we're actually doing this, can you?'

Alex grinned back. 'It is weird. Nervous?'

'Nervous and excited.' And a bundle of other emotions besides. These she didn't share with Alex. He'd proposed the trip because she needed to lay this ghost to rest. Ellie, of course, didn't really want to lay the ghost to rest. The thought of losing Harry was terrifying – something she didn't want to face. But Harry hadn't manifested in any form since the vision he'd shared in the theatre, the hour leading up to his death, five days before. Would this trip lay him to rest? Although Ellie allowed Alex to think this was her purpose, in truth, she was hoping it would bring him back to her. Violette might offer them another piece of the puzzle.

She had missed Harry so much these last few days. Memories haunted her, although the ghost did not. She thought about him constantly, a play performing in her mind even when she was outwardly preoccupied with other things. His absence hurt – a physical pain, an ache in her heart and body. Was this love, then? Long periods of anguish interspersed with brief moments of elation? So it seemed. How stupid to fall in love with a ghost. She had become part of an emotional equation which could never add up to the answer she wanted. On some level she knew this was true. On another level – a realm of wanting, loving, needing – she didn't believe it. She *had* to find a way to be with him. This was so vital, so real, a solution had to be possible.

Every night she lay awake, missing Harry. She played over the memories of their encounters over and over again. Her body ached to hold him, to feel the unique, perfect shape of him. Her hands yearned to touch his skin, the contours of his face. Her love for him was like a fire blazing in her mind, unquenchable, burning her away, taking away her capacity to think of anything else. He was her last thought when she fell asleep, her first thought on waking.

'Penny for them.'

'What?' She was jerked back to the present.

'A penny for your thoughts. That's what my grandma used to say when I was daydreaming.'

'Oh, I was thinking about Paris. I've only been there once – when I was fourteen. I told you – on our way back from a holiday in the south of France.'

Alex gave her a look. He didn't seem to believe she'd been thinking about Paris.

'It was the last big holiday we had together, me, Mum and Dad, before Mum got ill,' Ellie said. 'It was great.' Images of the holiday sprang into her mind. In truth, it hadn't been a total success. They'd had some wonderful moments, certainly. She remembered wandering along a promenade in the balmy evenings, watching the bronzed, beautiful French girls and boys in their stylish clothes, and swimming in the warm Mediterranean waters with her mum. At other times, she'd felt a bit restless and bored – lonely, even. She'd moved into stroppy teen mode that year, she recognised, no longer happy to make sandcastles and play games with her parents. She'd been a bit grumpy, wishing she had a friend of her own age to talk to and hang out with – especially on those evenings when her parents had seemed a little old and, well, embarrassing.

Ellie shook her head, wanting to banish this thought. Change was hard, and there was no avoiding it. Change was forced upon you, an inevitable part of life, any life. Was it always the same, even when you were old? So much losing. You lose your primary school to go to secondary school, then you lose that, and those friends you had, and then one day she would lose university. Her childhood was all but lost, and then she would lose her youth, and on and on, till the end when she would lose her life. Maybe it was weird for someone of her age to be thinking like this – but Ellie had seen her mother lose everything. She'd had to confront death and loss. She knew nothing was certain.

Ellie thought about her father. He'd lost his old life too. And he was forty-five, much further along the path of losing than she was. His image appeared in her mind: a tall, gaunt man with fine, white-blond hair retreating from his forehead, his warm, brown eyes, the elegant, capable hands that could play the piano or mend pretty much anything that needed mending. She pictured him walking along the promenade above the beach in France, hand in hand with her mother, talking and laughing with her, touching her shoulder or back from time to time with an affection and tenderness that demonstrated to everyone how lucky he felt he was, how much he cared for this woman who had chosen to share her life with him. Ellie had been walking ten paces behind them, a little sulky, making eyes at the glamorous French teenagers, and thinking how embarrassing her parents were. Odd to think of it now, to put herself back into the mind of her fourteen-year-old self and to see the situation with new eyes.

'Ellie?'

'Sorry. Miles away. I'm not great company, am I?' Then, to reassure him she wasn't obsessing about Harry, she said, 'I was thinking about my parents – you know, on the French holiday.'

Alex nodded. She still wasn't sure he believed her.

The arrangements for this trip had fallen so neatly into place – astonishingly so. At first her grandparents had resisted and worried – but Ellie reminded them she was eighteen now – an adult – and quite capable of making her own plans and taking a trip abroad. They were concerned about her health and mental state but Alex reassured them he'd take care of her. Neither he nor Ellie mentioned anything about Harry and their real motive for the adventure, telling them instead they wanted to take a break, see the sights and get away from it all.

Ellie and Alex had booked their tickets online, as well as two nights in the cheapest hotel they could find in central Paris. Nonetheless, the cost had added up, especially booking at such short notice. Ellie had some money her father had given her and she dipped into her savings to pay her share. They left details of the hotel and travel plans with Alex's parents and Ellie's grandparents, bought euros at the post office. Alex had exchanged several messages with Violette and made arrangements to meet her, and they'd bought a photo book about Lyme as a gift, as well as put together a folder of the information Ellie had gathered about Violet and Francois, and the Marine Theatre, for her.

At London they took the Underground to St Pancras Station. Ellie was jittery and a little stressed about the journey but Alex was efficient and relaxed when it came to guiding them from place to place and negotiating the Tube trains. At St Pancras they checked in, showed their passports, then settled at a coffee shop in the station's elegant glass and brick hall to sit out the hour until their Eurostar train arrived.

Alex grew restless very quickly. Ellie would have been happy to daydream, but he chatted a lot, then wandered off on his own to browse in the newsagent's shop. As he was standing at the front of the shop, browsing through the postcards, Ellie noticed a couple of other girls checking him out. He did look nice: tall and strongly made, with his blond hair sticking up in tufts, wearing his old jeans and a snug, flamboyantly lemon-yellow T-shirt. Alex came back with a paperback thriller and a postcard of London to send to his parents, wanting to share his adventure with them. He was very cheery and excited, like a little boy. Slowly the minutes ticked past – and then they were summoned onto the train.

Another two and a half hours of travelling: the end of England, then the dark passage through the tunnel, and suddenly they were roaring through France. The landscape altered – wide, cultivated fields without hedges, electricity pylons in an alien shape. Alex peered out of the window, thrilled by the new country, exclaiming at each passing settlement or perceived difference. Ellie felt sleepy and dozed for a short while. When she woke, they were drawing into the outskirts of Paris.

She felt momentarily afraid as they disembarked in Gare du Nord – fazed by the assault of the strange language, the crowd of people and the unfamiliarity. She was far from home. But Alex remained cheery and competent, looking out for signs and guiding them through the bustle of the Paris Metro, on and off underground trains, and finally into the late, hazy sunlight, into romantic, golden Paris, and to their hotel.

It wasn't a great place to stay: a small room with loud brown wallpaper and twin beds, an old television on a bracket screwed to the wall. But it was clean and the tiny ensuite offered a shower with plenty of hot water so they were happy enough. Ellie hadn't travelled to Paris to admire the inside of a hotel – they had the whole city lying around them, waiting to be discovered.

As soon as they'd settled in and unpacked, Alex was eager to be out again. He had a map of the city and a pocket guidebook. He and Ellie were meeting Violette in the morning so they had the whole evening to explore.

'Let's see the Eiffel Tower,' he said, poring over the map. 'I know it's the touristy thing to do, but, well, it's what you see in Paris, isn't it? Then we could walk along the River Seine to the Louvre. What d'you reckon?'

They had a glorious, enchanted evening. The dusty blue sky slowly darkened as they strolled along the Seine, admiring the architecture, taking photographs, marvelling at the elegant bridges. The air was hot and dry, gradually cooling as the sun disappeared. Ellie was wishing it was Harry beside her, and she kept up an imagined dialogue, the conversation she'd be having with him, but as time went by, Alex's company became so engaging she stopped thinking about Harry so much. Alex was so funny: he had a wry, quirky, self-deprecating sense of humour. He talked about his life and plans, the puppets he was making for the play, his struggle to learn his lines and act. He quizzed Ellie about her opinions and teased her, making her laugh. At ten o'clock, in a velvet darkness jewelled by hot yellow street lights, they stopped and dined on a restaurant terrace. Alex negotiated the menu, tried to speak French to the waitress, ended up making them all laugh. He was confident and good-humoured even when baffled and making a fool of himself.

They had an excellent meal of pork and peppers in a rich, savoury sauce, and afterwards dishes of chocolate ice cream, then bitter coffee in tiny white cups. At either end of the terrace, scarlet geraniums spilled from huge terracotta pots. The moon rose over the silhouette of Notre Dame on the other side of the river, and reflected in the dark water of the Seine. Ellie felt a moment of unexpected, glorious happiness.

Ellie had told Alex about her mother's engagement to Joe back in England. They talked about it again now. He hadn't seemed so perturbed about it. Surprised, yes, but not unsettled.

'You know you said life was all so random, like you even being born,' Alex said. 'You could look at it another way. I mean, if my dad and your mum hadn't split up, I wouldn't be here, and you wouldn't be here, in Paris, together, creating this moment. Maybe it isn't random. Maybe this was destined to happen.'

'Perhaps,' Ellie said, finishing her coffee. 'It might all be completely random or it might not. But somehow we can make up a pattern in it. We create the stories so it makes sense. Is that what destiny is? A kind of retrospective?'

They walked back to the hotel. Although it was a long way, Ellie enjoyed the chance to see more of Paris, but they were both exhausted by the end. Ellie brushed her teeth and washed her face, barely able to keep her eyes open, changed into her pyjamas in the bathroom then slipped into one of the twin beds. Alex went into the bathroom after her. He reappeared five minutes later wearing just his T-shirt and pants. For the first time they were both a little self-conscious about their intimate situation – sharing a hotel room. Alex turned off the light and Ellie sensed how close he was, his bed just an arm's length from hers. She could hear his breathing in the darkness. Alex moved restlessly.

'Don't like these blankets,' he said crossly. 'Wish they used duvets.'

'Yes,' she said. 'And it's hot.'

'Are you okay, Ellie? It was great to see you eating. You look like a sparrow. I like to see a girl enjoying her food – don't understand all this dieting and pecking at meals. Doesn't make sense.'

'I do like food,' she bridled. 'And yes, I am okay. Actually, I've had a brilliant day.'

Can you hear someone smile? Ellie couldn't see Alex in the dark, but she was sure he was smiling.

31

Violette Lefevre lived in a flat in the nineteenth arrondisement, a district in Paris's north east. Alex rang the buzzer outside the large, wooden main doors and they waited nervously.

'There's no one in. Are you sure you pressed the right button?' Ellie's voice was short.

'Yes, don't worry. She's at home – she said she'd be here,' Alex jumped back.

'Press the bell again. Perhaps she didn't hear.'

'Give her a moment, okay?'

They heard a voice in the speaker, though Ellie couldn't make out what it said. Then a loud buzzer sounded and the wooden door clicked open. Alex stepped inside. Ellie followed, into a dark hallway with a tiny elevator and a flight of stone steps – all very quiet.

'She's on the first floor, number three,' Alex said.

'I know. You don't have to keep telling me everything.' They were both edgy. Their boots clattered noisily on the stairs. No need to worry about door numbers – Violette was waiting for them on the landing. She smiled, and welcomed them in French, and afterwards, an awkward moment for her visitors, she kissed them on both cheeks, French style, before ushering them into her flat.

She had a tiny apartment. Violette guided them through a little hallway into a living room with a dark wooden floor and red-painted walls. Ellie glimpsed a miniature kitchen through another open doorway.

'Wow, what a lovely place!' Alex said. Despite its size, the room was a treat – with an old gold-framed mirror on one wall, several large oil paintings of nineteenth-century Paris scenes, a red velvet sofa, an ornate table with carved legs and a chandelier hanging from the ceiling. A large, elegant clock held aloft by tiny golden cherubs ticked on the mantelpiece and tall French doors opened onto a narrow balcony with black iron railings, above the road, crammed with pots of flowers.

Violette smiled and nodded, seeing how her young visitors admired the place.

'I'm sorry for my English. It is not good,' she said, gesturing for them to sit. 'I will try. And you will try to speak some French?'

Alex nodded. 'Sure, I mean, *oui*.'

Violette went to make refreshments, and returned five minutes later with coffee served in beautiful red and gold china cups, and a basket of croissants. She was a small, slender woman with lots of thick, very black hair (certainly dyed, Ellie thought) pinned up in a bun, pale, powdered skin and generous quantities of black mascara and eyeliner, making her look a little like an aged ballerina. She wore a midnight-blue velvet dress, elegant if rather old-fashioned, several jewelled gold rings and a large gold brooch in the shape of a scarab beetle, with a blue enamelled body.

Ellie took in every detail of her host, thinking this person was the closest she would ever come to a physical manifestation of Harry. Violette was his blood relative – his sister's granddaughter. That made her . . . what? His great-niece? They shared some of the same genes. Not many, but some. Ellie stared at Violette, drinking her in, trying to spot any resemblance to the man she loved.

'So,' Violette said. 'We start? Francois and his English Violet. What do you know?'

Alex looked at Ellie, and nodded for her to begin. Ellie felt a moment's panic. How much should she say? She and Alex hadn't discussed this in advance, whether she should talk about the haunting, the séance, her experience of Harry, the ghost. What would Violette think if she told her? Probably Ellie wouldn't be believed – Violette would think she was mad, or worse, feel insulted. Ellie glanced from Alex to Violette and back again. Alex gave her no clues – he was waiting for her to speak, leaving the decision in her hands. Ellie took a deep breath and turned back to Violette, whose expression was kindly, her eyes twinkling with anticipation.

I'll take the risk, Ellie thought. I like this woman. I'm afraid she'll judge me badly, or not believe me, but I'll take the chance.

It took a long time to tell the story. Violette's English was better than Ellie's and Alex's French, but it wasn't brilliant. Ellie had to repeat parts of the tale, or rephrase elements more simply. Violette interrupted frequently when she couldn't understand, and sometimes raised questions to be clear about what had happened, but she never once queried the truth of the story nor expressed, in her face, any doubt about Ellie's honesty or state of mind. In fact, she seemed to find the whole account engrossing.

When Ellie finally stopped talking, Alex handed Violette the book about Lyme-on-Sea and the folder containing copies of the documents and pictures. These Violette quickly scanned, exclaiming with interest and pleasure, making comments in French. Then she stood up and left the living room, returning two minutes later with papers of her own. She passed a photograph to Ellie, without a word.

Ellie looked at the picture. The room stilled, everything seemed to disappear, leaving her hanging in space.

Harry.

It was Harry: a perfect monochrome picture, his head and shoulders, against a white background. It must have been taken near the end of his life, because he was exactly as Ellie had known him. The photo was taken slightly in profile, with Harry looking away, into the distance. The portrait captured his beauty and pride, his passionate spirit, glimmers of his sensitivity. Or it did in Ellie's eyes, because she knew and loved him.

She took a quick breath, remembering where she was. She looked up at Violette and then Alex. Violette was staring at her intently. Now she gave a quick little nod, in confirmation.

'So this is the famous Harry?' Alex said. His voice sounded very loud and oddly clumsy. 'He's a handsome guy. I can see why you'd like someone like that.'

For the first time Ellie detected something forced in Alex's manner. He wasn't comfortable with the photograph.

'You see, it was all real. This is Harry. This is him.' She couldn't keep the note of triumph from her voice. She felt vindicated.

'You believe me?' Ellie said to Violette. 'You think my story is true?'

Violette's eyes shone. 'I've heard many strange stories in my life,' she said. 'And the history of Violet, Francois and Harry is a very strong one. I know about them already, these people. It does not surprise me to know that Harry doesn't rest easily in his grave. He hasn't properly passed on. And it doesn't surprise me that he woke up and fell in love with someone like you.'

Someone like you? Ellie looked down, embarrassed and pleased by the compliment. Then she stared at the photograph again, ravishing it with her eyes. She hadn't seen Harry in several long days, but now she had this new photograph and could gaze at it whenever she wanted.

'May I have a copy?' she said.

Now Violette began to tell them everything she knew. The French woman had been researching her family history and was particularly intrigued by the story of her paternal grandparents, the actors, and the grandmother who had fled from England to Paris for a life in the theatre with the man she loved.

She said both Violet and Francois had died when she was in her twenties. They'd been wonderfully affectionate grandparents who had continued to lead colourful

Bohemian lives, with lots of theatrical friends, many parties, and a lot of drinking.

'I regret I didn't learn more about them when they were still alive,' Violette said. 'My father – their son – was a very conventional, bourgeois kind of man – perhaps reacting against his parents. He certainly disapproved of them. But they seemed so wonderful to me. So much vitality. And even when they were very old (they always seemed very old to me, because I was young) they stayed in love. You can see it, when two people are in love, yes? They used to argue sometimes – shouting and throwing things – and then my grandmother would shout in English, and after she cried, and my grandfather cried, and I was afraid, but they would . . . how do you say?' She mimed tiptoeing, like a little mouse. Ellie supplied the word.

'Yes, they tiptoed together again, and embraced and kissed and cried some more, and all the rest of the day they held hands and whispered like little children.'

Violette smiled to herself, lost in the reminiscence. 'I wish I'd asked them to tell me more about their lives, but I was too young to think about it.'

'Did Violet talk to you about Harry?' Ellie said, waving the photograph.

Violette said her grandmother had treasured his photograph all her life.

'She never talked about him to me. I saw the photograph, and I knew he was her brother, that was all. Later, after she'd died, when I helped my father clear out their papers, he told me what he knew.

'Violet loved her brother very much, and she was very

sad to leave him in England. For many years, when my father was a child, he would find her crying for Harry. As soon as Violet arrived in Paris, she'd written Harry a long letter telling him she was sorry and explaining why she had left and how much she loved him. Then she received news that he'd died in an accident.

'My father said she always blamed herself for what happened. It made a . . . a shadow on her life. Of course, my father being my father, he didn't approve of the way she'd behaved, following her heart, not her duty. He thought duty was very important. I laughed at him, because naturally he would never have been born if she hadn't.' Violette gave a kind of 'pouff' sound, raising her eyes and waving her hands at the thought of her father's silliness. Ellie smiled.

'It was hardly her fault – Violet's, I mean,' Alex said. 'She should have been free to marry who she wanted, and to live how she wanted. It was her choice. He was trying to control her, wasn't he? And it was Harry's choice to chase after her, riding like an idiot along the cliff. I mean, sure it was a terrible accident, but it was his own doing.'

'What do you know about it?' Ellie demanded, ruffled by this criticism of Harry. 'Those were different times. He loved his sister! He wanted to protect her!'

Ellie saw something in Alex she'd never seen before – his anger, some kind of suppressed emotion. His body tensed and seemed to swell, making her nervous. But Alex mastered himself, taking a deep breath, letting the feeling ebb away.

Violette moved the conversation on. She was holding a

long, narrow envelope. Harry's name was written on the front, though the envelope was open.

'This is it,' she said. 'The letter Violet wrote to her brother before she knew he was dead. She couldn't bring herself to throw the letter away and I've kept it for years and years. Now I'd like you to take it. I want you to carry the letter to England and to read it to Harry.'

'Read it to Harry? How?' Ellie said. Alex had sat back in the chair, distancing himself from the conversation.

'His grave,' Violette said. 'Go to his grave and read it to him. I think it might help him. And help you, yes?' She fixed Ellie with an intense penetrating look. 'I can see why any girl would fall in love with Harry. Look at him!' She gestured to the photo, still held tight in Ellie's hand. 'Oh yes, he would steal any heart.' Her voice was fond and she sighed. Then she raised her head and said in a level voice, 'But he's not for you. You know that.'

Ellie's heart and face tightened. She didn't move or speak, letting Violette's assertion hang, refusing to agree. She moved the conversation on again.

They spent another half an hour in the apartment. She showed them several photographs of Violet and Francois. They made a strikingly handsome couple, both possessing a distinct and unusual beauty. Even in the pictures they fizzed with vitality and eccentricity. If Violet had stayed in England, done her duty as Violette's father had suggested, would she have become herself, this dynamic, lively woman?

'My father died last year,' Violette said. 'He was a hundred years old. Very small and weak at the end, but his voice was still loud. I wish he'd had the chance to meet you.'

'And you . . . you've never married?' Ellie felt nervous of asking such a personal question, but she was keen to know. Violette seemed so thrilled by the romance of her grand-parents. Had she enjoyed a grand passion of her own?

Violette shook her head. 'No,' she said. 'My mother left my father when I was in my twenties. He was very upset so I moved home to take care of him, for a while, and that was it. I never left. I met someone once, but I didn't want to leave Papa on his own.'

Did she feel regret about this? Hard to say. Ellie wanted to ask but didn't dare probe any further.

At the end of the visit, Violette explained how they could find Violet and Francois's grave in Pere Lachaise. They stood in the hall outside the apartment.

'I love your home,' Ellie said. 'How you've presented it, it's really beautiful.'

Violette smiled again, clearly pleased. 'You will not be surprised, most of it comes from my grandparents' house. I stored it after they died. My father lived in a very quiet, conventional place but when I had my own apartment,' she opened her arms in a welcoming embrace, 'at last, I could make it for me, just as I wanted.'

Ellie felt an odd mixture of affection and compassion for Violette. She'd spent most of her life living in the shadow of this bossy, conventional father and only now, in her sixties, was she able to create the home she desired. But she'd chosen that life, hadn't she? No one had forced her to live with Papa. Is that why Violette admired Violet, who, in contrast, had abandoned duty and bravely chosen her own path?

Violette looked sideways at Ellie, as though divining her thoughts. She touched Ellie's arm. 'I'm very happy,' she said. 'You think I am very old. Well, I am sixty-six and I suppose you are right. But I do not feel old. I can live exactly as I want now, and if I last as long as my father I have another thirty-four years to enjoy. Of course, it may be less.' Violette smiled.

'You know,' she said. 'I imagine my death is an open door I can see ahead of me. It is there, waiting, and I don't know what is on the other side, but every day is one more step on the path to this door, to my death.

'Perhaps you think this is sad or depressing, but not at all. Not – at – all!' She gestured again, and shook her head. 'It means I try to enjoy every – single – precious – magic day I have. Every little thing in every day! I know, sometimes it isn't easy when bad things happen, or boring times. But that's all we have – that path of days that will end. So make the most of them.'

She narrowed her eyes and gave a distinctly girlish grin. 'And maybe I'll have my love story yet. Who knows? Internet dating, perhaps?'

Ellie laughed, a surprised, happy laugh at the unlikely but pleasing idea of Violette engaging in a romance in her autumnal years. Violette laughed too.

'I hope it happens,' Ellie said. 'I really do.'

They promised to keep in touch and invited Violette to visit Lyme. She said she would email copies of other pictures and documents for the exhibition at the museum, but allowed Ellie to take the photograph of Harry. She had other copies. Finally Violette handed Ellie the letter Violet had written to Harry. She had sealed the open envelope.

'I don't want you to read it till you are standing at his grave,' she said. 'It will be stronger like this, for you and for him. When you have finished reading, give him the letter. Bury it. And we will see what happens.'

Violette kissed her visitors goodbye and this time gave them each a hug too.

'Take care of one another,' she said, twinkling again. 'You have a wonderful friend, Ellie.' As she spoke she was looking at Alex, another perceptive glance.

'Enjoy the rest of your stay in Paris,' she called as they made their way down the stairs. 'And visit me again one day. Come and stay!'

'*Au revoir!*' Ellie called up the stairs. '*Merci beaucoup! Au revoir!*'

32

The cemetery of Pere Lachaise lay before them. Cloud covered the sky. The air was warm and still, vaguely oppressive.

'What a place,' Ellie said. 'My God, it's beautiful.' She held a pretty posy of flowers, purchased from a florist's they'd passed on the way.

They wandered through the necropolis, Ellie a little ahead, marvelling at the huge, elaborate cemetery. A multitude of curious upright tombs lined the paths, like ornate stone sentry boxes with pillars and tiny stained-glass windows. Trees grew here and there, weeping rust-and lemon-coloured leaves though it was only August. The place was dried and bleached by the summer sun. Dust, stillness, dry weeds bursting through cracks in paving stones and untended graves.

Few people – just a handful of tourists, with cameras and one solitary reader dressed in gothic black, a beautiful Asian boy of about eighteen, sitting in the shade of a mausoleum with a novel. Statues and angels carved in white marble, some broken, wrapped about with ivy or mantles of moss. A crow, silken black and appropriate, hopped from one cross top to another, ruffled its feathers and watched them pass.

'Here it is.' Ellie stopped and pointed. 'Their names – look. Violet and Francois LeFevre. He died a year before she did.'

The memorial was relatively simple – a black stone plinth, a tapered column, like Cleopatra's needle, standing on top. No weeds or evidence of damage: Violette had probably been taking care of it.

'This is it,' Ellie said. 'Where they are buried. She's in the ground, here, Harry's sister. Those people we saw in Violette's pictures. Isn't that strange?' She paused, then said, 'It freaks me out a bit.'

Alex made a small sound, but said nothing. Ellie placed her posy at the base of the plinth then gazed at the memorial. What did she feel? Unnerved and impressed by the cemetery, unsettled by the reality of the grave and the knowledge of whose bones lay decomposing in the ground beneath her feet.

She took out her phone and took a couple of pictures.

'Let's go,' she said. 'Oscar Wilde's grave next, yes?'

Oscar Wilde, author of *Salome*, the play in which Violet had famously performed all those years ago. It was easy to find as half a dozen tourists were lingering close by. Ellie saw a big stone block, in which Oscar's name was carved, and on top of it, a large, and to her eyes, rather graceless angel. More impressive were the lipstick kisses decorating the stone, hundreds of them, like rosebuds in various shades of red and pink, and the notes and gifts left for Oscar on the ledge at the bottom of the plinth.

'Don't you think he'd be delighted?' she murmured to Alex. 'Oscar, I mean – if he could see this. To think he was so loved – to know that all these people want to leave him lipstick kisses, and poems and notes and things.'

Ellie took pictures of this memorial too. When she'd finished, Alex was sitting on the edge of a low grave on the other side of the path. Ellie sat beside him.

'What's the matter?' she said. 'You've hardly said a word. I mean, you went all quiet when we were at Violette's. Are you upset? Was it something she said? Or have I done something? If I have, I'm sorry. It's just – well – I've never seen you like this. I don't like it.' She was, after all, used to him taking care of her, thinking about her feelings. Now he was the gloomy one.

Alex rubbed his face with both hands. He didn't look at Ellie, but at the ground.

'I'm sorry, it's not your fault,' he said. 'No, you haven't done anything. And I'm spoiling your Paris afternoon, and I apologise for that. I'm just not in a good mood, that's all. It's my problem. Not yours.'

'If you're not happy, that *is* my problem. You've listened to me and helped me when I've been upset. Won't you let me help you? What's up? I've never seen you in a bad mood before. You're always so positive and resilient.'

Alex raised his head. 'It's okay. There's nothing you can do. And I don't want to talk about it. But thanks for the offer. I'll shake it off, this mood, just give me a little time.'

They took the Metro back to the hotel. It was the end of the afternoon. Tired out, Ellie announced she would take a

298

nap before they went out in the evening. Alex said he wanted to take another walk, and set off on his own.

Lying on the bed Ellie took out the picture of Harry and gazed at him. He was so unspeakably gorgeous she wanted to stare at him forever. But a few minutes later she fell asleep, the photo resting on the pillow beside her.

The sound of Alex taking a shower woke her at seven. He emerged a few minutes later, hair damp and tousled, face fresh, fragrant with fruity shampoo. She watched him, anxious to gauge his mood, but Alex gave a big grin.

'Wake up, dress up,' he said. 'It's our last night in *la belle Paris*. We're going to have a ball. Can't waste any more time. We're back on the train tomorrow.'

'You feeling okay?'

'I'm fine,' he said. 'Sorry about earlier. All's well.'

Ellie felt a huge sense of relief. She jumped off the bed and into the shower. She put on a dress – a light, flowery, flimsy thing with spaghetti straps – and a pair of sandals with heels, and even painted her lips with a little gloss. She observed herself in the mirror. A day in Paris, even with the hidden sun, had brought some colour to her skin. Her chocolate brown hair glistened. She looked, she decided, rather nice. She thought of Harry, and wished he could see and admire her.

'You look lovely,' Alex said gruffly, as she emerged from the ensuite. 'Gorgeous. Really.'

'So do you,' she said. And indeed he did. She'd never seen him in a shirt before. How had he contrived to carry it in a rucksack, with only a minimum of creases? A cream, linen shirt – appropriate for the balmy evening – and trousers, not jeans. He looked older, dressed like this: a man, not a boy.

Alex, with the help of his guidebook, took them to Le Marais, a lively maze of narrow streets with art and designer boutiques. Ellie enjoyed the spectacle they presented, a good-looking young couple, all dressed up. Even in stylish Paris they attracted a few glances, from men and women. They found a tiny restaurant with a courtyard, and dined from a table lit with candles, another excellent meal. Alex ate chicken, Ellie chose fish. They shared a bottle of chilled white wine, and tore into pieces of fresh, white French bread.

Alex didn't seem unhappy any longer. He talked and listened, teased and joked, made her laugh, just as he had before. Except – except what? Something had changed, she sensed it. A very subtle difference. He was holding back. She perceived a guardedness – so although they had another lovely evening she felt a bit sad. Their relationship had altered. What had changed it? Or changed him? She wanted the old Alex back. The old connection.

After the meal, a tiny bit tipsy, they strolled through the Paris streets, taking in the atmosphere, staring into the lighted windows of the shops. They had one more drink in a tiny bar full of very loud music where a young French guy in a Gucci suit tried to chat Alex up. Then they walked back to the hotel and Ellie took Alex's arm. She didn't like this distance between them, however imperceptible the change might be. So she clung to his arm as they walked, willing everything to be as it had been.

When they got back to the hotel, tired by heat and

walking and overindulgence, Ellie fell asleep straight away. Alex woke her at eight in the morning. Dry-mouthed, still sleepy, she packed her stuff and they vacated their hotel room, ready for the long journey home.

33

A pale moon hung in the early twilight, in a sky of lilac and violet, a ribbon of dusty cinnamon on the horizon, above the sea. Ellie stood alone in the graveyard, behind the solid body of the church, staring out across the water. She had the letter in her hand, still unopened. She wanted to read it to Harry, and she was afraid to. What if she lost him? Perhaps he'd already abandoned her: she'd heard nothing from him – no word, no perfume, not a glimpse of the man she loved.

They'd arrived home the previous afternoon, exhausted by the travelling and the excitement of the weekend. Ellie's grandparents were waiting at the station, with anxious, hopeful faces. They'd dropped Alex off, at his parents' house. He gave Ellie a polite, perfunctory farewell hug, a grin to her grandparents, then he was off, hefting his ruck-sack along the garden path to the little house in its wild garden.

Once at home, Ellie's grandparents asked her a hundred questions about the trip. Had she enjoyed it? Did she feel better? How did she and Alex get on? What did they do, and see? Ellie supplied the right answers but she was eager to be alone.

When she stepped into her room, the stalker wall confronted her. After this short absence, she realised properly why it had shocked Alex. The sheer storm of paper, covering the wall from top to bottom, certainly screamed obsession. Well, I *am* obsessed, Ellie thought wearily. At the same time, she realised she was growing tired of it, her mind, body and heart bruised and aching. Today she wanted some peace and calm.

Everything had changed, everything was the same. The town, its tide of holidaymakers, the beaches of pebbles and sand, the immemorial buildings – as they'd always been. But Ellie felt different. Hard to say exactly how, but the town seemed smaller. How could it not, after a weekend in grand Paris? Violet's letter waited on her bedside cabinet. She couldn't bring herself to read it to Harry that first evening. She put off the task, had a bath instead, wrote all about the trip in her journal, then curled up on the sofa in the living room, watching television with her grandparents.

The day after her return, Ellie attended a play rehearsal. She and Alex had only missed one while they were away but something had clicked into place during their absence. Before, the production had seemed like a haphazard, ragged patchwork of incompetent acting, unlearned lines and unconnected scenes – with huge gaps in the narrative, because so many chunks had yet to be practised. Now this was no longer the case. The play had coalesced into a whole. Lines were learned. The young actors were growing into their roles. Ellie could see, finally, how the play would look. It might – possibly – hold together after all. Mike was thrilled, but he worked them harder than ever. They still had so many rough edges to polish, holes to fill, scenes to practise.

For a few days, the theatre had been closed off to everyone and they'd had to rehearse in a scout hut. Surveyors came in to check the integrity of the building after the incident in the room beneath the stage. Nick the reporter wrote about it in the newspaper with a dramatic headline: THEATRE SUBSIDENCE SHOCK! What if the play had to be cancelled altogether? But the surveyors said the building was safe – for the time being – as long as the lower room was shored up and off limits. But what about the long term?

The situation had moved on for Warren and Daisy too. They'd obviously had a good weekend together and were clearly a couple now, all loved up, Warren gazing at Daisy adoringly whenever he had the opportunity. And Daisy had a happy glow – enjoying the attention.

What had Daisy thought of Ellie's and Alex's going away to Paris? Was she jealous? Ellie hadn't spoken to Daisy since that day in the theatre when the building shifted and Ellie passed out, having witnessed Harry's fall from the cliff top. They'd exchanged a couple of texts, Daisy anxious to find out if Ellie was okay, but afterwards she had maintained her distance. What had come between them? Perhaps Daisy was just wrapped up in her new romance. Surely she wouldn't mind now she had Warren. Of course nothing was that clear-cut.

If Daisy was harbouring any bad feeling because Alex had taken a trip to Paris with Ellie, his behaviour at the rehearsal would have given her evidence enough that romance was not remotely on the cards, Ellie thought. Alex was perfectly friendly but he paid Ellie no more attention than anyone else. In fact, when he wasn't on stage, he spent most of his time talking to Carly – about the fairy puppets, Ellie gathered, and her performance, Titania, and fairies in general. She remembered Daisy telling her that Alex had someone he liked . . . could that person be Carly? This possibility made her uncomfortable. Why, when she had Harry?

So after a couple of weeks enjoying delightful, intense new friendships, Ellie felt a little on the outside again. The rehearsal was okay – but she felt – what? She'd lost something. But she had Harry, she reminded herself. He was the most important.

When she wasn't needed, Ellie wandered alone around the theatre, aching for Harry, willing him to appear to her or give her some small sign of his presence, his love, his interest. She tried to go down to the little room beneath the stage, but the staircase had been blocked off with chipboard and tape, and a danger sign. Had Harry gone now? Had she lost all of them? The thought created a dreadful emptiness inside her – a sense of utter desolation.

'Alex? I thought I'd read the letter tomorrow night.' She accosted him on the way out of the theatre. She heard the slight pleading note in her own voice.

'You are? Best of luck with it, Ellie. Tell me what happens.' He was friendly enough but Ellie realised she wanted him to offer to accompany her to the graveyard. This he did not do.

*　*　*

And so – twilight, in the graveyard. Alone. A view over the endless sea. The letter in her hand.

The wind tugged her hair. Far away, on the sea, she saw a boat with a dark sail, coming towards the harbour. The night crept a barely perceptible step closer.

Dressed in black – jeans, T-shirt, light jacket – she went to the grave with its angel.

Ellie sighed. She stood in front of the angel and opened the envelope containing the letter Violet had written to her brother, not realising he was already dead. As Ellie drew out the single sheet of paper, a seagull swooped over her head and then away, over the cliff edge and the sea.

Ellie took a deep breath and unfolded the paper. For a moment the looped, archaic, black-ink handwriting swam in an illegible mass. Her eyes blurred with tears so she wiped them with the back of her hand then looked at the letter again.

"My dear brother,' Ellie read aloud. *"I am travelling to Paris with Francois Lefevre, where we shall be married. I understand you will be grieved and angry, that you think I am making a mistake, but I appeal to you to forgive me for any hurt I cause you or our parents. It is not, nor ever has been, my intention to injure or dishonour my family – I love you all far too much.'*

Ellie looked up from the letter. She pushed a strand of hair from her face. The wind had risen. High up, on the spire, the weathervane creaked as it swung to north-east. Another degree of darkness.

'I love you, Harry – but I love Francois too. I love him truly and passionately. I never realised it was possible to feel this way, to want something so much, and I believe he feels as I do. We intend to spend the rest of our lives together, and for that reason

we are leaving England for France, which will serve two purposes. First, I hope our distance will save my parents from the embarrassment of my elopement, and second, Francois has a greater chance of professional success in the theatres of Paris. I hope to pursue my own acting ambitions too – something our parents would never support. As a married woman, independent of my parents, I will be free to work as I please. Again, living and working in Paris, in a foreign country, I may spare my family some of the embarrassment they fear."

Ellie broke off again. Her words echoed strangely in the graveyard, perhaps bouncing from the walls of the church. The angel loomed palely. With every passing minute, as night drew on, it grew harder to read the letter. Only one paragraph more. Ellie's pulse galloped. Her hands and lips were cold.

'Most of all, dear Harry . . .' The wind snatched her words away. She raised her voice above it. *'Most of all, dear Harry, I want you to know how much I love you and how sincerely I want you to be happy. I know too well how angry you will be, how fiercely you wish to protect me, but do not blame Francois for my free choice. I hope and wait for the day when you will forgive me for leaving you, when we shall be friends again, you will visit me in Paris, and all will be as it was between us. Please let that day be soon. Violet.'*

Ellie finished speaking. She lowered the letter. Her throat was dry, her mouth numb. She folded the letter, squatted, and scraped at the soil near the foot of the marble plinth. The ground didn't yield easily, baked hard by the summer sun. Ellie broke her nails digging so she found a piece of flint to hack into the earth, finally making an impression into which she could lay the letter. She covered it in soil and little stones.

'Well, Harry, what now?' She stood in front of the mourning angel, in the dark. In front of the church, the street lights popped on. The wind died for a moment. Ellie heard the sea, waves spilling on the pebbles.

'Those were Violet's last words to you. She asks for your forgiveness. She wants you to understand why she ran away.' Ellie glanced behind her. For the first time, she worried someone might hear her, talking to no one in the graveyard – some passer-by in the street.

'Do you forgive her?' She spoke more quietly. 'She loved you. All her life, she mourned the loss of you. She blamed herself.'

Ellie waited. The angel glimmered. Ellie thought, randomly, of the boat with dark sails. By now it would be safe in its harbour. Hot tears fell over her cheeks and ran under her chin.

'Harry?' Ellie said, in anguish. 'Can you hear me? Please – give me a sign. I love you. I love you so much. I can't bear to be without you.'

Light played oddly on the angel. It stirred. Ellie tried to make sense of what she was seeing. No, the angel hadn't moved. Something was standing between Ellie and the angel, a partially transparent form, hard to make out in the darkness.

'Is that you?' she whispered. The form seemed to rise from the ground, like a vine, twisting, filling out, blossoming, as though it had grown from the bones in the grave, buried a hundred years before.

'Harry?' There he was, standing before her. She rushed towards him, put out her arms – but they passed through Harry and pressed against the angel instead.

'I can't touch you!' she said. 'Harry, I can't touch you! Take me with you again, into your world, like you did before. Take me away from here.'

He hadn't spoken yet. She could see his face clearly, as though it were sculpted from light. He was so utterly, unspeakably beautiful that Ellie's heart hurt.

'Speak to me, Harry. I want to hear your voice.' She tried to touch him again, but he had no substance. Her hands grasped at the air. He was looking at her, with an intent burning gaze, a mirror for her own longing.

'Ellie, I'm here,' Harry said. His voice was gentle. 'Please, be calm. All is well.'

'I saw you die,' Ellie said. 'I was with you! I saw it. Then you disappeared and I thought you'd gone, and I couldn't bear it if that happened. I don't want to be without you Harry, not ever.'

She saw a change. Something in his face had softened. 'I'm sorry I inflicted that on you. I'd forgotten it, the reason for my waiting and the time of my death. I was trapped – and you connected me with the past, and my future,' he said. 'Thank you for bringing me Violet's letter,' he said. 'And yes, I do forgive her. I understand now. I understand everything.'

'What do you understand?'

'I fell in love with you, Ellie. I love you – how did Violet describe it? Truly and passionately. I'd never loved anyone like that, until now. Did they marry? Did they always love each other?'

'I met their granddaughter and she said they did,' Ellie nodded and sniffed. But it was hard to think about Violet and Francois. Her every atom yearned to be close to Harry, to hold him, to hear him telling her how special she was to him, how much he loved her.

They remained as they were for a time, gazing at each other. Harry's face beamed love and calm. Ellie still wept. He seemed peaceful but she was distraught.

'You're going to leave me,' she said bitterly. 'You've got what you needed, and now you'll move on. Isn't that right?'

'Yes,' Harry said. 'I don't belong here. I can't stay here. We can't be together. I'm dead. You're alive.'

'As simple as that.'

'Yes. As simple as that.'

'You've used me,' Ellie said. She could hear the whine in her voice. 'You've had your experience of love, so you can let go and pass on to wherever it is you'll go. What about me? How can I live without you? You say you love me, but you don't even seem to care that we can't be together.'

'Oh, Ellie, that's not true. Please don't be angry. I can't bear to see you so unhappy. You've given me something rare and precious. You've helped me escape from a hundred years of imprisonment in a moment of dark and rage and torment. No one has ever done so much for me. That will stay with me forever. You're a part of me, and I'm a part of you, your life, for as long as you remember me. I love you, Ellie. I love you. Please accept the gift of it.' He sounded so different now. The hurt, arrogant boy had gone.

Ellie sank to her knees and covered her face with her hands, mirroring the attitude of the angel on the plinth.

'I have to go now,' Harry said.

'I can't touch you,' she sobbed. 'I can't hold you.'

Harry drifted towards her. His incorporeal form passed slowly through her body. This time she felt it, as though the motes of him penetrated her skin and flesh and bones, and set her nerves dancing. She closed her eyes, seeing patterns of brilliant stars. Within her, a multitude of tiny lights seemed to swell and expand, filling her body, making her radiant, till all she could feel was obliterating joy and peace and fulfilment.

The moment stretched – and then finished.

Harry was gone.

Ellie remained as she was for a time, breathing slowly, head bowed, savouring the last lingering moments of Harry's passing.

Ellie looked up. The angel reared over her. The scroll at its feet caught a faint dusting of orange street light. She read his name, the dates of his birth and death.

Always loved.

34

Ellie walked down to the beach, where she sat in the dark on a bank of pebbles, staring out to sea. Far away, in warm, lighted pubs, people were drinking and talking. In the huddle of homes, families dined, watched telly, leading their lives.

Little waves uncurled on the stones, over and over again. The feeling of bliss slowly dissipated, leaving in its place a terrible vacancy. Ellie confronted the fact that she would never see Harry again. He'd gone. Everything was over.

Some part of her had always known this would happen, but another larger, hungry part had refused to heed the quiet warning. She'd fallen for him. Totally and utterly – fallen and fallen – and now she'd crashed on the ground. Somehow she would have to live without him, or more accurately, without the thoughts and dreams and imaginings and hopes that had obsessed and sustained her over these last weeks. She had to let it all go.

What was left then? Pain and forebodings of pain.

The church clock chimed ten times. Waves unfurled, rattling the pebbles. Ellie rose to her feet and headed out of town.

She ran along the cliff path, uphill, stumbling in the dark. If she ran fast enough and hard enough, perhaps she could avoid these thoughts, this sense of utter despair, the visceral pain of Harry's loss. She pushed herself, bounding up the slope, forcing her legs to work. Soon she was sweating. Her muscles ached, her breath was laboured, but the incline levelled out and Ellie continued to run.

She got a second wind, her body adjusting to the exercise. She took long strides, covering the ground. The moon was bright so she could see reasonably well, if she concentrated on the path. This focus filled her mind, distracting her. If only she could keep moving, she would perhaps escape the intolerable pain and – worse – the overwhelming sense of despair.

So much emotion crashing down, all the wanting and yearning for Harry, who had gone away forever. Ellie's feelings were tearing her to pieces. She had to keep running.

On and on. Downhill and up again the other side. She leaped a tiny stream, stumbled again on a stone, starting to tire. Muscles, lungs and heart protested. She was reaching her limits. She tripped, falling heavily to the ground and scraping the skin on her hands. But she stood up again and ran on.

Ellie stumbled more and more often. Her pace slowed. She couldn't see very well. Shadows everywhere. The path seemed to jump up and catch her feet. Down below, as though part of another world, the silvered sea pushed at the base of the cliffs.

Ellie stopped. She'd run right up to the edge of the

precipice. The momentum of her run and the sudden halt left her teetering above the abyss. Several tiny pieces of stone fell from the cliff top, bouncing on the rocks, disappearing into the darkness and the sea. Ellie didn't move. Sweat plastered her hair to her neck and forehead. Her body was shaking, her muscles burned. She gulped for breath.

This was it – the place she'd seen through Harry's eyes, the night he galloped after Violet. Surely it was. Without conscious thought, she'd found the place where he'd died.

The night was huge all around her – the high cliffs, the ceaseless sea, the wide fields, the sky, and stars, spreading away into measureless space. She was a tiny point shivering in an infinite space. The rocks beneath her feet were millions of years old. The sea had heaved and flowed for long eons. The stars twinkling so kindly in the sky were older still. Ellie felt it more keenly than ever before, how small and brief and fragile she was.

Harry was gone. Her mother was dead, her father had left and even her fledgling friendships seemed to have fallen away. She had no burning ambition for the future, no path laid down for her to follow. Did all people feel like this? It was the same for everyone, each solitary individual, cast onto the earth, not knowing where they'd come from or where they were going, trying to work out what to do and how to live and the reason for it all.

Ellie could see no reason, only drift and emptiness. For a short time Harry had been her reason, her all, the need for him embedded in heart and mind and body, but he'd gone. She felt like an empty shell, sucked off life and substance. And it hurt. *It hurt.*

'I can't bear it,' Ellie said aloud. The wind rose again, climbing over the cliff. She started to sob as she spoke, addressing the elements like a madwoman. 'I can't bear this pain. I can't, I can't.' Another billow of wind, blowing the words back into her face.

'Harry! Harry, why did you do this? I want you! It's not fair, it's not fair!' A frenzy of words and tears and snot: the indifferent universe did not respond. She balled her fists and pressed them against the side of her head. Her life was in pieces.

She inched closer to the edge of the cliff. Another shower of stones and soil tumbled to the sea. The wind whirled around her. Its cold was keen as a whip on her sweaty face. Way down, the sea crashed against the cliff, its surface wrinkling and dressed in foam.

'Ellie?' A voice – level, warm, masculine. 'Ellie, come back to the path. It's dangerous. Step back, okay?'

Ellie didn't look round, but she knew who it was. The intrusion of this friendly, familiar voice broke into her cataclysm of grief and hurt. So the universe wasn't indifferent. Alex, who was a part of it, was talking to her. Ellie waited.

'It's me, Alex. Step back, please. You're worrying me. I'd love to talk with you. And Daisy's coming too, only she's slower than me. My God, you can run fast!'

Even in her unbalanced state, she detected how hard he was trying to stay calm. His voice soothed, holding her attention.

'Please, step back,' he repeated. 'And then – well, we can talk all night if you like. Or walk, or whatever you want.

Only I'd rather not run any more, you wore me out. I need to do more exercise, I'm not as fit as I think.'

Ellie's breathing slowed. She still hadn't turned round but something had altered inside her mind. When Harry had gone, a door had opened inside her, leaking Ellie's soul from her body. Now, thanks to Alex's presence and words, this door had closed, keeping her together.

Ellie suddenly realised how close she was to falling, on the precarious, crumbling cliff edge. She gasped in panic, tottered and then fell backwards onto her bottom. Alex leaped forward and grabbed her.

'Oh my God, oh my God,' Alex said, pressing his face into her shoulder, all calmness gone. 'Oh my God, Ellie, I thought you were going to fall or jump or something.' He continued to babble, shocked and relieved, including one or two surprisingly colourful words.

'I'm so sorry, I'm so sorry,' he said. 'I was so hurt and upset, I was determined to get over you, to rein back a little. So I let you go to the graveyard on your own. My God! What happened? Is that why you're here? I let you down, I should have stayed with you. And then I was worried, and Daisy was worried too, and your grandparents said you weren't at home, and it was late and dark, so I went down to the graveyard and when you weren't there I went to the beach and I saw you running off along the cliff path. I was so scared! What if something had happened, what if you'd hurt yourself!' He held her tight, almost hurting her himself. The flow of words stopped. He loosened his grip, drew back, and looked into her face.

'Please, come over here – the other side of the path – the

316

safe side. Sit on the rock, beside me. It's sheltered, out of the wind.'

Ellie looked into Alex's face, indistinct in the moonlight, but she could see it well enough. He was sweating, as she was. A picture loomed in her mind, of Alex seeing her from afar and chasing after her.

'Are you okay?' he said, voice quiet.

Ellie nodded.

'What happened? D'you want to talk about it?'

Ellie hesitated. 'Harry's gone. Gone forever. He doesn't need to be here anymore. He forgave Violet. He finally understood why she needed to be with Francois.'

'Because he'd fallen in love with you?'

Ellie nodded, leaking new tears.

'So you helped him – gave him a gift.'

Ellie nodded again. 'That's kind of what he said.'

'But you lost him. And it hurts.'

'I feel like I've lost everything. It's all . . .' She struggled to explain her feelings: 'It's all tumbled on top of me – Mum, my dad and Louise, being on my own, and then losing Harry. I can't tell you how strong my feelings were for him. I know it sounds mad, being in love with a phantom, but I wanted him so much.' More tears and sobs. Surely she would soon run dry. Ellie pressed her face against Alex, putting her arms around his strong, warm neck, breathing the comforting smell of him.

'Oh, Ellie.' He comforted her, letting her lean on him. 'I thought you were going to jump. I was afraid you would die. Is that what you were thinking?'

Her sobs quietened. 'Not consciously. I just wanted to

get out of that place – you know, the emotional place. The hurt. I'd have done anything.'

'Well, if you're ever in that place again, don't stand by any cliffs. Call me instead. Any time – day or night. Ring me. Okay?'

'Okay. Thanks.'

'Promise?'

'Promise.' Ellie shivered. Alex untied a jacket from his waist and offered it. Ellie slipped inside, the sleeves hanging over her hands. 'Did you say Daisy was coming? Did you tell her? Does she know – about Harry?'

Alex nodded. 'I told her. I hope you don't mind. I had to, so she'd know how important it was to find you. But she might be a while.' He allowed himself to smile. 'She's not a great runner and you came a long way. I went on ahead to try and catch you.'

'Shall we start walking back? We'll meet her.'

'Sure, if you're up to it. We can sit a bit longer if you like.'

'No. Let's go.' Ellie stood up. 'And thank you. For coming after me. For caring. I really appreciate it.'

'No problem. Only please . . .'

'What?'

'Don't do it again.'

They began to walk, Ellie hugging Alex's jacket around her. She still felt the keen hurt of Harry's loss, but just for now it was tolerable. She tried to focus on the moment, and not the pain, looking out at the night and the friend walking by her side. Her mind cleared enough to remember something Alex had said when she'd fallen back from the cliff edge. He'd said he was hurt and upset, trying to get over her, reining back . . . And something entirely obvious occurred to her, a state of affairs that had been staring her in the face and which she'd failed to notice, because her attention was so focused elsewhere. This realisation opened like a tiny, sunny flower in the wasteland of her heart.

She didn't say anything or pay this flower too much attention. She simply noted it and then left it alone.

'There she is. Look – sitting on the step of the stile. It's Daisy!' Alex waved his arm. 'Daisy! Here we are! We're coming! Everything's okay!'

Daisy stood up. She was carrying a torch and wearing unsuitable pink court shoes. Nonetheless she hurried over to Alex and Ellie and embraced them both, and for a moment the three stood close together without saying a word, holding tight, while the wind gusted around them.

35

Applause. Whoops and cheers from the younger members of the audience, the stamping of feet. The curtains closed. They had had a full house for the last performance. Word of the show's brilliance had spread through the town.

Members of the cast looked at one another, stupid grins on their faces. They hugged and kissed, danced and jumped up and down, high on adrenalin and success. They were thrilled, all of them. All the hard work and frustration and hours of rehearsals had culminated in this triumph, a five-performance run, a glowing review in the local paper (thanks, Nick), and jubilation from Mike, who had worked harder than all of them.

Ellie threw her arms around Daisy, then Alex, who looked splendid – if a little comical – in his robe of patch-work velvet, in brown, green and gold. He was wearing stage make-up, dark around his eyes, a sprig of leaves painted across his forehead. This made him mysterious and exotic. Daisy was delicate and maidenly in a long gown of turquoise with a layer of diaphanous silver on top, a coronet of white flowers in her hair.

Daisy had designed and created many of the costumes.

Ellie had helped. Her sewing skills were minimal but had improved. The girls had spent a lot of time working together in the week and a half since Harry had gone; hours of cutting, stitching, embroidering and talking. It was oddly absorbing and therapeutic. Ellie felt a bit like an invalid, recovering from her broken heart, and this medicine of making and conversation helped her to heal.

Beyond the curtains, the crowd roared louder.

'Another bow?' Mike called out. 'Get back in line, everyone! Last time!'

They hurried back into place. Mike joined them, a smile beaming from his face. The curtains swung open and they stepped forward to the front of the stage for a final bow. The noise poured over them, lifting their spirits. Ellie had never experienced anything like it – the thrill, the pleasure of the audience, the profound sense of accomplishment. *I might have missed this.* The thought passed fleetingly through her mind.

The other actors pushed Carly forward to take a bow on her own. She'd shone like a jewel in the play. She had, as they say, stolen the show. Daisy had conjured up a spectacular costume for Carly as Titania, the fairy queen: a dress like a bloom of jade and pearl, pale silver threads and tiny, blinking gems, an emerald bodice stitched with swirls of leaves and buds, a sweep of net for her wings, pleated and artfully ragged, an odd, high coronet of ivy and gauze and wild roses. When she performed, Carly enchanted the audience. Everyone seemed to hold their breath – mesmerised – as she spoke with Alex's strange, beautiful fairy puppets, when she cooed, love-struck, over

Alex playing Bottom the Weaver, when he wore his donkey's head. The others didn't begrudge her her success – on the contrary, she'd cast a radiance over the entire production.

Ellie's eyes scanned the crowd. Her grandparents had already seen the play. They'd attended on the second night, then raved and enthused about everything – her acting, the stage set, the puppets, costumes, direction, the cast, the fairy queen.

Ellie didn't tell her grandparents about the escapade on the cliff top, and she extracted a promise from Alex and Daisy that they wouldn't either.

Her friends had escorted her home the night of the cliff-top flight, after they'd comforted her over coffee in a late-night café. Ellie went straight to bed and slept a long time. When she woke the following morning, she'd dismantled her stalker wall, putting everything in a file. Then she took the model theatre to pieces, and stored it in a box along with the *Romeo and Juliet* script and Harry's shirt, from the theatre. She asked her grandfather if he would take them all to the Lyme museum, for safe keeping, until they were used in the exhibition about the Marine Theatre.

Daisy and Alex had called round in the afternoon and stayed for an hour. They sat in the garden, drinking glasses of elderflower cordial, talking idly. From then on Ellie saw one or other of them, sometimes both, each day. And she attended rehearsals, helped make costumes with Daisy and painted scenery with Alex. The pain of Harry's loss, of all her losses, endured, but it wasn't constant. She sat through the bad times knowing they wouldn't last forever and focused on taking pleasure from any possible moment of happiness; being with her friends, the play, odd things like hanging up clean washing on the line in the sunny garden or choosing a different icecream flavour from the stall on the front. She went on long walks every day, sometimes alone – when she thought about what had happened, trying to make sense of it – and sometimes with Alex or her grandmother. She asked Jean about Sophie, but also about her own life, youth and plans for the future. Jean was delighted.

'I know you're not, well, entirely happy, but I'm glad you've come back to us,' she said.

Another roar from the audience.

There she was! Grandma! And her grandfather – sitting one row from the back. They'd come to see the play a second time – without telling Ellie. She caught her breath: beside them, applauding with gusto, she saw her father. What a shock – that most familiar of faces in the sea of an audience. For a moment she didn't hear the clapping. Her ears didn't register the sound. Her gaze locked on her father's face. How strange that he could seem like a stranger and still be so known and loved. And she did love him – from the pit of her belly, through her heart, into her mind and memory. Her love for him was rooted and firm. It always had been, despite the hurt and rage.

My dad.

I love you, Dad.

Tears filled her eyes. He was clapping a little too enthusiastically she noticed. A bit embarrassing. But she could see how proud he was. She swallowed, not wanting to cry.

Carly stepped back. They all retreated from the front of the stage. The curtains closed. Finally the applause died away and they heard the murmur of people talking, standing up and leaving the auditorium. The cast members left the stage to change, clear up and head for the after-show party at Alex's house.

But Ellie could only think about her father. He'd come to see the play. He'd returned early from America for the performance. Her grandparents, presumably, had told him about it. Ellie hadn't contacted him these last weeks, wanting space to think and build herself up. Yet – how moved she was to see him, and actually, how delighted he'd watched the play. She was proud of it – not just her own role, but the whole production. She'd invested so much time and energy and creativity in it.

She wiped off her stage make-up, undressed automatically and pulled on her ordinary clothes. The following day they would return to the theatre, dismantle the set and clear up. Now everyone was excited about the party – everyone except for Ellie.

'Hey, Ellie!' Daisy pirouetted into the room. 'Party party!' She looked into Ellie's face. 'Something wrong? You've gone all quiet.'

Ellie stood up straight. 'It's my dad. He's here – in the audience. I didn't know.'

'That's good, isn't it?' Daisy said softly. 'Really. He must be so proud of you. W-as that him, sitting by your grandparents?'

'Yes. You saw them?'

'Yep. Near the back.'

A knock on the door. Alex stepped in, with Warren and Carly and a couple of the others.

'You ready to go?' Alex said. His gaze skipped from Ellie to Daisy and back again. 'What's up? Problem?'

'Ellie's dad's here. He watched the play.'

'Oh. I see.' Alex looked at her. 'How do you feel about that?'

'I'll have to talk to him. You know, say hello. I don't know if I can come to the party. I'm really sorry.'

'Don't worry,' Alex said. 'This is important. Go and talk. And come along later if you like. Bring him along.'

'Yeah, sure,' Ellie said, rolling her eyes. But inside she was nervous. More than nervous.

She walked from the dressing room to the theatre foyer, heart thundering. How would she feel when she met her dad again? They were standing near the door, her dad and grandparents, chatting to some other people. Her father was standing in profile but he turned and looked directly towards her. He looked both familiar and strange. He was so much a part of her life, but now she saw him with new eyes. He was not just Dad – that towering presence – but a man, cast into the world as she was, to make his way as best he could. And, just now, he was evidently nervous too.

'Ellie?' He stepped towards her and held out his arms. She gave her dad a tense hug. He was shaking.

'How are you? The play was brilliant! I'm so glad I didn't miss it. You were brilliant. The whole production – it was something else. And the puppets – wow! Better than professionals. There are some talented kids in this town.'

He kept his arm over her shoulder, relaxing a little bit, his face anxious but shiny with happiness. Her grandparents looked on.

'We're off. Maybe see you later.' Alex had arrived. He and the others were on their way to the party.

'Dad, these are my friends. This is Alex. Alex Sullivan. He made those puppets. This is Daisy, and Warren and Carly.'

Her father smiled, surveying the gathering. Then he turned to Alex and shook his hand. 'Absolute genius,' he said. 'I don't know how you did it. They were so . . . real.' Then he said, 'Alex Sullivan? Joe's boy?' A peculiar expression flickered across his face.

'That's right,' Alex nodded. 'I know you'll want to talk to Ellie, but if you want to join her at the party later please come. It's at my parents' place.' Then he and the others were gone, focused on the party and each other.

The place quietened. 'You want to go for a coffee?' Ellie's dad said.

'Okay, yeah.' Ellie tried to be nonchalant. Her grandparents had edged away, leaving the two of them some space. Her dad waved. 'We're off. See you later.' They smiled and waved back, almost visibly sending them helpful, hopeful vibes.

'Where's Louise?' Ellie said. They were sitting in the bow window of a pub overlooking the night-time harbour. Lights twinkled on the tethered boats and along the curve of the sea wall.

'Probably at her place by now. We flew back together – arrived at Heathrow this afternoon. I made my way here on the train.'

'To see the play?'

'Yes. Your grandma said I couldn't miss it. So we cut the trip short by a few days, changed flights and here I am. And I am very, very glad we did. The play was fabulous.' He took a sip of coffee, replaced his cup, and added, 'Do you mind that I came? I mean, you didn't tell me about it. Not a word. Maybe you didn't want me to see it?' She sensed the brew of feelings behind these words. She'd hurt him with her silence. She'd chosen not to share this important part of her life.

'No, it's fine. I'm glad you came. It was a shock seeing you in the audience. But I'm glad.' Another silence. Then Ellie said, 'How was your trip?'

He studied her face, not sure what to say. They were both so sensitive of the situation, and each other. But he sat up straight, looked her in the eye and said, 'I missed you a lot, and I wish you had come, but setting that to one side, it was great. Actually, it was fabulous. Business-wise, more than I could have hoped for. Personally, I had a wonderful time. We both did, Louise and I.'

Now Ellie sipped her coffee. Then she put her palms face down on the table, stretching out her fingers. She studied the backs of her hands and then raised her eyes to her father's face.

'You love her, don't you?'

'Yes, very much,' he answered simply. No excusing or apology, no reassurance of how much he'd also loved her mother, or still loved her: just a yes.

'Will you get married?' Her voice was level and curious.

'Yes. We talked about it only yesterday, before we left the US. You are, naturally, the first person I've told.'

'And if I disapprove?' She said it lightly.

'Then we'll still marry. But – more than anything – I'd like your approval. It would be such a blessing. That's what Louise wants too.'

Her father had changed, Ellie realised. He was stronger, and calmer. She studied his face, noticing the signs of age – the deep lines across his forehead and under his eyes, threads of grey in his fair hair, now growing thin at the front. She thought of Violette's path of days. Most likely, her dad had more behind him than ahead of him. Did he think about that too?

'It's okay,' Ellie said. 'If you're sure this is right for you. If you're happy together, then yes, I do approve. It will be weird, for sure, so it might take me a while to get used to it.' She paused. 'I do want you to be happy, Dad. I want you to have a good life.'

Her father smiled. He had tears in his eyes.

'Thank you, Ellie,' he said, voice choked. 'You have no idea what that means to me. Thank you.' He blinked and sniffed. 'I've missed you so much. Really, I can't tell you how much. Maybe you needed this time, but I have missed you.'

'I've missed you too,' she said.

'Please give Louise a chance. I can't ask you to like her – obviously that's up to you and her. But I am asking you to give her a chance.'

'I understand. And I will.'

Rob hesitated – then said, 'So, what's happened for you? Apart from the play.'

Ellie smiled, gazing at her coffee cup. 'I fell in love,' she said.

'You what? You fell in love? With who? What happened?' His words fell over each other. He looked agog. His little girl? The words were written all over his face.

Ellie laughed.

'Is it that Alex boy?' Rob asked.

Ellie shook her head. 'Nope. Not him. No one you know. And anyway, it didn't work out. It's over now.'

Rob was still staring, mouth open, obviously bursting with questions he refrained from asking, except to say, darkly, 'I hope you weren't hurt or upset – by this boy, I mean. The one you fell in love with.' She could still hear the note of incredulity in his voice. Despite everything he couldn't quite believe his girl was grown up enough to be falling in love.

'Please, don't worry.' She smiled and placed her hand over his, giving it a little squeeze. 'Everything's good now. Difficult, yes, but okay.'

An hour later they wandered up the hill to Alex's house. They'd talked about the America trip and the play. Ellie didn't tell her father what she knew about her mum's youthful relationship with Joe Sullivan but, judging from his reaction to Joe, she divined he already knew about it. She wondered how he would feel, visiting the Sullivans' house. Would Joe be there? Yes. Indeed he was – sitting in the garden with Sue, enjoying the mild summer evening while Alex and the rest of the cast celebrated noisily in the house.

Ellie pushed open the garden gate and led the way along

the path. Joe stood up and walked towards them. The chimes tinkled.

'Joe, this is my dad, Rob. Dad – this is Joe Sullivan.'

Joe stretched out his hand. They were both tall men. They looked one another in the eye and slowly shook hands.

'It's good to meet you at last,' Joe said. 'A great pleasure. Please, come and meet my wife. Ellie – I expect you want to join the noisy party. Rob – can I get you a beer?'

Ellie went to the house. At the door she looked back, to see her dad chatting to Sue while Joe fished in a crate for a bottle. He seemed relaxed, she thought. No need to worry about him. He could take care of himself.

36

Dear Mum,

I ran away to Lyme-on-Sea to escape everything, but ended up having a very difficult, painful time. I thought I could hide in the place you and I used to share, where we had so many wonderful adventures, but it hasn't worked that way. In some ways this has been the most painful time of all – falling in love with Harry opened the door on all sorts of feelings about you and Dad and me. I'm recovering now, slowly. But I still feel bruised. Thinking and remembering certain things makes me hurt all over again.

But sometimes I'm happy. You know, I almost feel guilty for being happy, because you're dead, but I imagine your voice in my head telling me you want me to be happy. I know you do. You don't want me to be miserable forever. And I want to enjoy life. I'm choosing to be happy. You know, working at it. And that does get easier.

Ellie put down her pen. She was writing a letter to her mother in her journal, sitting on the café terrace on the seafront, in the shade of a parasol. Kids and parents played on the stretch of sandy beach by the harbour. The usual

assortment of holidaymakers mooched along the promenade. Sunlight glittered bright white on the surface of the
level sea. Ellie sighed. She felt happy right now, taking in
the scene, enjoying the voluptuous heat and the process of
writing down her thoughts.

*I've learned some surprising things about you, too. You and
Joe – how he broke your heart. I wondered why you never told
me about that, but then again, why would you? It was a part
of your life before I was born. It's weird to think of it. You and
Dad, as a couple, were all and eternal for me – the usual child's
perspective, I know.*

*Dad met Joe at a party – and afterwards I asked him what
he thought about you having been engaged. It wasn't easy
asking him something like that – not easy for Dad, either. But
we've kind of renegotiated our relationship. He knows he has
to let me create my own life, and I can see I have to let him do
the same. Don't worry – it doesn't mean I love him less, and I
know he'll always be there for me too. It's made things a little
bit easier, freed things up. I don't want us to end up like
Violette Lefevre and her Papa. I mean, I am very fond of
Violette and she seems happy now, but the thought of her life
makes me shudder – being controlled and stifled by her needy
old dad. Nope, no thank you.*

*Anyway, Dad and Joe. They seemed to get on, actually.
Perhaps your ears were burning, wherever you are, because
Dad said they talked about you a lot. Sharing memories,
laughing about funny and exciting things from your youth,
appreciating you. Actually I think it was good for Dad to talk
to someone (someone who wasn't family) who knew you when*

you were young, and who cared for you. I wonder what Sue thought about it, but Dad said she didn't seem bothered and soon left the two of them to it. I don't suppose Sue feels she has anything to worry about. She and Joe seem very attached.

So the next day, when I talked to Dad, he said he'd known about Joe and the engagement from the beginning of his relationship with you, because you'd talked about Joe a lot. Dad said he'd loved you passionately and devotedly from the start, and he'd felt ordinary and unworthy, very much in the shadow of the wonderful, brilliant, artistic Joe.

But as time went on, things changed. He said you seemed to forget about Joe and fell more and more in love with him instead. Dad recalled the time you finally told him that he'd become your soulmate and how overwhelmed he was, that he proposed on the spot, and you married, and I came along and . . . well, obviously you know the story. Then Dad said a strange thing. I'll try and remember it:

'I'm very glad to have met Joe, even after all this time. I never entirely lost the feeling that I was second best for your mother, that Joe was the special one for her. She never mentioned him again after those early months of our relationship, but she'd obviously thought he was marvellous. And running into him now, after all these years, even though Sophie has gone, it was like – oh, actually this Joe is another ordinary, middle-aged bloke like me. Sure, he's a great guy, but really, he isn't the irresistible love god after all.'

Well, he said something like that. I hope you don't mind me telling you, Mum. And they did both love and appreciate you a lot . . .

I'll have to meet Louise again soon. Not looking forward to

333

it. She's not a patch on you. I told Dad I'd give her a chance,
but it's going to be difficult. I'm not sure what he sees in her.
Maybe Louise is always going to feel she's living in your
shadow.

Ellie had been writing fast. Her hand ached. She slid the
pen and journal into her bag. It was the first time she'd
written a letter to her dead mother. It had been Alex's idea.
She'd often had imaginary conversations with her mother
and this way she could release them, get them out of her
mind. Probably she wouldn't do it often: just from time to
time, when the need arose. And the odd thing was, Ellie
could usually imagine what her mum would say or how
she'd respond. After all the years of growing up, her mother's thoughts, quirks, worries and values had become a
part of her. Ellie could refer to them, whenever she wanted.

'Ellie! Ellie!'

She looked up. Alex was jogging towards her, dodging
the amblers on the promenade. He grinned and waved. A
big smile spread across Ellie's face too. Alex was so handsome and healthy and full of vigour, and at the same time,
so natural and lacking in self-consciousness.

'Sorry I'm late. Lost track of time.' He'd leaped up the
step onto the terrace. Paint and varnish stained his hands.
Sawdust sprinkled his hair. Alex ordered an orange juice.

'I've got some news,' Ellie said.

'What? What is it?'

Ellie smiled, pleased to have him on tenterhooks. 'I've
got a university place, for October.'

'What? Fantastic! I told you something would happen!

334

Where? Doing what?' Alex was beaming, evidently delighted.

'History and theatre studies – joint honours. At Leicester. They had a place. I have to be there in two weeks.'

Ellie hadn't been thinking about her A-level results. She'd had too many other things on her mind. And perhaps she hadn't wanted to think about them. She knew she hadn't done very well. But the results were waiting in the post at home, and her father had sent them on to her. True enough, she hadn't achieved the necessary grades for the offer to study English and Drama at Warwick, but she'd gone through clearing and received notification of this alternative that morning.

'You know, this is actually better for me,' Ellie added. 'It's been a tough summer, you know that better than anyone. But I've discovered some new interests – the research for the exhibition, the set design stuff I did with you, and helping Daisy with the costumes. This course actually touches on all those things. I think it's going to be great.'

'But in just two weeks? Are you nervous? You'll have a lot to sort out.'

'Nervous, and excited.'

Ten minutes later they were walking along the coast path, eastwards, through patches of scrubby woodland and out into the sunshine.

'Do you think falling in love is selfish?' Ellie said.

'In what way selfish?'

'I mean, that all-consuming being-in-loveness, wanting and needing and aching and obsessing. It's so powerful, isn't it? What the poets write about. *Romeo and Juliet* stuff: ignoring their families, dying for love. I mean, I fell in love with Harry, and I didn't want him to go. I wanted him to stay, for me, to make me happy. And my dad fell in love with Louise and put his need to be with her above my need for him to stay alone for me.'

Alex laughed and shook his head.

'Yeah, okay.' Ellie laughed too. 'Fair point. Some kind of battle of different selfishnesses going on there. It's tricky, isn't it?'

'Tricky, yes.' Alex brooded for a moment. 'But, if you could have held on to Harry, stopped him passing over or whatever he did, would you have done that?'

'I've asked myself that question – and to be honest, I don't know the answer. I'd like to say I'd have released him and taken the hit, but at the time? I'm not sure.'

'Okay, another question. If you could go back in time, rewind, and not buy the model theatre and miss this whole episode, would you do that? Basically, do you regret it? Wish it had never happened?'

Another hard question. Ellie pondered.

'I don't regret it,' she said. 'Even losing him. Even the hurt of everything. I'm glad it was a part of my life, because, anyway, everything's finally changed for the better. It's like falling in love with him so violently was the jolt I needed to shake up all the broken, frozen pieces of my life and put them together in a new way.'

They walked through a kissing gate then along the edge of a field of stubble, the ground beneath their feet baked hard and riddled with cracks. Butterflies rose from the dusty hedges as they passed. A hundred metres further on, Alex led the way over a stile, to a wooden bench by the coast path. He sat down and signalled for Ellie to join him. The hedge now reared behind them and sea pinks trembled in the wiry grass at the cliff edge.

'What an incredible view,' Ellie said. She gazed at the sea, with its varied stripes of blue, spreading to the horizon.

'Look!'

'What?'

'There, at the base of the cliff – that tiny little patch of pebbles. A seal! See it?'

'No. Where? Where is it?'

'There!' He pointed. 'And there's another one in the water. You can just see its head poking out.'

Ellie squinted and shaded her eyes. Could she see? She wasn't sure.

When she looked back, Alex was holding something in his paint-flecked hand. He cradled it tenderly. She looked quizzically into his blue, blue eyes.

'What is it?'

'For you.'

Ellie could tell he was a bit nervous. Alex uncurled his fingers and slowly handed the object to her.

A box, like the ones she had seen in his room all those weeks ago. A box about twenty centimetres square, made of many tiny fragments of driftwood, with a hinged lid. Perfect, exquisite, the fragments fitted together beautifully, were sanded to a fine finish and waxed, revealing the various, rich colours of the wood and its complex grain. How had he contrived to find and match these pieces so precisely?

Ellie took the box, lost for words. She was so moved by its unique beauty and the care he had taken in making it for her. How many hours, how much thought and effort had Alex invested in creating this marvellous thing? She turned it round and over, appreciating the gift. Then she opened the lid. Inside, on a moss-green velvet lining, was a piece of sea-glass, pale green, made smooth and opaque by the sea, and shaped like a heart.

Ellie swallowed, and looked at Alex. Tears filled her eyes.

'That is the most amazing present anyone has ever given me,' she said. 'I'm sure I don't deserve it. It's lovely. Perfect. I don't know what to say.'

'Then don't say anything. I can see you like it. That's enough.' Alex relaxed and grinned, clearly pleased.

Ellie lifted out the heart and held it up to the sun. She enjoyed the sensation of its smoothness on her fingertips. Then she put it back into the box and closed the lid.

'You know what I said earlier, about falling in love being selfish,' she said. This was difficult. They hadn't talked about Alex's revelation that night on the dangerous cliff but they both *knew*. The topic had hovered around them.

'It wasn't selfish of you, was it?' she continued. 'I mean, I didn't realise – how you felt about me. And in Paris, all that Harry stuff, you seeing that photo, realising how real it all was, how much I loved him. I hurt you, didn't I? That's what you meant. And so you stepped back. But even though you knew I loved someone else, you still cared

338

about me, for my own sake. You came after me, chased me on the cliff in the night, to make sure I was okay. That wasn't selfish, was it?'

Alex didn't answer right away. He stared out at the sea, the warm breeze ruffling his dusty hair.

'I'm not in any hurry,' he said. 'I don't want to be your rebound. You recover, get happy, go to Leicester, have some fun. I'm not going anywhere. Keep in touch. Call me up if you ever need to, and if you want, come down to Lyme-on-Sea in the Christmas holidays. We'll see what happens, yes?'

Ellie leaned her head against his warm arm. 'Yes,' she said.

They went into the Marine Theatre that night. Daisy had the key, ostensibly to collect the last items of scenery from the play. In truth, they had another motive.

Daisy, Warren, Carly, Alex and Ellie. In a bag Carly had half a dozen little candles in glass jars. They went straight to the stage, lit the candles and arranged them in a circle. Warren turned off the electric lights and the five of them sat at the edge of the warm, yellow pool of candlelight.

'We're here to say goodbye and farewell to Harry Weatherstone, who haunted the Marine Theatre,' Warren said in a nervous, rather pompous-sounding voice. 'He has passed on to the next world, and we wish to close the veil.'

Warren went on about cardinal points and invocations and closings. Ellie watched the four still faces of her friends, softly painted by candlelight. They would be parting soon:

Warren was also off to university. Carly was applying to drama school. Only Daisy and Alex would remain in the town. Alex had just started his art foundation course at the local college.

The fate of the theatre was front page news in the local paper this week – reporter Nick's big scoop. The council had finally decided to pull it down. A developer had submitted plans to build in its place a range of little apartments, and a smaller, modern arts centre with a modest performance space, some recording studios, meeting and rehearsal rooms.

Although local people were mourning the loss of the old building, most realised this was the best option, Nick had opined. He'd asked Ellie out for a coffee the previous day, to talk about the exhibition. He'd also flirted outrageously.

'Really, it's in a terrible state – I'll send you a copy of the council report. The theatre was already starting to crumble when the sixties revamp took place. They just sort of patched it up and covered over the problems,' he said. 'It would have cost an absolute fortune to shore it up, fix and restore it, and the council doesn't have that sort of money. This way, the developers will pay for the new arts centre in exchange for permission to build and sell the apartments. Planning gain. Everyone's happy.'

Ellie's attention returned to the present – the closure of the séance. Warren was still talking. Everyone seemed to have drifted off into their own thoughts. She'd told Carly and Warren a little about Harry and the haunting, though she wasn't sure they really believed her, and she hadn't gone into her love affair with the ghost. Only Alex and Daisy knew about that. And Violette, of course. Violette had sent her an email that evening, asking how Ellie and Alex were, talking about a date she had lined up that evening with a sixty-year-old French gentleman, an artist. Ellie could hear Violette's excitement in the email. She imagined them, the elegant twosome, wandering arm in arm along the Seine in the twilight. Ellie sent a reply, saying how romantic it sounded and that she hoped all would go well.

'Spirit of the west, we invoked you for our protection, now we release you. Move freely, take our gratitude with you. Spirit of the south, we invoked you for our protec-tion . . .' Warren continued.

Really, where does he get this stuff? Ellie wondered. Warren looked so serious. She caught Daisy's eye but had to look away again as they were both about to burst into giggles. Warren had suggested this little closure to their earlier séance, a formal farewell to the theatre ghost, and with the end of the theatre itself on the cards it had seemed the proper thing to do.

Ellie found it hard to connect this ceremony with Harry. She had already said her goodbye to him, in the graveyard that night, and then the grief of the days that followed. Now, after the play, seeing her father and developing this fragile, tentative connection with Alex, Harry seemed further away. This ceremony-game with Warren and her friends was more a farewell to their summer together than to her lost love.

The theatre exhibition, for which Ellie had done so much

work, was scheduled to take place in the spring, coinciding with the demolition. The museum staff would continue with the research. Ellie had agreed to help out when they set up and opened during the Easter vacation. Violette had agreed to open it, as guest of honour.

'The circle is closed. Harry Weatherstone, farewell. Your spirit flies free into the land we cannot visit, and from which no one returns.' Warren stopped talking. He gestured for the others to blow out the candles, which they did, one by one. They sat, silent, in darkness.

Harry Weatherstone, farewell. For one moment Ellie felt again a piercing sadness, a cold finger pressing on the bruise of loss.

Then Daisy giggled. 'Are we done? Can we go now?'

The moment passed. Ellie let it go.

They wandered down to the beach and scrunched over the pebbles to the water's edge. Ellie and Daisy sat side by side on the stones, wriggling to get comfortable.

'So – you and Alex,' Daisy said. 'About time.'

'He told you? I mean, nothing's really happened yet. You don't mind?'

Daisy looked away and shook her head. 'I've known for weeks that he liked you. When he told me he liked someone – I thought it might be you. And yes, I was pretty cut up about it to start with. And I could see that you didn't even realise! Of course I know now you were all wrapped up in this Harry stuff. No, I honestly don't mind anymore. I'm very happy with Warren. He's great. We have a lot of fun – and him being new, I'm enjoying finding out all about him.'

'Thanks. You've been – well, all the times we've shared. All the help. Your friendship – I mean . . .' She stumbled over her words.

Daisy threw her arms around Ellie, planting a kiss on her cheek.

'Sure – I know what you mean. I love you too. Make sure you come back at Christmas. And Alex – well, you're very lucky to have him. Take care of him. Otherwise I might just have to kill you.' She drew back, giving Ellie a wicked grin.

Later, they walked along the promenade to the pub by the harbour. Alex and Ellie walked behind the others, side by side. They passed the little bookshop where she'd bought the model theatre, those long weeks ago, and where she had first met Alex.

'How are you feeling?' Alex said. 'Were you okay in the theatre? Did it upset you?'

Ellie shook her head. 'No. It was kind of nice, actually. Not just for Harry – all of us being part of a farewell ritual. I liked that.'

'You're happy?'

'Very happy. And lucky.'

Alex stopped walking and took her hand. He drew her towards him and said, 'I know I should wait, but I can't . . .'

Ellie snuggled against him. Falling in love with Harry had been an emotional explosion – a devastation. With Alex it was something different: like a fire that slowly kindled and grew, a love that warmed and nourished, filling her with happiness.

Light from the street lamp spilled around them. Further

up the path Warren shouted something that made the girls laugh. Waves turned over on the pebbles. The perfume of fresh fish and chips drifted on the evening air.

Ellie raised her face and Alex bent down to kiss her.

SARAH SINGLETON

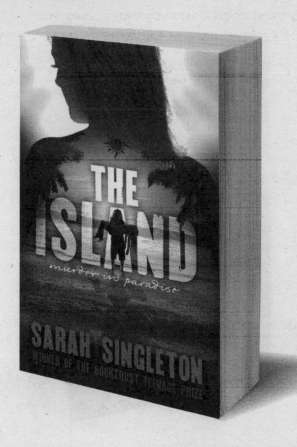

Three friends, Otto, Jen and Charlotte have planned the trip of a lifetime to India for their gap year, but what starts as a fun adventure soon turns terrifying when Otto discovers the body of a girl on the beach, and finds himself the prime suspect for her murder. Can Charlotte and Jen discover the truth and clear Otto's name?

"a compelling and intense whodunnit... a genuinely satisfying mystery thriller with three utterly credible, imperfect central characters, and in which Goa, its landscapes, its dangers, and its joys rise vividly from the pages... an unnerving, completely absorbing read." **The Bookbag**

ISBN: 978-1-84738-296-2

SARAH SINGLETON

Charlotte is working at a tiger sanctuary, but another traveller staying
there is starting to make her feel uncomfortable. When things start going
wrong at the sanctuary, Charlotte fears a vendetta against her could be to
blame. She asks Otto to come and pretend to be her boyfriend, but when
their 'fake' relationship seems to be developing into something more
serious, things take a sinister turn…

*"Singleton knows exactly how to create and maintain suspense.
Deftly and delicately, she also weaves emotion into the mix, evoking
through the relationships between the central characters the unforgettable
intensity of teenage friendship and first love."* **The Guardian**

ISBN: 978-0-85707-073-9